Praise for *Some Boys*

"Blount hits home with this novel...Some Boys belongs in every YA collection."

—*School Library Journal*

"You will be satisfied at the end of this powerful work."

—*RT Book Reviews*

"A largely sensitive treatment of an emotionally complex topic."

—*Kirkus*

"A bold and necessary look at an important, and very real, topic. Everyone should read this book."

—Jennifer Brown, author of *Thousand Words* and *Hate List*

"Some Boys is an emotional and heart wrenching story that sheds light on rape and bullying."

—Christy's Book Addiction blog

"Some Boys is smart, heartbreaking, horrifying and courageous... A must read."

—Confessions of an Opinionated Book Geek blog

"This book did quite a number on me...made me FEEL, and feel really strongly."

—The Eater of Books blog

Praise for *Send*

"Dan's likable first-person voice rings with authenticity . . . this offering may be relevant for those looking for more books on the ever-important topic of bullying."

"Blount's debut novel combines authentic voice with compelling moral dilemmas...raise(s) important questions about honesty, forgiveness, the ease of cyberbullying and the obligation to help others."

—VOYA

"A morality play about releasing the past and seizing the present...the ethical debates raised will engage readers."

—*Publishers Weekly*

"Read. This. Book."

—Fiction Folio blog

"Emotional, dark, and real, Send will not disappoint."

—Singing and Reading in the Rain blog

Praise for *TMI*

"A great page-turner to savor during the last days of summer."

—Seventeen.com Book Club

"[A] tech-driven cautionary tale...Blount addresses the potential perils of online relationships and the sometimes-destructive power of social media without proselytizing."

—*Publishers Weekly*

"Blount has a good handle on teen culture, especially the importance of social media...realistically expressed... [and] honestly portrayed."

—*School Library Journal*

SOME BOYS

PATTY BLOUNT

sourcebooks fire

Published by Sourcebooks Fire, an imprint of Sourcebooks, Inc.
P.O. Box 4410, Naperville, Illinois 60567-4410
(630) 961-3900
Fax: (630) 961-2168
www.sourcebooks.com

Library of Congress Cataloging-in-Publication data is on file with the publisher.

Printed and bound in the United States of America.
VP 10 9

To Kelly Breakey, with my eternal gratitude for encouraging the first because without that, there couldn't have been a second and a third.

Chapter 1
Grace

No Monday in history has ever sucked more than this one.

I'm kind of an expert on sucky days. It's been thirty-two of them since the party in the woods that started the battle I fight every day. I step onto the bus to school, wearing my armor and pretending nothing's wrong, nothing happened, nothing changed when it's pretty obvious nothing will ever be the same again. Alyssa Martin, a girl I've known since first grade, smirks and stretches her leg across the empty seat next to hers.

I approach slowly, hoping nobody can see my knees knocking. A couple of weeks ago during a school newspaper staff meeting, Alyssa vowed her support, and today I'm pond scum.

"Find a seat!" Mrs. Gannon, the bus driver, shouts.

I meet Alyssa's eyes, silently beg her for sympathy—even a little pity. She raises a middle finger. It's a show of loyalty to someone who doesn't deserve it, a challenge to see how far I'll go. My dad keeps telling me to stand up to all of Zac's defenders, but it's the entire bus—the entire *school*—versus me.

I gulp hard, and the bus lurches forward. I try to grab a seat back but lose my balance and topple into the seat Alyssa's blocking with her leg. She lets out a screech of pain.

"Bitch," she sneers. "You nearly broke my leg."

I'm about to apologize when I notice the people sitting around us stare with wide eyes and hands over their open mouths. When my eyes meet theirs, they turn away, but nobody *does* anything.

This is weird.

Alyssa folds herself against the window and shoves earbuds into her ears and ignores me for the duration of the ride.

The rest of the trip passes without incident—except for two girls whispering over a video playing on a phone they both clutch in their hands. One of them murmurs, "Six hundred and eighteen hits," and shoots me a dirty look.

I know exactly what she means and don't want to think about it. I look away. As soon as the bus stops, I'm off. On my way to my locker, most people just ignore me, although a few still think they've come up with a clever new insult. An elbow or the occasional extended foot still needs dodging, but it's really not that bad. I can deal. I can do this. I can make it through school unless I see—

"Woof! Woof!"

My feet root themselves to the floor, and the breath clogs in my lungs. And I know without turning who barked at me. I force myself to keep walking instead of running for home, running for the next town. I want to turn to look at him, look him dead in the eye, and twist my face into something that shows contempt instead of the terror that too often wins whenever I hear his name so he sees—so he *knows*—he didn't beat me. But that doesn't happen. A foot appears from nowhere, and I can't dodge it in time. I fall to my hands and knees, and two more familiar faces step out of the crowd to laugh down at me.

"Hear you like it on your knees," Kyle Moran shouts, and everybody laughs. At least Matt Roberts helps me up, but when Kyle smacks his head, he takes off before I can thank him. They're two of *his* best buds. Nausea boils inside me, and I scramble back to my feet. I grab my backpack, pray that the school's expensive digital camera tucked inside it isn't damaged, and duck into the girls' bathroom, locking myself into a stall.

When my hands are steady, eyes are dry, stomach's no longer threatening to send back breakfast, I open the stall.

Miranda and Lindsay, my two best friends, stand in front of the mirrors.

Make that *former* best friends.

We stare at one another through the mirrors. Lindsay leans against a sink but doesn't say anything. Miranda runs a hand down her smooth blond hair, pretends I'm not there, and talks to Lindsay. "So I've decided to have a party and invite Zac and the rest of the lacrosse team. It's going to be epic."

No. Not him. The blood freezes in my veins. "Miranda. Don't. Please."

Miranda's hand freezes on her hair. "Don't, please?" She shakes her head in disgust. "You know, he could get kicked off the lacrosse team because of you."

"Good!" I scream, suddenly furious.

Miranda whips back around to face me, hair blurring like a fan blade. At the sink, Lindsay's jaw drops. "God! I can't believe you! Did you do all of this, say all this just to get back at me?"

My jaw drops. "What? Of course not. I—"

"You *know* I like him. If you didn't want me to go out with him, all you had to do was say so—"

"Miranda, this isn't about you. Trust me, Zac is—"

"Oh my God, listen to yourself. He breaks up with you, and you fall apart and then—"

"That is *not* what happened. I broke up with him! I was upset that night because of Kristie, and you know it."

She spins around, arms flung high. "Kristie! Seriously? You played him. You wanted everybody to feel sorry for you, so you turned on the tears and got Zac to—"

"Me? Are you insane? He—"

"Oh, don't even." Miranda holds up a hand. "I know exactly what happened. I was there. I know what you said. I figured you were lying, and now there's no doubt."

Lindsay nods and tosses her bag over her shoulder, and they stalk to the door. At the door, Miranda fires off one more shot. "You're a lying slut, and I'll make sure the whole school knows it."

The door slams behind them, echoing off the lavatory stalls. I'm standing in the center of the room, wondering what's holding me up because I can't feel my feet...or my hands. I raise them to make sure I still have hands, and before my eyes, they shake. But I don't feel that either. All I feel is pressure in my chest like someone just plunged my head underwater and I tried to breathe. My mouth goes dry, but I can't swallow. The pressure builds and grows and knocks down walls and won't let up. I press my hands to my chest and rub, but it doesn't help. Oh, God, it doesn't help. My heart lurches into overdrive like it's trying to stage a prison break. I fall to the cold bathroom floor, gasping, choking for breath, but I can't get any. I can't find any. There's no air left to breathe. I'm the lit match in front of a pair of lips puckered up, ready to blow.

Minutes pass, but they feel like centuries. I fumble for my phone—my mom's phone since she made me switch with her—and call her.

"Grace, what's wrong?"

"Can't breathe, Mom. Hurts," I push out the words on gasps of air.

"Okay, honey, I want you to take a breath and hold it. One, two, three, and let it out."

I follow her instructions, surprised I have any breath in my lungs to hold for three seconds. The next breath is easier.

"Keep going. Deep breath, hold it, let it out."

It takes me a few tries, but finally I can breathe without the barrier. "Oh, God."

"Better?"

"Yeah. It doesn't hurt now."

"Want me to take you home?"

Oh, *home*. Where there are no laughing classmates pointing at me, whispering behind their hands. Where there are no ex-friends calling me a bitch or a liar. Where I could curl up, throw a blanket over my head, and pretend nothing happened. *Yes, take me home. Take me home right now as fast as you can.*

I want to say that. But when I glance in the mirror over the row of sinks, something makes me say, "No. I have to stay."

"Grace—"

"Mom, I have to stay."

There's a loud sigh. "Oh, honey. You don't have to be brave."

Brave.

The word hangs in the air for a moment and then falls away, almost like even it knows it has no business being used to describe me. I'm not brave. I'm scared. I'm so freakin' scared, I can't see straight, and I can't see straight because I'm too scared to look very far. I'm a train wreck. All I'm doing is trying to hold on to what I have left. Only I'm not sure what that is. When I say nothing, she laughs too loudly. "Well, you're wearing your father's favorite outfit, so just pretend it's a superhero costume."

That makes me laugh. I glance down at my favorite boots—black leather covered in metal studs. My ass-kicking boots. Ever since Dad married Kristie, Mom lets me get away with anything that pisses him off, and wow does he hate how I dress.

"Grace, if you feel the pressure in your chest again, take a deep breath, hold it, and count. Concentrating on counting helps keep your mind from spiraling into panic."

"Yeah. Okay." But I'm not at all convinced. "I missed most of first period."

"Skip it. Don't worry about getting in trouble. Where are you now?"

"Bathroom."

"Why don't you go to the library? Relax and regroup, you know?"

Regroup. Sure. Okay. "Yeah. I'll do that."

"If you need me to get you, I'll come. Okay?"

I meet my own gaze in the mirror, disgusted to see them fill with tears. Jeez, you'd think I'd be empty by now. "Thanks, Mom." I end the call, tuck the phone in my pocket, and head for the library.

The library is my favorite spot in the whole school. Two floors of books, rows of computers, soft chairs to slouch in. I head for the nonfiction section and find the 770s. This is where the photography books live—my stack. I run a finger along the spines and find the first book I ever opened on the subject—*A History of Photography*.

I pull the book off its shelf, curl up with it in a chair near a window, and flip open the back cover. My signature is scrawled on the checkout card so many times now that we're old friends. I know how this book smells—a little like cut grass. How it feels—the pages are thick and glossy. And even where every one of its scars lives—the coffee ring on page 213 and the dog-eared corner in chapter 11. This is the book that said, "Grace, you *are* a photographer."

I flip through the pages, reread the section on high-key technique—I love how that sounds. *High-key*. So professional. It's really just great big fields of bright white filled with a splash of color or sometimes only shadow. I took hundreds of pictures this way—of Miranda, of Lindsay, of me. I practiced adjusting aperture settings and shutter speeds and overexposing backgrounds. It's cool how even the simplest subjects look calm and cheerful. It's like the extra light forces us to see the beauty and the flaws we never noticed.

I unzip my backpack and take out the school's digital camera. It's assigned to me—official student newspaper photographer. I scroll through the images stored on the card—selfies I shot over the last few weeks. Why can't everybody see what I see? My eyes don't sparkle. My lips don't curve anymore. Why don't they *see*?

I shove the camera back in my bag. With a sigh, I close the book, and a slip of paper floats to the floor. I pick it up, unfold it, and my stomach twists when I read the words printed on it. A noise startles me, and I look up to see Tyler Embery standing at one of the computers. Did he slip this paper into my favorite book? He's had a painfully obvious crush on me forever. Every time he gets within five feet of me, his face flushes and sweat beads at his hairline. Tyler volunteers at the library during his free periods and always flags me over to give me the latest issue of *Shutterbug* that he sets aside for me as soon as it arrives. He grabs something off the desk and walks over to me. I smile, thankful there's still one person left in this world that doesn't think Zac McMahon is the second coming of Christ. But Tyler's not holding a magazine. He's holding his phone.

"Six-eighty-three." There's no blush, no sweat—only disgust.

I jerk like he just punched me. I guess in a way he has. He turns, heads to the magazine rack, and places this month's issue, in its clear plastic cover, face out, in a subtle *fuck you* only I'd notice. I stuff the paper into my backpack and hurry to the exit just as the bell rings.

I make it to the end of the day. At dismissal I make damn sure I'm early for the bus ride home so I can snag an empty row. I plug in my earbuds to drown out the taunts. *It's not so bad*, I tell myself repeatedly, the taste of tears at the back of my throat familiar now. I don't believe me.

Once safely back in my house, I let my shoulders sag and take my first easy breath of the day. The house is empty and eerie, and I wonder how to fill the hours until Mom gets home. Thirty-two days ago I'd have been hanging out after school with Miranda and Lindsay or shopping at the mall or trying to find the perfect action photo at one of the games. In my room, I stare at the mirror over my dresser, where dozens of photos are taped—photos of me with my friends, me with my dad, me at dance class. I'm not welcome at any of these places, by any of these people anymore. I don't have a damn thing because Zac McMahon took it all. I think about Mom killing all of my online accounts and switching phones *just until things settle*. But now that the video of me that Zac posted on Facebook has 683 Likes, it's pretty clear that waiting for *things to settle* is a fantasy.

I rip all the pictures off the mirror, tear them into tiny pieces, and swipe them into the trash bin next to my desk. Then I pull out the slip of paper I found in the photography book, and after a few minutes of staring at it, I dial the number with shaking hands.

"Rape Crisis Hotline, this is Diane. Let me help you."

Chapter 2

Ian

Thank God it's Monday.

The entire weekend sucked, starting Friday night when I got grounded for denting my dad's car, and then it just circled the toilet from there. All the crap with Grace Collier is really messing Zac up, so I took him to a party in Holtsville to get away from the rumors for a while. I only had a couple beers, and on the way home I swerved to avoid hitting some dude who just came out of nowhere and I plowed into a mailbox.

I told my dad somebody hit the Camry while it was parked and that I had no idea how it happened.

It didn't matter. I got tossed into solitary confinement except for the hours of lectures on responsibility and how my sisters never did anything like this when they were my age. Pretty sure Dad's got about 365 separate lectures by now. He could publish the damn things in one of those flip calendars they sell at kiosks in the mall. *365 Days of Motivating Your Teen to Get Up Off His Ass!*

A roar of laughter from down the hall interrupts my thinking time. I follow the noise, spot Grace Collier on her hands and knees while

Kyle and pretty much everyone else laugh like hyenas. I freeze where I stand. Grace is just about the hottest girl I've ever seen. Amazing body she likes to show off in tight black leather and metal studs, wild dark hair that goes all the way to her ass, and these intense silvery gray eyes she loves to paint like Cleopatra that practically see right through a guy. It took me two months, two *solid* months to work up the guts to ask her out, and just when I had it all planned out, Zac beat me to it. Now after everything that went down I'm almost glad I never got my shot.

Almost.

Matt helps her up, but when Kyle swats the back of his head, they take off. Before she disappears into the girls' bathroom, I get a glimpse of her face and see more than just those bright eyes.

I see pain.

I wait for a minute and then head to my first class, world history. Yay. I slide into my seat at the back of the room. Zac's already there, surrounded by his fans.

"Thanks, bro. Appreciate it." He clasps hands with Tommy Rao, a kid on the basketball team. Tommy jerks his chin in acknowledgment, takes his seat over near the window.

"Hey, Ian," Zac nods at me. "Your dad still pissed?"

I roll my eyes. "You have no idea. I'm grounded. Again."

"Sucks." Zac tenses when Miranda Hollis and Lindsay Warren, Grace's best friends, rush over to him.

"Oh my God, we just want you to know we don't believe her. You're such a great guy, Zac." Miranda puts a hand on Zac's arm.

Zac shrugs and smiles. "Thanks. It helps to hear that." Miranda smiles, lowers her eyes, and twirls her hair in that universal signal that says, *I am totally into you.*

I swallow a grin. Damn, he's good. The girls take their seats, and I ask, "Zac, what's going on?"

His smile widens. "You didn't see Facebook?"

"No, grounded, remember?" No phone, no computer, no TV. It was just me and homework.

"Right." He pulls out his iPhone and hands me his earbuds. "Here. Take a look." Then he laughs. "Six hundred and seventy-two. Sweet."

I click the video he's got on screen and almost drop the phone. It's Grace. Holy hell, it's Grace Collier, and she's—Jesus. I rip the buds from my ears and hand him back the phone. "Wow."

He laughs. "I know, right? She doesn't know who she's messing with."

The bell rings, and the class quiets down. But I can't concentrate on imperialism after seeing that video. I've talked to Grace maybe three times total, but she never struck me as a girl who'd twist the truth to get back at somebody. By the time the bell rings at the end of class, I'm seriously happy I never got around to asking her out.

"Ian, you're free now, right?" Zac asks. "I need to stop at my locker first. And then I'll meet you in the library, and we can review the math stuff."

"Oh, God, thanks, man."

Zac has the highest grades in the class, and Coach Brill won't keep me on the lacrosse team if I don't ace the next math test. If I get booted off the team, my dad will deliver yet another lecture on how I'm failing my own future by not living up to my potential. I can already hear it. "Your sisters managed to earn scholarships while working part-time jobs and playing basketball," he'll say and fling up his hands. Claudia got a degree in architecture, and Valerie's studying to be a pharmacist. But I'll probably be living in a double-wide, collecting welfare.

I blend in with the stream of foot traffic changing classes and head for the stairwell. Dad thinks—actually believes—that I like not knowing what I want to be, but I've got a couple of ideas I've been thinking over. It might be cool to build stuff. Maybe engineering. It started with LEGO blocks, and then I moved on to building models and rebuilding stuff around the house. I just took apart the blender and rebuilt the motor, not that he cares about that.

Probably never even noticed.

Could also be fun to teach. I wouldn't mind coming back to school as a teacher instead of a student. I'd be cool. All the kids would love me. I'd listen, really listen to them instead of talk *at* them. I shake my head and snag a table in the library. There's no point in even telling my dad any of this. He'd just shake his head and warn me I'd need better math grades.

I may not be perfect like my sisters, but I'm not the loser my dad thinks I am either. I don't get high. I don't steal money from their wallets. Okay, so I dinged the car—big deal. It's not like I killed anybody.

My chest tightens when I remember the guy walking his dog that I almost hit Friday night.

Zac slides into a chair and throws his backpack on the table. "Jesus." He scrubs both hands over his blond hair. "Heard the collie missed the entire first period. That girl's got issues, man. Glad she's not my problem anymore."

Grace Collier's the furthest thing from a dog there is. But I get why he calls her that. As he finishes the sentence, I look up, and there she is, standing in the non-fiction section, looking seriously wrecked.

Zac doesn't see her. He's busy opening his pack and pulling out books. But I do, and I don't know what to say, what to do. They hooked up last month after the game against Holtsville High School, and now Zac's done with her. It happens.

But Grace doesn't look pissed. She looks devastated.

I open my notebook and grab a pen and just pretend I don't see her. "Thanks for the assist, man. If I get kicked off the team—"

"Won't let it happen, bro. We need you." He punches my shoulder. "Hey, after we win the game today, what do you say to a little cruising?"

I snort out a laugh. Cruising is Zac slang for *get laid*. "Sure, if I get a free pass tonight."

"When we win today's game, your dad will have to let you celebrate with the team, right?"

I lean back and smile. "Hope so. Thanks again. Really."

"No problem." He grins and flips my math textbook to the problem that keeps tripping me up.

I glance back the non-fiction shelves, but Grace is gone now.

Zac and I get to work, and I can't help thinking he's wrong—the problems are just beginning.

————————

We opened the scoring at barely two minutes into the game against the Shoreham Sharks. But at 4:53, the Sharks fire a shot into the cage, and Zac practically breathes fire. Now the score's tied at one all, and we aren't gonna just sit back and take it. Coach Brill sends me in just as we force a turnover. I join the battle, but the Sharks' goalie has the net sealed tight. When the goalie slings a breakout pass to a midfielder on a fast break, I run all out—this is my skill, my talent. I'm a blur on the field.

Zac's watching, sizing up our opponents. I'm so fixed on my target, I don't see one of the Sharks attack men. By the time I do, I can't stop, can't adjust, and *bam!*

Circle of stars.

Dimly I hear a whistle blow, hear muffled shouts and curses and another whistle, but it's all jumbled like one long bleat. It takes me a long while to figure out I'm sprawled on the turf, and then I notice the hands pressing and probing me.

"Ian! Ian, talk to me, son."

I open my mouth, but my tongue just sits there, limp.

"Give him a minute, Coach."

I blink a few times, but that does nothing to make the circle of stars disappear. Hands tap my face. "I'm okay," I try to say, but it comes out, "Mmmay."

I figure out which strings control my limbs and manage to roll to my hands and knees, sucking up oxygen and finally clearing my vision.

"Come on, Ian. Get up." Kyle Moran shouts. Slowly I figure out how my legs work, get them back under me. The coach and the EMT each grab an elbow and walk me off the field to *glad you're not dead* applause from both teams.

I'm forced to sit out the rest of the game. We win six to one, and the Panthers celebrate with pizza, which I miss because I'm sitting in the emergency room. Couple hours later I'm still in the emergency room with my parents, waiting for the doctor to come back with my films. I've been poked and stuck, x-rayed, and even MRI'd. I feel fine except for the worst headache of my entire life. Dad's checking his watch. Mom keeps checking me. Suddenly Dad jumps to his feet. "How is he, doctor?"

"Good news is there's no skull fracture."

Could have fooled me.

"Bad news is there *is* a concussion. You're benched for a while, son."

What? No way. Before I can protest, he turns to my parents and continues, "Keep him home from school tomorrow. Nothing more exerting than TV on the couch."

Dad rolls his eyes. "Oh, that won't be a problem for him."

"Dad, jeez." Am I really gonna have to sit through a flip-calendar lecture at the hospital? "I feel fine. I can go to school."

The doctor shakes his bald head, flips open one of those metal chart thingies, and scrawls something on my paperwork. "Sorry, Ian. Concussions are tricky, and this is a serious one."

"It is?"

Dad frowns. "Ian, you were hit from the side, spun around in midair, and landed hard. You were out cold for at least a minute."

I don't remember any of this.

"You may feel fine now, but tomorrow or the next day something may worsen it—like another hit to the head. I want to give this some time, see how you feel in a few days."

"There's another game on Saturday. Will I make that one?"

"Let's see how you're doing on Friday, and if everything looks good, I'll clear you."

I blow out a relieved sigh.

"If you feel dizzy, sick, or have any headaches, trouble concentrating, I need to know about it." He tears a slip of paper off a pad and hands it to my dad.

Dad nods, pockets the paper. We drive home in silence, the glare of headlights doing strange and uncomfortable things to my concussed head. I know I'm going to spend the night getting awakened to answer stupid questions like what's my name, who's the president, and what year is it.

"Tomorrow you'll stay home and in bed. No video games. I don't want you straining your eyes. You can call Zac or Kyle to get notes and homework after school."

I don't answer. I don't feel up to getting into another argument.

"Can you work from home tomorrow?" Mom asks Dad, and I cringe. *Please, no.*

"Yeah. I may have to run out for a couple of client meetings, but most of the day I can keep an eye on him."

Looks like I'm back in parental prison.

Chapter 3
Grace

Tuesday morning.

Day thirty-three.

Mom drops me off so I don't have to deal with the bus crowd calling me names. I arrive at school, and the second I step into the building, it starts. Insults. Shoves and elbows. Whispers and giggles. Comments loud enough to hear. *Slut. Liar. Bitch.*

I have no classes with Zac McMahon—about the only thing I can think of that's good. But I have to endure one with Miranda. She's chatting with two girls near the window when I take my seat.

"Can't believe she tattled to her mommy."

Her audience laughs and looks at me.

"She called my mother, and now I'm the one in trouble, even though she's the one who started the lie in the first place."

I sigh heavily. "Miranda, I'm sorry you think I stole Zac from you—believe me, I don't want him—but I am not lying."

She glances at me like I'm a pile of poo she just stepped in. "Then why did you tattle to your mommy that I made you cry?"

"What are you talking about?"

"Oh my God, seriously?" She rolls her eyes and takes out her phone. "This text? The one your mother sent to my mother, and now I'm in trouble?"

I glance at her screen and see what she means. She sent me a text which my mom intercepted. With another sigh, I dig out my mother's phone. "This is my mother's phone. She has mine. So if you texted my phone, *she* got the message."

Miranda's eyes go round, and her jaw drops. There's a tiny part of me that cheers.

"Guess it's your own fault you got in trouble."

"Grace, if you're through riling up my class, I'd like to begin."

I glare at Mr. Brown while Miranda shoots me a look of pure malice.

And the day just keeps getting worse. My social studies teacher, Mr. Reyes, asks me to stay after class. "I heard what happened and hope you're okay."

I nod, stunned to hear a kind word.

"Um, so I was wondering if, now that you understand the risks of teen drinking, you'd be willing to talk to some eighth-grade students I mentor at my church. Sort of a *what not to do* thing."

Frowning, I think about that for a moment. He wants to use me as some kind of before picture? Hell, no! I didn't do anything wrong. Zac did. "Mr. Reyes, did you ask Zac McMahon to speak to your group too?"

Mr. Reyes blinks and adjusts his tie. A dark flush creeps slowly up his face. "Um, no. He didn't—"

"Yeah. He did."

With his hands up in surrender, Mr. Reyes shakes his head. "Grace, what I mean is—"

"Yeah. I know what you mean. My answer's no." I stalk out of his class before I smack him with my way-too-heavy textbook, and somewhere deep in my belly a fire starts to smolder. To stay safe, I wait for my mom to pick me up from the safety of the main office, but even the secretaries are having a hard time not looking at me with that same level of disgust I keep seeing in everybody's eyes. I pull out my mom's phone, but there are no text messages to read, nobody to call. I put that away, take out the digital camera, and snap a few shots of the secretaries doing their thing. Maybe there's a feature Mrs. Weir, the editor, can use them for, but I don't know.

A loud sigh interrupts my boredom. "Miss Collier, could you please stop tapping that foot?"

My foot? Right. I glance down and my knees are bouncing. "Oh. Sure. Sorry." I shift positions and notice the semester abroad sign tacked to a bulletin board. Mom's been chattering about this all month. The brochure is glossy and full of color pictures of happy students wandering around famous spots across Europe.

For the serious student interested in escaping the confines of traditional study, a semester abroad immerses you in culture and language. Instead of hiding in classrooms, you'll explore museums and experience local customs, gaining a deep appreciation for the world outside your comfort zone.

It looks amazing—Rome, Paris, London. Maybe I could stay for more than a semester and not come back until graduation. I close my eyes and imagine it. Sipping cappuccino at a sidewalk trattoria, wandering around the Louvre or maybe even watching a parliament debate. I could make new friends, maybe date a boy with a sexy accent.

My stomach kinks, and I let my eyes slip shut. Date a boy? No. No way. Who'd want me now? A tsunami of regret flows through me, and Ian Russell pops into my head. I've been crushing on Ian for months. He was the only reason I went to that stupid party last month, and he didn't even show up. But the thought of dating him—even seeing him—after Zac makes me sick.

The burn in my belly gets hotter, bigger. Mrs. Reynolds, the school nurse, walks in, puts some file folders in a basket, sees me sitting on a hard plastic chair, and angles her head. "Grace, you okay?"

I shrug.

She sits next to me and peers at my brochure. "Europe, huh?"

"My mom thinks I should go until this 'blows over.'" I make finger quotes.

"And you? What do you think?"

"It sounds great."

"But?"

Another shrug. "I'd have to come home sometime."

Mrs. Reynolds pats my arm. "Hold your head up, Grace. Even when you're dying inside—especially then—hold it up." She smiles and walks out.

I consider her words. What she said echoed what Diane, the rape counselor, had said. Maybe I should go to one of those meetings, see if it helps. The brochure in my hand keeps taunting me with smiling faces and cowardly words until I finally crumple it up. No, I'm not going to Europe. I'm done avoiding people, and I am *so* done with being called names. I stare at the camera still in my hand until something in my brain goes *click*. I can reclaim everything Zac McMahon stole from me. A month ago I wanted to die. Now I have a plan. And I'm mad enough to put my plan into action.

Zac thinks it's fun to post pictures online? Fine. I'll give him pictures.

The phone in my pocket vibrates. Mom's finally here. I stride to the door and pitch the brochure in the wastebasket on my way out, head up high.

Chapter 4

Ian

Big mouths and short fuses are a bad combination.

I struggle against the iron arms of my teammates keeping me from choking Coach Brill. "You can't bench me! You're not a fucking doctor."

Sound stops. Air is sucked out of his office, out of the entire locker room, leaving the funk of sweat and wet towels to hang somewhere around nostril level. Jaws drop, and every eyeball in the place bounces from me to him and back again.

Coach Brill stands up, all six feet four inches of him. Two paws the size of dinner plates land on his desk hard enough to make pens jump. His eyes narrow, and he leans close enough for me to count the whiskers on his chin. I'm too mad, too blinded by my rage to consider all the ways this can get bad, really bad. "I *can* bench you. Know what else I can do? I can send you to Mr. Jordan's office. Know what *he* can do? Suspend you."

Suspend me? Is he fucking kidding me? "This is the last game of the season! It's a concussion, not a brain tumor."

He leans in even closer. The arms holding me back quiver. "Mr.

Russell, I don't care if it's a broken toenail. Your family doctor needs to sign off on it before you play on my team, you got that? You'll miss tomorrow's game if you shut up now. Want to sit out the All Long Island Tournament too? Keep flapping that big mouth."

Kyle Moran squeezes my arm. "Jesus, Ian, just shut up."

"Yeah," Matt Roberts adds, squeezing my other arm. "We need you."

I glare at my coach, practically breathing fire.

"We're done here. Get your butt to Mr. Jordan's office." Coach picks up his phone. "Now," he barks.

I jerk out of Kyle and Matt's grip, slam the door on my way out.

Cursing all the way to the principal's office, I throw myself into a chair and wait for Mr. Jordan to summon me into the inner office. When I get home later, I'm going to freaking kill my parents. They knew the last lacrosse game of our season was this Saturday. Was it really so hard to schedule my follow-up appointment *before* the game? My dad's always going on about giving my all to the team because it's so important to win a scholarship, and then he drops the ball.

"Ian Russell, I hear you've become a neurologist since we last spoke?" Mr. Jordan stands in the door frame, frowning at me over his glasses, beckoning me with a finger.

"Mr. Jordan, it's not fair." I leap to my feet. "I feel fine. My parents just didn't get the appointment to clear me, but they will and—"

"Mr. Russell, I understand your disappointment, but what you don't understand is that Mr. Brill is not doing this to be a pain in your you-know-what. He's following the policies that make it possible for this school to have a successful sports program that—as hard as this may be to accept—benefits all of us rather than just you. Sit down."

I roll my eyes and slide into the chair in front of Mr. Jordan's spotless desk. Rumor has it he has a pit crew standing by to scrub it down after every meeting.

"You will not play in Saturday's game. You will not play at all until you procure the required medical clearance from a qualified doctor. As for the outrageous way in which you spoke to a member of this faculty, you will not participate in next week's lacrosse camp. You will apologize to Coach Brill. And you will ride the bench during the All Long Island Tournament."

"No!" I jump to my feet. "Come on, Mr. Jordan. You can't punish the whole team for my temper."

He waves a hand at the chair I just vacated. I sit back down, mentally kicking my own ass while simultaneously trying to think up a way out of this.

"Look, I'm sorry for what I said. But the team needs me. Some of these guys are graduating. This is their last shot at a win."

"You have a point, Mr. Russell." He steeples his hands and thinks for a minute. "Tell you what I'll do. Next week is spring break, and since you're not going to be playing lacrosse with your team, perhaps you'll consider donating that week to cleaning lockers on the second floor? Cutbacks, you know." He winks.

I lean forward. Clean lockers? I'd scrub the toilets if that means I get to play. "You mean if I agree to clean lockers this week, I get to play in the tournament?"

"I think that's a fair exchange."

"Agreed. Thank you, sir."

He holds out a hand to shake. "Clean out your locker, report here tomorrow at eight a.m."

Wait, what? "Tomorrow?"

"Yes, Ian. Tomorrow's Saturday, I know. You'll work tomorrow plus Monday through Friday."

I sigh. "Fine."

I stalk to my locker, cursing and grumbling. I scare a tiny girl so badly she flattens herself against a locker as I go by. A locker I'll most likely have to empty of all its pink notebooks with little hearts in the margins and—oh, Jesus—feminine supplies and who knows what else. Not how I planned to spend my spring break. I was really looking forward to lacrosse camp, our weeklong skills-building event. The damn concussion wasn't enough punishment, I guess. When Dad hears about this, he'll probably make me clean all the windows on the house just to piss on top of shit. I'm still in trouble for denting his car.

My steps hitch. As long as I stick to the story, Dad will never know what happened.

The phone in my pocket buzzes. I pull it out, unlock it, not surprised to see who's calling me instead of texting. "Hey, Dad."

"Ian, have you lost your mind?"

I sigh. Guess Mr. Jordan has my dad on speed dial. "No. Lost my temper and already apologized. No biggie."

I can practically hear my dad's blood pressure spike. "No biggie? Cursing at your coach, the man who can write the letter of recommendation that either gets you a scholarship or doesn't, and you think this is no biggie? Jesus H. Christ."

Where does the H come from anyway? Is there some obscure gospel buried someplace under the Vatican that said Jesus had a middle name and it's Hiram or Horatio or something? Why does nobody ever swear his whole name instead of just the H? I was about seven before I figured out my name was just Ian and not Ian Alexander Russell with three exclamation points at the end.

"Ian, are you listening to me?"

"Uh, yeah, Dad." Oops.

"Way to go, son. You get to spend your entire week off scrubbing lockers instead of working on your cradling and passing skills. Oh, and by the way, your follow-up appointment *was* set for Tuesday morning, but we'll have to change it because of your inability to control your temper—again."

I don't bother reminding him of the time he slammed a door off its hinges because we ran out of milk. Or the time he dented the dishwasher because the dishes weren't clean. "Okay, Dad, I get it. I messed up. I'll clean the stupid lockers and apologize to Mr. Brill again, okay?" I stop walking when I reach my locker, fumble with the combination for a few seconds, and finally pop it open just as he starts another flip-calendar speech. Wish he'd just publish the damn things. Then we'd be rich, and I wouldn't have to risk my brain stem on the lacrosse field for a slim shot at a scholarship along with every other player on this team.

"Yeah, sure, you do that. If it were me, I'd kick you off the team. You need a good lesson in responsibility. You can't just sail through life, saying whatever the hell you want and apologizing for it later."

Oh my God, it's not like I bombed the school or something. Get a grip. "I get it, Dad."

"No, Ian, you don't. If you got it, we wouldn't always be having these conversations, would we?"

Gotta love my dad's definition of a conversation. *I talk, and you listen while I tell you you're lazy and ungrateful and will never succeed.*

"And when you get home, you're going to wash and wax my car."

At least it's not all the windows on the house. I swipe all the crap from my locker—might as well make this the first one I clean—and slam the door. "Dad, I gotta go. I'll be home in twenty minutes, and I'll get started on the car then." I end the call without waiting for his reply.

For a long moment I stare at the phone in my hands and wish I could crush it to powder, grab the keys, and just drive until I run out of road. I could work fields, bus tables, or wash cars when I need to eat or fill the tank. And when I run out of road, I could just hang on a beach, with nobody to tell me what a screwup I am, no older sisters casting their perfect little shadows over me, no raised voices in the next room complaining about my every action like I'm some supervillain with an evil plan to make my parents crazy on a daily basis.

"Yo, Russell!"

I whip my head around. Zac and Jeremy are heading my way, cleats clacking on the linoleum. Zac strides straight up to me and shoves me. "What the hell's wrong with you, man? We have a shot at the title. You already missed one game, and now you're benched. Jesus, Ian."

I hold up my hands. "I know, I know! I fucked up."

Zac rolls blue eyes toward heaven. "Fix it. Apologize. Write a damn essay or something."

I shake my head. "I tried. Jordan's got me cleaning out lockers over the break."

Zac throws a punch at a locker. I wince. I'll probably get blamed for that too. "Are you kidding me? You're gonna miss the skills camp too? Ian, I swear to God if we lose tomorrow, I'll kill you."

If we lose tomorrow's game, I'll do it myself. I know how much Zac has riding on this game. If we win tomorrow, the Laurel Point Panthers play in our first class-A championship game ever. With Zac as captain and our school's first title under his name, he'll be able to pick which scholarship to accept from a list of D-1 schools.

Jeremy clears his throat. "So, um, cleaning lockers, huh? That blows."

I nod. "Tell me about it. There's no damn air conditioning." It's been warmer than normal for April on Long Island, which is awesome if you're not me and won't be trapped indoors.

"Hi, guys!"

All three of us turn, see two giggly girls watching us from behind veils of hair. Jeremy's freckles immediately go darker, and my throat closes up. But Zac? He smiles and nods with a quick chin jerk, slicks a hand over his sweaty hair, and drops his voice low. "What's up?"

The girls giggle again and come closer. "Dance practice just ended." One says with a wave of her hand down the hall. Right. The dance squad practices in the large group instruction room. Both girls wear the same huge T-shirt with the sleeves cut out, knotted at the hip, shoulders exposed, *Laurel Point Hyperactive* written in some frenetic font across the chest. Um, not that I'm looking at their chests.

Zac scans her from head to toe. "Sorry I missed it. Bet you have some moves."

"I'm pretty good."

Her friend steps up. "I'm better."

With Zac's attention captured by the second girl, Jeremy catches my eye and grins. When it comes to women, Zac is a god, and the rest of us are mere mortals.

"We think she's lying." The second girl rushes to say, hoping to keep Zac's attention focused on her for as long as possible. I shift my weight from one foot to the other. Jeremy looks at his shoes. But Zac just grins wider. We all know who she means.

"Good to know. So what's your name?" He leans in, lifts the shirt that slid off her shoulder back into place.

"Ashley." She smiles. Her friend glares. I don't know either of them. Probably sophomores. But they sure know Zac.

"I'm Zac. This is Jeremy and Ian."

"We know," they giggle in unison.

"You're what? Juniors?"

More giggles. "No, sophomores."

Too young! I put a warning hand on Zac's shoulder, but he shrugs it off.

"I'm hungry. Let's go eat."

Zac never asks. He just announces his intentions, and girls topple like dominoes. Even sweaty from lacrosse practice, chicks can't resist his blue eyes, blond hair, and ripped body. I lean on a locker, flex a muscle. Nobody notices.

Ashley's entire body lights up with joy. The first girl looks like she's about to go thermonuclear until Zac turns back to me and Jeremy and asks if we're coming too. I'm about to say yes until I remember my dad's car is waiting for me to wash and wax it.

"Can't, man. I'm grounded. Have to report home in fifteen."

"Sucks." Jeremy offers, his eyes on the girls. I think the only reason Jeremy hangs with us is for the girls Zac casts aside. Zac likes variety, so when he moves on, Jeremy moves in. Me? I do my own hunting, but it's hard to score when girls can't take their eyes off Zac.

"Wait for us outside the locker room," he orders. The girls giggle again, take off with a squeak of tennis shoes and a few looks over their shoulders. Wish I could hear their conversation as soon as they're alone. Pretty sure Ashley is about to get bitch-slapped.

"Sweet," Jeremy comments.

Zac shrugs. "Good enough. Let's go shower. Later, man." He clasps my shoulder. "Have fun scrubbing. I'll leave you something special in my locker. Be cool, okay?" He lightly taps my cheek, and I shove him off, laughing.

"You too. Watch yourself with Ashley and her friend. They're under sixteen," I remind him.

"Relax, Russell. Just being friendly. Helps to have friends in my corner as long as the collie is barking up my ass. Later." He grins once more and heads down the corridor.

I collect my pile of locker crap and start walking. I hate that he keeps calling Grace a collie. But I keep quiet. I was late to the party that night—grounded again. Big surprise, right? By the time I got to the woods that paralleled the train station, everyone was gone—fled in panic because somebody thought he saw a police car patrolling the area.

I don't think the police patrol was true. If it were, they'd have been the ones to find Grace Collier unconscious and bleeding instead of me.

Chapter 5
Grace

A lot can change in a month.

Thirty-six days, to be exact.

Am I still Grace? Or am I what everybody says I am because I was drunk, because I believed him? I hoped Mom was right—that this would blow over.

Thirty-six days. It's not better. It's worse.

There was one bright spot. Mom let me take the car today so I wouldn't have to wait around for her to pick me up.

Every Friday after school the newspaper staff meets. A few weeks ago I was in the middle of the action, the middle of the conversation and…well, the fun. Now I'm shoved to the periphery. I can feel all the eyes in the classroom boring a hole through me, but I do what Mrs. Reynolds said. I keep my head up high.

Lindsay hasn't talked to me since Zac posted his video. Instead, she pouts and has other students or Mrs. Weir, our editor, talk to me on her behalf. Fifteen minutes ago she tried to get Alyssa to ask me something, and Alyssa said, "I'm not talking to her. You talk to her."

They went around the entire classroom like this—all five staff members refusing to speak directly to me until finally Mrs. Weir threw up her hands and said, "Grace! I'm sure you've heard the request half a dozen times by now. Can you just send Lindsay the file name, please?"

I did, but that didn't stop their antics. It just made things worse.

Now Lindsay's standing near Mrs. Weir's desk, shoulders hunched, sucking on the inside of her cheek. I can see her poor, suffering face reflected in the monitor displaying our photo-editing software. I look over my shoulder, raise an eyebrow to challenge her, and she immediately lowers her eyes. She leans down, says something to Mrs. Weir, who rubs her temples and sighs. "Lindsay, just tell Grace you need to use the computer, and I'm sure she'll move."

Lindsay shakes her head, sending her ponytail swishing.

The smell of pencil shavings and paste hangs heavy in the air. Mrs. Weir likes to do newspaper layouts the old-fashioned way. Drafts of stories in progress are tacked to a board with the pictures that will run with those stories—pictures I shot—beside them. There are six of us here today, working on the spring issue. Everybody stops what they're doing to watch Lindsay quietly stab me. With a click of my mouse, a new photo fills the screen. It's one of her I took the night of the party. Her face just falls apart—eyes fill, lips turn down. I wonder how she'd like it if this picture were plastered all over Facebook with SLUT written under it. There's a part of me just begging to do it. But I can't.

I can't be that mean.

"Mrs. Weir! She's not even doing real work." Lindsay whines in a soft, wounded voice that tells everybody she's just the poor victim in all this.

Mrs. Weir sighs again and crosses to me, saying nothing about the unflattering shot of Lindsay dancing in the woods and holding a beer. "Grace, would you please finish your work so Lindsay can use the computer?"

"Sure, Mrs. Weir." I close the photo-editing program, back up my pictures to the flash drive I've started carrying since some of my work mysteriously disappeared off the hard drive, and offer Lindsay my chair, the smile never leaving my face. She scurries over to the classroom door, where the germ-killer gel dispenser is fastened to the wall, squirts some in her hands, and then takes the chair I just used. Jonah Miller and Alyssa Martin snicker while they slice up layouts.

Mrs. Weir says nothing, and I try not to let my mind fill with revenge fantasies.

I move to the board, examine the layouts. Jonah and Alyssa scoot away. I shoot them a glare because this routine is getting stale now. I pull the school's camera out of my bag, take some shots of the expressions on their faces, and they suddenly remember they've got work to do. Lindsay's clicking on keys, and then I hear her whine again. "See, Mrs. Weir? She didn't even upload the shots she was supposed to get."

Mrs. Weir leans over Lindsay's shoulder, reviews the pictures I took of the last lacrosse game, and calls me over. "Grace? Where are the shots of Zac's last-second save?"

"Right here." I join them at the computer, lean over Lindsay to point to the folder where I saved the pictures. Lindsay recoils like I'm an acid bath she doesn't want to fall into.

"These are useless," Lindsay murmurs from the vicinity of Mrs. Weir's armpit.

I shrug.

"Grace, Lindsay's right. These pictures are blurry and too far away to be of any use."

I cross my arms. "Those are the shots I got."

"She did this on purpose," Lindsay says, and she's right. I did. Just not for the reasons she's thinking.

Mrs. Weir turns to the other students. "You all can leave for the day. You too, Lindsay. Thank you for your help."

Their eyes dance with humor that they can't hide behind their hands like the whispers that hiss at me every time I walk by. When the door closes, Mrs. Weir turns back to me. "Grace, what's going on? You were supposed to get pictures of the game, but these look like you stayed in your car and tried to shoot them with the high-powered zoom."

"That's as close as I am willing to get to Zac McMahon."

"Grace, regardless of what you think Zac McMahon did—"

"I don't *think* he did anything," I spit out before Mrs. Weir can finish her sentence.

Mrs. Weir presses her lips into a tight line and finally looks at me. "I can't take sides, Grace. And without evidence, that's what I'd be doing. The fact remains you're the photographer the school trusted with its only camera. If you won't take the pictures, give Lindsay the camera so she can take them herself. Turn off the computer and lock the door when you leave." Mrs. Weir gets up, leaves the room.

Out in the corridor Lindsay blocks my path. "I can't believe you, Grace. You knew this article was a big deal for me and totally ruined it because Zac broke up with you."

I sidestep her. "You really believe that? You really believe all of this is about a stupid breakup? Lindsay, you were there. You know what happened." But she looks away, squirms, and tugs on her ponytail. There's no hope, no point in trying to convince her. "Lindsay, believe what you want, but I can't be near Zac. You don't like the pictures I edited, go take your own."

Mrs. Weir is halfway down the hall and doesn't hear Lindsay's next round of insults. "You stole him from Miranda. You knew she liked him. Now you're making up lies because you hate that he likes her more than you! You're a whore. You'd do anybody just so they wouldn't ask Miranda out. Everybody sees what you are."

Everybody's blind. "Back off, Lindsay, or I'll hurt you," I say way too loudly.

That's when Mrs. Weir stops and turns around. "Grace, did I hear you threaten Lindsay?"

Oh my God, are you freaking kidding me? "Mrs. Weir, did you hear the things she just said to me?"

"Lindsay, go home. Grace and I need to have a chat with Mr. Jordan."

The glee on Lindsay's face breaks the leash on my temper, and I viciously kick one of the lockers behind me. Mrs. Weir strides back to me, examines the locker I left a pretty decent-sized dent in. "Okay, Miss Collier. I guess we *definitely* need to meet with Mr. Jordan now."

Sure. Why not? What's one more adult in my world telling me how wonderful Zac McMahon is and what a loser I am?

Fifteen minutes later I'm sitting in front of Mr. Jordan's desk. His office smells like coffee and Old Spice. Mr. Jordan's pretty cool, but somehow Mrs. Weir knew I'd freak out if she left me alone with him. I can see that knowledge in her eyes. Both are looking at me, wearing twin looks of disapproval. Luckily I've had plenty of practice with those looks over the past week.

I'm immune now.

"Miss Collier," Mr. Jordan takes off his glasses and pinches his nose. "I think you should take a break from the paper and hand in the camera."

No way. "Mr. Jordan, I need it for my social media project." There is no social media project. But they don't know that.

"I'm sorry, Grace. You've left me no choice. You threatened a student."

My hands tighten on my bag. I *need* this camera. It's the only hope I have left. "I defended myself from a physical attack by that student, Mr. Jordan. Mrs. Weir knows Lindsay hates me, did nothing when she called me names in her classroom, and then left us alone."

Mr. Jordan sends Mrs. Weir a questioning look, and she squirms.

"Be that as it may, there's still the little matter of damaging school property."

"Is there something else I can do? Detention. A paper. Anything. I really need the camera."

Mr. Jordan glances at Mrs. Weir and shrugs. "Well, I just got another student cleaning lockers during the break. You can work together."

To keep the camera, I'd clean the entire building with a toothbrush. "Fine, I'll do it."

"Start tomorrow. Be here at eight a.m. and report to the custodian."

"But Mr. Jordan, tomorrow's—"

He holds up a hand, cutting me off. "Saturday. Yes, Grace, I know. There are a lot of lockers. Do we have a deal?"

I sigh and nod, disgusted with the whole bunch of them. Rules, regulations, rights—what about my rights? Zac McMahon belongs behind bars. I don't care how bright he is, how high he scored on his SATs, or how many saves he makes. I stalk to the door and fling it open.

"Miss Collier?" The principal stops me. I turn around, trying not to glare. "I'm very sorry for what happened. I wish there were a way I could make this right, but I can't. You should know Zac complained to me about you. You need to stop—"

I don't care if Zac's heir to a throne. He's still a slimeball. I just barely manage to stop myself from slamming the door on my way out before he can finish that disgustingly insulting sentence, breathing fire all the way to my car. If one more person tells me to be careful about what I say about Zac, I'll lose it.

I head to the student lot, still fuming. The few students I see put their heads down, refuse to make eye contact with me. Thanks to Zac and the video he posted on Facebook, I'm the school slut, and they don't want to catch what I've got. It doesn't matter that I've never slept with any of them. It doesn't matter that I've never even dated any of them. All that matters is *Zac said Grace is a slut.* Therefore, it's fact. I don't fully understand the biology of slut germs, but apparently they infect anybody who talks to me, so nobody does. I hear the coach's whistle, the guys' hoots, and cheers from the athletic field and try not to cringe. The student lot is almost empty. My car—correction, my mom's car—is all by itself. Apparently even the car has my slut cooties.

I slow down, squint at the car.

Oh, God.

The way the sun glints off the car looks weird. Dull. I angle my head, move a little closer, and see it. Keyed into the metallic beige paint are two words in eight-inch-high letters:

LYING SLUT

Could Lindsay have done this? Jesus. The adrenaline rush from my earlier rage at Mrs. Weir and Mr. Jordan evaporates, and my shoulders drop. I unlock the car, toss my stuff inside, and start the car.

Nothing happens.

"No. No, no, no," I chant as I crank the key again. Nothing. Not even a whine. I unlock my cell, call my mom.

"Hey, Mom. I have a problem."

"Panic attack?" There's a weariness in her tone.

"Car won't start."

There's a loud sigh. "Does it try to start and won't turn over?"

"No, nothing happens at all."

"Sounds like the battery is dead. I'll call your dad for you."

"Great. Um. Thanks."

She didn't reply. She'd hung up.

I stare at my phone for a minute and then drop my head against the seat.

Ten minutes go by, then twenty. I hear laughter, loud and raw. From the side-view mirror, I watch Zac McMahon and Jeremy Linz stride to Zac's car, a black Mustang. Two girls from the dance team are already waiting near it. I slink lower in my seat, lock my doors. The Mustang starts and with a squeal of tires, leaves the lot. I watch it until it's out of sight.

I'm not afraid. I am not afraid. He's a coward, a spineless coward who smiles at you while he lies. I know what he is. I know the truth, and I am not afraid. I shut my eyes and keep repeating it.

It doesn't work.

No matter how many times I say it, I can't make my body stop shaking when I see him. Or hear his voice. Or smell his brand of soap.

At the forty-minute mark a minivan pulls into the lot, and I sigh in relief. It's my dad. But the look on his face when he gets out of the van kinks me up all over again. He taps on my window, makes a rolling gesture.

"You okay? What's wrong?"

"Won't start."

"I thought—" He presses a hand to his chest. "Okay, let me see."

He's wearing running pants and a golf shirt emblazoned with a team logo. Right. Forgot he's the coach now. I get out of the car so that we can switch places. He scans me from head to toe, his face tight. "Your mother let you wear this to school today?"

I look down at my outfit. Leggings, boots, skirt, studded cuffs. "What's wrong with it?"

He shakes his head, but I see the way his eyes lock on the scratches in the paint. "Christ, Grace, you look like a groupie for some rock band."

Funny. Everything's covered, and yet I'm still a slut.

"Do you see this?" He waves a hand at the ruined paint job. "Don't you get that you're making yourself into a target?"

I've been dressing like this since ninth grade. I cross my arms, shoot out a hip, glare at him without once calling bullshit. The only reason I'm a target is because Zac McMahon made me into one.

My dad shakes his head, climbs behind the wheel, and cranks the key. Nothing happens for him either. He tries shifting the car into neutral, still nothing. Finally he pops the hood. While he sticks his head under it, a voice whines, "Kirk! We're going to be late."

I glance at the minivan. Great, he brought the whole family. The Four K's. Kristie's in the front seat, pissed off. Keith and Kody—that's Kody with a K—are in the backseat. The boys wave, and I wave back. My dad's vicious stream of curses has me whipping around to see what's wrong.

"Your battery's not dead. It's gone. Somebody took it right out of the car. Jesus, Grace." More cursing. "Get in. I'll drop you home."

Wow. "Are you sure it's not too much trouble? Wouldn't want to make you late for Little League or T-ball."

"It's soccer, Grace. We have time if we leave right now."

Fine. I tug on the van's sliding door, climb in next to Keith and Kody, ignore Kristie's loud sigh. She flips her hair, and I get a whiff of strawberries. I wish I could cover my nose, but that would just be rude.

"We're supposed to be on the field in twenty minutes," she reminds Dad through a tight jaw.

"I am not leaving her out here alone, Kristie."

Kristie turns and stares out the passenger window.

"Hi, Grace! Look what I got!" Kody shows me an action figure I don't recognize. I take it, examine it, and look impressed.

"Wow, he's pretty cool. What does he do?"

"He's Captain America. He fights the bad guys and saves people and works with Iron Man."

Iron Man, I know. "Iron Man's awesome. Do you have him too?"

Kody shakes his blond head, a gene he got from Kristie. "No. But maybe I'll get him for my birthday!"

Perfect. I haven't bought him a gift yet, so now I've got an idea. Kody's having a big party at the end of the month. Dad and Kristie hired a petting zoo that comes right to your house with a bunch of caged animals. Kody's been revved about it for weeks.

"Grace, you could say hello to your stepmother." Dad frowns at me in the rearview mirror.

She could say hello to me too instead of staring straight ahead, pressing her lips together like she's sucking on lemons. "Hi, step-mother!" I wave in an exaggerated motion.

The boys both laugh. Kristie frowns at me in the passenger-side mirror. I'm two for two.

"Grace, are you gonna watch our soccer game? I'm good. Daddy says so, and he's the coach." Kody's eyes, the same silvery blue as mine—as our dad's—shine with excitement.

"Not as good as me," Keith shoots back. Keith favors Kristie blond hair, blue eyes.

It's funny. Zac has blond hair and blue eyes too. I don't seem to have a great track record with people who have those genes. I shake it off and laugh. "I would love—"

"Grace is busy, sport. Maybe some other time." Dad cuts me off before I can promise anything, which is a shame because I would have gone. I adore these boys. It's their parents I have issues with. Actually *they* have issues with *me*. I wonder where they play. Maybe I'll show up one day. Bet Kristie would love that. The boys chatter all the way to my house. Dad pulls into the driveway, presses the sliding door button before the van even stops.

"Here we are. Say good-bye, boys!"

"Thanks. What about my car?"

"You need a new battery. I'll pick one up after the boys' game, drop it in, leave the keys under the mat."

I smile my thanks. Kristie makes a sound of annoyance.

"Bye, Grace! See you at my birthday party!"

"Captain America couldn't keep me away," I promise before Kristie can say anything.

I slide my bag on my shoulder and walk up the drive to the front door, imagining the discussion they're going to have later over me, a nasty little part of me hoping it will be just like the last time I instigated a "discussion." *"Daddy licked Kristie's lips,"* I'd said on the car ride home from my first—and my last—dance performance. I just wanted to know if she tasted like the strawberries she always smelled like. I didn't know it was a big deal. There was a loud fight that night. He moved out the next day. I didn't see him again for almost two weeks.

People adore Kristie (except my mom). With her cardigans and pearls and perfectly smooth blond hair, nobody can believe she seduced a married man and got herself pregnant. People adore Zac too. With his blond hair and laser blue eyes and lacrosse skills, nobody can believe he assaulted me. Then there's me. With my wild dark hair, boots, skirts, and studded wristbands, I'm obviously the anti-Krist who cried rape to get even with a guy for dumping me. Everybody can believe that.

People are idiots.

I unlock the door, call out, "Mom? I'm home."

She's standing just beside the window, lips pressed together, eyes still full of betrayal, and it's been years now. "Where's the car?"

"Oh. Sorry. Didn't know you were there. It's stuck at school."

As she stares after the minivan driving away, she shakes her head. "What did Kristie have to say about being forced to help you?" she asks with a smirk.

I shift my weight and look away. "She wasn't thrilled."

Mom nods, pleased. She's been more ticked off than usual at Dad and Kristie. I know she blames him for what happened to me the night of the party, which is kind of funny because *he* blames her.

"God, you look so much like him," she whispers. It's melancholy and wistful and proud all at the same time, and I can't stand seeing her in pain, so I flee to my room, where my copy of *The Taming of the Shrew* waits. I try not to remember the woman who used to twirl me around the living room when her favorite song came on. She has the best laugh. A loud, infectious belly laugh. Some nights when I was in bed, I'd hear her giggle with my dad and laugh too. I had no idea what was so funny, but that's how it was with her. When she laughed, so did everybody around her.

Mom doesn't really giggle anymore. I don't know if that's my step-mother's fault—another Kristie Kasualty—or mine.

Chapter 6

Ian

"Hey, little man."

I crack open the one eye that's not stuck to my pillow, find my sister grinning down at me, and groan. "Go away, Val. And stop calling me that." I flip over, turn my back to her, sink back into sleep.

Valerie bounces on my bed, nearly breaking one of my ankles. I kick her off.

"Ow, Ian! Come on, get up, or the Millennium Falcon gets it."

I crack open my eye again, watch her study the models I keep on a shelf over my desk. I consider her threat for a moment. Oh, she'd do it in a heartbeat. But I was never all that happy with how that model turned out, so I close my eye and sigh.

"Ian, for God's sake, get up! You told me to wake you up early today."

Right. I did. I roll onto my back.

"Ugh, jeez, little man. There isn't enough mouthwash in the world for that morning breath."

Oh, really? I grin and sit up and say, "Hi!" right in her face. She turns an interesting shade of green and flees.

"Oh, God. Bathroom. Gonna be sick. Get up! If you're late, Dad will kill us both."

She's right. But my bed is really comfortable, and a few more minutes won't matter—

"Ian! Get your ass up."

"I'm up! I'm up. Okay. Right." I jackknife upright, eyes saucers, heart pounding.

Dad strips the covers off me.

"Downstairs. Five minutes. You were supposed to be up twenty minutes ago. And for God's sake, do something with this room. It should be condemned." He waves at my laundry pile and glares.

I climb to my feet, but a wave of dizziness tosses me right back to bed.

"Ian?" Dad's voice loses its edge. "What's wrong?" He presses a palm to my forehead.

"A little dizzy. It's okay now." I try leaving the bed for a second time and this time succeed.

"Look here." Dad turns me to face him, stares into my eyes. "You're pale. Does your head hurt?"

"Not really. Just need to wake up, and I'll be fine."

"Okay. See you downstairs." He manages a tight smile and leaves my room. I stare at the door he closes for a full minute, wondering who the hell that was.

Ten minutes later I shuffle into the kitchen, pour some cereal and a pain reliever chaser. When I look up, four sets of eyes watch me.

"Ian, your father said you felt dizzy?" My mom's wrapped in a fuzzy bathrobe, giant mug of coffee in her hands. Her hair is still bed-messy. Right. It's Saturday. Mom's off today. Valerie's in sweats, her dark hair in a ponytail, and Claudia's in a pair of pajamas with giant red lips on them.

I lunge for the newspaper sitting on the table. "I'm okay. Just a little headache."

"I want you to take it slow today. Those lockers will still be there the next day."

"He's fine, Mary." Dad waves a hand. "You ready?"

I freeze with the spoon halfway to my mouth.

"For what?"

"I'm driving you."

"I can drive myself."

"You could…if I were letting you use the car, which I'm not. So I'm driving you."

There's no point in arguing. I swallow a few more spoonfuls of my cereal, turn a few more pages, and follow him. We're both completely silent on the ride to school. It's a nice change from the lectures, so I roll with it.

"Call me when you're ready to go home."

I nod and open the car door. Before I can move, he grabs my arm.

"Ian, call me if you get dizzy again. You hear?"

"Yeah, okay."

Dad smiles. It's a real smile. Not one of his constipated or sarcastic ones. "Ian, I'm proud of you for choosing good hard work like this instead of letting down your teammates."

I shift, look away. "Um. Thanks."

"Ian?"

I turn back, wait.

"Do you know where the camera is? The good one. One that uses film?"

I shake my head. "No idea."

He presses his lips together and shakes his head. "I know we have one somewhere."

I get out of the car and watch him drive off. Weird. Very weird.

Fifteen minutes later I'm standing in the main second-floor corridor, staring at the janitorial cart with disgust.

"Just dump whatever stuff students left in their lockers in the trash bin," Bob, the janitor, instructs me.

"Books too?"

"Not textbooks. Those should go here." The janitor indicates an empty shelf on the cart. "When the locker's empty, make sure you disinfect it thoroughly. We don't want to be the cause of some outbreak."

My eyes pop, and my breakfast nearly comes up. "Yeah. Got it."

Bob looks at his watch. People still wear those things? "Your partner's late. Guess I should report that to Mr. Jordan." He shakes his head with a sigh.

I've got my head inside a locker when the squeak of canvas on linoleum catches my attention.

"Oh, here she is now," Bob states the obvious.

Oh, fuck. It's Grace Collier. I sigh and wonder what the hell I did to piss off the universe.

She sees me and halts in the middle of the corridor, one leg twitching like she's dancing except I don't see any earbuds, and those freaky silver eyes of hers stare at me like I'm holding a whip and chains. At least she's not wearing her usual Cleopatra eyeliner or black lips.

"You Grace?" Bob asks, and she nods. "You're late. I'll have to report that to Mr. Jordan."

She shrugs but says nothing, not even an apology. She slides off a heavy-looking backpack and props it across the hall. While Bob gives Grace a master key and the same locker-cleaning lesson he just gave me, I study her. She looks different. Grace usually wears a lot of black leather biker-chick stuff. But today the only thing familiar about her is the nose ring through one nostril. She's got all that wild hair tied back in an elastic, and she's wearing running pants and a baggy T-shirt that keeps falling off one shoulder. Reminds me of the dance chicks from yesterday. Wonder if Zac got lucky with both of them. I swallow a smirk. Wouldn't surprise me if he did.

"Ian? Any questions?"

Bob's tap on my shoulder gets my mind out of Zac's business. Grace is staring at me with disgust. I shake my head.

"Okay. I already unlocked the bathrooms on this floor for you. You can take an hour for lunch. That's it. Use the door near the athletic field to get back inside the building. I'll come check up on you about four o'clock."

Grace snaps on a pair of rubber gloves and adjusts her shirt and opens the locker next to the one I'm cleaning. Bob stops her. "Why don't you work on the other side?"

"No."

"Excuse me?"

"I said no."

Bob frowns at her for a moment and finally shrugs. "Okay. Fine." He disappears down the corridor, and I return to my work, spray the disinfectant inside the locker, and let it sit. It kind of smells like oranges. I use my master key on the next locker, spray it, then return to the first locker, and start wiping, scrubbing, rinsing.

The second locker has a glob of sticky, tarlike, mystery goo that I can only guess used to be gum. I grab a scraper from the cart, attack the goo, muttering curses the whole time. From the corner of my eye, I notice Grace move to my right about two lockers down. She sprays the interior but can't reach the top of it. Without her biker boots, Grace is actually shorter than me. I never noticed that before. She puts one foot inside the locker, hauls herself up to reach the top, but still can't make it.

"Here, I got it." I reach over her to wipe up the spray from the top shelf, catch her scent. Lilacs. They're my mom's favorite flower. I turn back to her with a smile, but she's three feet away, looking at me like I'm a dog foaming at the mouth. "Oh, um. Sorry. I was just trying to um, help, I guess." I hold up my hands. What the hell is her problem? You know what? I don't really care. I move back to my locker and leave her to her own business.

We work for what feels like hours, two lockers at a time, leap-frogging over each other as we make our way down the corridor. By 11:00 a.m., my head aches, and my throat feels scratchy from inhaling the disinfectant. I peel off my gloves, toss my cleaning supplies to the cart, and head down the corridor to the bathroom Bob left unlocked for us. Splashing some cold water on my face helps. By the time I get back, Grace is nowhere to be seen. I shrug. She's probably in the bathroom too. I clean two lockers, then four, but she's not back yet.

The backpack she'd put on the floor when she got here this morning is gone. If she took off, I am *so* reporting her. I go back to my work, and when I open up the next locker, I discover it's still full. I curse loudly. The echo that bounces around the deserted corridor is so satisfying that I do it again. I start removing the books—textbooks on the shelf, personal stuff in the trash bin. Then I see the owner's name written in wide bubble-shaped letters—Danielle Harrison.

Danielle's in my math class. She's been out all week. Hear it's chicken pox.

Aw, hell.

I pull her stuff out of the trash bin. I'm not dumping it now that I know it's hers. It must suck being sick during spring break—even more than cleaning out lockers. I pile all her stuff up on the corner of the cart and then spray her locker. I have to let the spray sit for a few minutes. When I move to the next locker, I bump the cart, and all of Danielle's crap hits the floor. I don't bother cursing. It's not as much fun when nobody's around to hear it. I just crouch down, start cleaning it all up.

That's when a wave of dizziness drop-kicks me. I grab my head, fall to my knees, wait for my world to stop spinning. Shutting my eyes helps me not hurl all over the clean floors. My body is convinced it's in high-speed motion. Shit, this is worse than being on that roller coaster at Six Flags.

"You okay?"

Slowly I open my eyes, relieved to find the school has stopped pitching. Grace is about four feet away, her eyebrows raised.

I shut my eyes again. "Headache. Dizzy."

I hear a zipper open. "Here."

When I open my eyes, Grace is holding out a small bottle of pain relievers. I take it gratefully, tap out two capsules, and dry-swallow them. "Thanks."

I crawl to the lockers, put my back against one, stretch out my legs, and rub my temples. Plastic rustles.

"Here. Eat something. You look sick." Grace is holding out half a sandwich to me.

I blink up at her, wondering what the catch is.

She shifts her weight to one leg and cocks her head. "For God's sake, it doesn't have cooties."

A laugh bursts out of me against my will. Grace has a seriously hot voice. It's not high-pitched and whiny like pretty much every girl I've ever met. It's...well, it's soft but *direct*. Hell, all I know is I want to keep her talking so I can listen to that voice. "Cooties? Did you make this sandwich back in second grade or something?"

I take the half from her hand, sink my teeth into it, and oh, God! I expected chick food—grilled vegetables or alfalfa sprouts or something—but it's roast beef and cheddar smothered in mayo, and I moan because it tastes amazing. "This is really good." I swipe an arm across my mouth.

"Really good for something made back in second grade or just really good in general?"

I could be seeing things, but for half a second there's a tiny bit of a smile twitching Grace Collier's lips. "It's really good, period. Thanks." I take another bite.

"Yeah." She shrugs. "No problem." After a minute she drops to the floor across from me, takes a bite out of the other half, and starts collecting all of Danielle's stuff that I had dropped.

"So what'd you do to get stuck on locker-cleaning detail?" I ask.

"Kicked one. Put a dent in it. It was either this or surrender the camera I borrowed."

"For what?"

"Um, an internship application."

"Who with?"

"*CityScape Magazine.*"

I nod. My mom gets that magazine. It's a big monthly with glossy pictures and ballsy articles. I can totally see Grace on their staff. "Writing or taking pictures?"

She shrugs. "Whatever I can get." She takes another bite of her half of the sandwich.

56

"So, um, you're not mute then." I gobble up what's left of my half.

She snorts. "There're a lot of people who wish I were." She picks up the whole pile, puts it in the trash bin.

My grin fades. Jesus, what is wrong with me? Sitting here, sharing a sandwich with the girl who almost ruined my friend's life. I crumple up the plastic wrap, toss it in the trash, and start wiping up the disinfectant from Danielle's locker. Grace stands, brushes the dirt and dust off her truly amazing ass, and moves to a locker four or five spaces away from Danielle's. I pry my eyes off her anatomical assets and reach into the bin to retrieve what Grace tossed.

"I thought we were supposed to throw out what we find?"

"We are. But this is Danielle Harrison's locker. You know her?'

She shakes her head.

"She's been out sick with chicken pox. That's why her locker's not empty. So I'm not tossing her stuff."

Grace gives me this weird look and then sprays another locker. We don't talk for the rest of the day.

Chapter 7
Grace

Ian freaking Russell. I should have asked. I should have asked who I'd have to work with.

When I woke up this morning, my mom was already out for her run. The car's still stuck at the school parking lot, so I figured I'd have to walk to school. I grabbed clothes—a pair of sweats and a ratty T-shirt—tied my hair back in a ponytail, and headed to the kitchen to pack food. It was nice this morning, already warm by 7:30. The walk to school was uneventful until a car zipped by me and my throat closed up. Panic attack. I called my mom, and she met me on Main Street at the bus stop, where I had my head between my legs, trying to breathe through the block of ice lodged in my lungs.

"Oh, baby, it's okay. I'm here. You're not alone."

When it finally stopped, we walked the rest of the way to Laurel Point High. In the parking lot we stared at the words carved into the passenger side of the car. Mom put her hands on her hips and sighed. I opened the door, found the key where Dad said he'd leave it. The car started right up.

"Do you need me to come in with you?" she asked, but I shook my head.

"No. I think I'm good now."

"Good. Grace?"

She looked ready to cry. "Mom, what's wrong?"

"I'm sorry, honey. I'm so sorry. I haven't really been there for you since all this started, have I?"

I sighed and looked away. Not just since all this started. Since Dad took off. But I shrug it off. "I'm okay, Mom. Really."

"Except for the panic attacks, you mean?" she said and smiled sadly. "What time will you be done?"

"Um, about four, I think. Not sure."

"I'm taking the car." She smiled, and I laughed. She waved and drove out of the lot.

I watched her until I couldn't see her car anymore. I wanted to chase after her, throw myself into her arms and sob, "I'm not okay, and I really don't think I ever will be." How do I tell her I'm scared of everything, every waking minute? How do I tell her I hate her and hate my dad for using what happened to me as another weapon in their favorite game, *You Suck and Here's Why*?

The ice ball bounced against my chest again, and I stared up the street. But Mom's car was gone, and I couldn't stop silently screaming for her to turn around and take me home.

Across the lot the sound of a whistle blowing jolts me from my pity party, and my head whips to the ball field. The lacrosse team is practicing. I'm at school during a weeklong vacation—just me and the lacrosse team. Just me, the boy who raped me, and a few dozen of his closest friends.

There.

I said it.

The R word.

Part of me fears I'll break into a million pieces every time I have to say that word. I back away from the grunts and shouts and sticks clashing and climb the steps, slip into the school before any of the players see me. I am supposed to meet the janitor in the second-floor west corridor at 8:00 and—Oh, crap, I'm late. I'm freaking late. I jog up the stairs and turn west and skid to a halt.

No. No, no, no!

Please let this be a mistake.

Mr. Jordan said he'd assigned locker cleanup to somebody besides me.

Oh my God, I'm cursed.

They both turn when they hear me. I look for it—the expression on their faces that matches the expression on every other face when I walk by. The expression that says, *Here comes the lying whore!*

"You Grace?" the janitor asks, and I nod. "You're late. I'll have to report that to Mr. Jordan."

Knock yourself out, pal. Principals don't scare me.

Students do.

I pay only the slightest attention to the instructions the janitor provides. I'm watching Ian Russell out of the corner of my eye. Tall and lean. Great mouth, dark hair, and dark eyes that have their own gravitational pull, Ian's easy on the eyes, but that's not all. There's something about him, something that's always been there every time I've looked at him.

I've looked at him a lot.

He's got this restlessness, this energy that practically sizzles, and I don't understand it, even though I always wanted to.

He's on the lacrosse team. Why isn't he on the field with the rest of the team? What did he do to get stuck with this job?

But none of those are the *real* questions I'm asking. I don't want to think about the real questions. But how can I not? How much did Ian *see*? How much does Ian believe? Why did he help me that night?

The janitor gives me the master key and instructions on what to put where and then points to the lockers across from Ian.

Hell no.

He's deluded if he thinks I'll turn my back on any friend of Zac McMahon's.

The janitor leaves, and I grab a pair of rubber gloves, anxious to get started. I keep Ian in my visual field, ready to defend myself if he so much as raises a hand to me, but all that dark hair hides his face. I spray a locker and can't reach the top. And suddenly Ian's right there, and my arms are too busy holding me up to fight.

"Here, I got it."

Shit. I jump so hard I hit my elbow. He mumbles some apology, but I can't hear him over the rush of panic. He backs off and returns to his own locker, and for a long moment I think about climbing inside one of the lockers—who cares if it's clean—and just hiding inside until the shift is over. Six days. How the hell am I going to get through six days of this? I take some more deep breaths and scrub the hell out of the next locker.

Ian leaves me alone, and I'm grateful. We work in tandem and in silence, moving down the corridor. It's not until Ian disappears down the hall that I look up and discover hours have passed. I grab my bag and duck out, make my way to the athletic field, where the big-shot lacrosse team is playing. Sticking to the tree line, I move fast until I'm in range of the goal.

Where Zac is.

I swallow hard and take the digital camera out of my bag. I power it on, aim, zoom in, and start clicking. The angle's wrong. The light is wrong too, but it's the best I can do. I have to get this shot.

I *have* to.

The coach blows his whistle and action halts. The players all head to the side of the field, and my heart stops. I'm trapped here. They'll see me. Zac will see me. I shove the camera back into my bag and hide behind the trees, panic snapping at my heels. I fold myself into a ball, hoping nobody notices me, nobody asks why I'm here. I crouch there for five minutes, then ten, and the coach's whistle blares. I peek around the tree. The players are in position again. I wait another minute, and then I run for it, blend in with the relatives and fans milling around the bleachers, and finally make my way back inside the school.

As soon as I'm inside, I fall against a wall and put a hand to my chest. My heart's hammering against my ribs and my throat's closing up like the aperture in my camera. I hurry up the stairs and down the corridor, duck into the girls' bathroom, and hide in a stall. Jesus! I can't do this again. I don't think I'll survive it. I get myself together again, splash water on my face, and head back to my row of lockers.

Ian's on the floor, sheet white, holding his head, surrounded by a pile of books, and I don't think twice. I run to him, almost drop my bag. He's breathing. He's okay. There's a pang in my chest, and I figure it's my heart telling me, *Enough already!* I approach him slowly. Quietly.

"You okay?"

He doesn't move. "Headache. Dizzy."

Relief rises up in me, but so does concern. Seeing Ian without his sizzle scares me, so I rummage through my bag, find a bottle of pain reliever. "Here."

He murmurs his thanks and then crawls to the lockers, puts his back up against them with a loud sigh. His color is still way too pale against his dark hair. I dive back into my bag, pull out the sandwich I made this morning, and unwrap it. "Here. Eat something. You look sick."

I offer him half, and instead of taking it, he stares at it—at me—and then it hits me. He doesn't want to catch my taint—the girl who cried rape. "For God's sake, it doesn't have cooties."

He laughs. Oh my God, Ian Russell actually laughs. And then he's talking to me and eating the sandwich I gave him, and I have to be dreaming because nobody's smiled at me without hurling insults in more than a month. I can't believe it. Words come out of my mouth. I don't even plan them. He talks, and somehow I reply. Somehow I don't shut up. I tell him about kicking a locker, and then I make up this whole lie about applying to a magazine's internship program because I don't want him to know why I *really* carry the school's camera. And it's amazing because I'm happy, I think. It's been so long since I felt happy. I'm not entirely sure, but I think that's what I am. Until Ian says something about me not being mute, and I try to be all confident and funny and self-deprecating all at the same time and say, "There're a lot of people who wish I were."

And when the light goes out of his eyes, I think, *There it is!* There's the look I was waiting for, the look that never lets me forget what I am.

Loser.

Liar.

Slut.

I want to tell him I'm not any of those things. I want the ground to swallow me alive. I want to run and hide. I want this day to end. I start throwing out the mess of locker guts Ian spilled all over the floor, but he stops me, saying something about chicken pox. When he carefully piles all the stuff back into the clean locker, I pretend I'm not watching him, not picturing him as the knight who rescued me with a white Toyota Camry. I gulp back the scream that's building up in my chest, this hideous powder keg of insistence that he—the guy who's so carefully replacing some sick student's One Direction notebook back in her locker—knows I'm not what everyone says I am, knows and isn't talking.

He ignores me the rest of the day.

Chapter 8

Ian

I head outside to hang by the door for my dad. Grace is nowhere to be seen. That's good. Real good. Don't want to see her. Shouldn't have talked to her. And she knew it. She ran out like the hounds of hell were on her heels.

Guess that's my fault. I forgot. Damn concussion. Sitting there, talking to her, looking into those bright eyes, it was so easy to forget what she did. What she said Zac did. But I remember now. I got grounded that night. The team was partying in the woods by the railroad station. I was supposed to be there at 7:30, but my dad got ticked off because there was no gas in his car and wouldn't let me out of the house. I didn't even use his car, but he didn't want to hear it. We had a big fight, and I got into more trouble for mouthing off. An hour and a half later Claudia confessed that she'd taken the car and didn't fill the tank.

And even then I still wasn't allowed to go because I had a poor attitude or some shit like that. Mom finally appeared as a witness for the defense, and just before nine o'clock I got sprung. Headed to the tracks, but by that time nobody was around. Tried texting a few people, but nobody replied. Walked into the woods, practically tripped over Grace's body sprawled next to a railroad tie, surrounded by beer bottles.

Her underwear was around her ankles.

Thought she was dead. Jesus, I was sure of it. I panicked. I shook her, shouted at her, and she moaned. I tapped her face, shook her some more. Her eyes opened, silver clouds, and then they popped wide when she focused on me. She started crying, and then she puked. She begged me to take her to the hospital. What could I do? I thought she had alcohol poisoning or something. But she said she was raped, and then everybody looked at me like I was the guy who did it.

"Zac," she said.

I almost hurled. No way. There's just no way. But the hospital called the police and her parents. Her dad showed up with some trophy wife. Then her mom arrived, and the three of them screamed and cried while Grace was processed for evidence.

I called Zac.

"She says I did what? No way, man. She came on to me. She was totally into it."

He proved it to me with that video he showed me. I guess I wasn't enough because he put it on Facebook. I can't get the image of Grace moaning and panting out of my brain. It's like thirty seconds long, but I only watched about five. Five seconds were all I could handle.

I don't have a thing for her anymore.

Zac got there first. They only went out twice, and I thought it was over. Done. No chemistry. Whatever. Thought I'd make my move since it didn't work out. But now that they did it, I can't.

Guys don't move on a friend's woman.

The cops talked to me, to Zac. To Jeremy. To Grace's friends, Lindsay and Miranda, and anybody else at the party that night. They said Grace was drunk, stumbling and sloppy drunk. Zac had his hands all over her, and she never complained. Miranda said Grace was flirting with Zac. At some point they'd disappeared together. Nobody was sure when. Everybody fled when somebody thought they'd seen a patrol car.

Except Grace.

A horn honks. I climb into the passenger seat and nod to my dad. "Hey."

"Hey." He rolls his eyes. "So how many lockers did you clean?"

"Stopped counting when I hit twenty." I yawn. "I still smell the cleaner. Stuff's foul."

"How's your head? Any dizziness?"

I hesitate a moment. "Yeah. Had a bad headache, and Grace gave me some pain reliever and half her sandwich."

"Grace who?"

Crap, why did I say her name? He's never gonna let this go now. He'll start the lecture about teen drinking and how lucky I am that he decided to ground me that night. "Collier. She got in trouble too."

"Grace Collier? Isn't that the—" He turns right on red when we reach the street.

"Yeah."

"How is she doing?"

Not the question I'm expecting. I check out his expression, and he seems concerned instead of outraged. "Um. Okay, I guess."

"You guess? You just spent the whole day with her. You didn't ask?"

No. I didn't. Because I don't want to know.

We cruise down Main Street. "Ian, did you talk to her at all?"

"Yeah, Dad, I did. I thanked her for helping me."

"That's it? You never asked how she's been doing since...since that night?"

"No, Dad, I didn't, okay? I don't talk to Grace, not after what she said about Zac."

"Ian, there are two sides to every story."

"Yeah, I know. I just don't believe hers."

We're quiet for a few blocks. Dad brakes for a red light. "You weren't there. How do you know what really happened?"

"Because I know Zac, Dad." I slink low in my seat, impatient for the light to change so I can escape. It finally turns green, and Dad turns left into our neighborhood.

"You know Tracy and Al, right?"

I nod. They're like my parents' best friends. Their daughter, Amy, is the same age as Claudia, my oldest sister.

"Years ago before you and Valerie were born, Tracy was married to somebody else. Joe. We met at the playground, hit it off, and started hanging out so the kids could play together."

Holy crap. Al's not Amy's dad? I never knew this. I stare out the passenger window, wondering how many bones I'll break if I jump out.

"One night we had just put Claudia to bed when someone starts pounding on the door. I mean pounding with fists. I grab my bat, head downstairs, open the door, and find Tracy standing there in a blood-stained nightgown."

What fresh hell is this? A new spin on the lecture series?

"I'll give you the condensed version. Joe beat his wife. For a year, one solid year, I hung out with these people. Went to their house. Had them to ours. Never saw a single hint that Joe had this kind of temper. Or that Tracy feared him in any way. Not a single clue. That's what I told the cops when Tracy had Joe arrested."

Dad pulls into our driveway, cuts the engine, opens the door. That's it? What's the point of all this?

"So what happened?"

"They let him go. And the next time it happened, Tracy needed surgery to repair the damage."

"I don't get it. Why are you telling me this?"

I follow Dad up the walk to the front door. "Just that you can't know somebody unless you live with them to tell what they're really like. Zac's your friend, and it's great that you want to be loyal to him. But you don't really know what he's capable of. So don't be so quick to judge Grace, okay? Even if it wasn't rape, that boy still left her in the woods, alone. That's got to say something to you, Ian."

I look down at my shoes. "He was scared, Dad! Everybody

freaked out when they thought the police were coming. He panicked. That's all."

Dad's quiet for a long moment. "Maybe. But I'd sure think twice before I let him date one of your sisters."

I fly upstairs to my room. I don't want to hear another word. Zac didn't rape anybody. They were just messing around. They had too much to drink, and things went too far. It happens. Grace will get over it.

I flip on my computer, check in with my crew. Jeremy's status says the team is meeting at Pizza Hut at 7:00. I grab some clothes, duck into the bathroom, and shower off the stench of disinfectant.

———

"Yo, Russell!"

I spot Jeremy's wild red hair in the middle of a group of my teammates sitting at a bunch of tables shoved together in the corner of a Pizza Hut and head over.

"What's up, man?" I high-five Kyle Moran, one of our attackers, a tall, skinny guy with a Mohawk, and drag over another chair.

"Ian, what the hell happened with Mr. Jordan?"

"You didn't hear, Kyle? Ian's scrubbing lockers," Jeremy slings an arm around my neck, rubs his knuckles over my head. I laugh and elbow him in the gut, hoping like hell nobody asks me about Grace.

I shouldn't have worried. Zac slaps Jeremy's arm away from my head. "Dude, are you mental? Concussion."

"Sorry, man." Jeremy immediately goes serious.

Our server arrives and sets a few baskets of breadsticks on our table. Conversation and laughter stop for a few seconds as we check her out. She is hot—I mean off the charts. Blond hair in a long braid down her back, tight T-shirt showing off some very nice assets, and a smile that's a little shy, a little sexy. Her name tag says she's Addie. Jeremy's jaw practically smacks the table. Kyle's eyes dart right to her tits. And Zac's running his hand over his hair, messing it up the way chicks seem to like it.

When she walks away, ass wiggling just right, our table erupts in a series of groans, sighs, and an *Mmmm* from Jeremy.

"Back off, boys. That girl is mine." Zac stares after her and grins.

"No way, McMahon." Kyle shakes his head, the points of his Mohawk blurring. "Up for grabs," he says and lunges for a breadstick.

"I wouldn't mind grabbing some of that," Jeremy says and squeezes the air to demonstrate.

"Like you have even half a shot," Kyle retorts.

"And you do?" I ask.

"Boys, that's a real woman, not CGI. You wouldn't know what to do with her without a console." Zac shakes his head, amused.

Kyle's laugh booms across the restaurant. "Bet she likes my joystick!"

"That's what she said," Jeremy says and snickers. Jeremy's still stuck at age thirteen.

"Dude, the key to scoring with a chick like that is to show her what you can do for her—not *to* her."

A chorus of laughs rises up like a wave. "Oh, class is in session, guys!

Professor McMahon is gonna school us!" Matt Roberts shouts from the other end of the table and pulls out his wallet. "Twenty says you don't even get a phone number." He slaps a bill to the center of the table next to the breadsticks in a tiny puddle of moisture from the pitchers of soda.

There's a split second of hopeful glances, and then everybody's pulling out money, with three betting against Zac. Not me.

I never bet against Zac.

"Okay, here are the rules." Matt leans in. "All you have to do is get her to make a date with you."

Zac scoffs. "Please."

"Here she comes. Here she comes." Jeremy shushes us as Addie and another server approach our group loaded down with trays of deep-dish supremes and stuffed crust. The other server, a curvy brunette, locks eyes with me. Zac leans back in his chair, angles his body toward Addie, cocks his head, and pins on the smile—the one that says, "I know what you like, and I can give it to you."

Trust me, it works.

Addie ignores him.

Undaunted, Zac tilts his head to…read her name tag. I roll my eyes. "Addie. What's that short for?"

She looks down at him, doesn't smile. "Addison."

"Pretty."

Now she smiles. Here we go.

"So, pretty Addison, how old are you?"

"Old enough."

Jeremy's *Whoa* is quickly shushed by an elbow from Kyle. Zac leans forward, puts his hand on Addie's back, rubs it up and down. She doesn't slap him away, so I figure he's in.

"Me and my guys are celebrating. Our lacrosse team went undefeated this season. The title game's next and after that, tournament. It's kind of like an all-star game, and…well, I got picked."

I try not to snort at his false modesty. Everybody at the table was picked.

"So why don't you help us celebrate?"

"Sure. Few more pitchers of soda?" she asks sweetly, and I wonder if Zac realizes he's just been asked how old *he* is.

"Not what I had in mind." He stands slowly, his hand still rubbing her back, eyes never leaving her face. "I was thinking you…me…a nice quiet drive over to the beach…watch the sunrise."

Oh my God, it's like watching a magician at work. Zac's tall—about six-foot-two. When he stands, Addie has to tilt her head back to maintain eye contact, unaware that he's totally invaded her personal space and is close enough to kiss her. Genius.

"Um. That sounds nice."

"Is that a yes?" Zac presses, and the entire table holds its breath.

"Uh. I'll think about it."

And the entire table exhales.

Zac leans closer, whispers something in Addie's ear that has her blushing and smiling and nodding. When she walks away, Jeremy is the first to crack. "Come on, bro! What'd she say?"

Zac kicks back, hooks his hands behind his head. "You heard her. She's thinking about it."

"Well, what did you say?"

Zac grabs a slice of deep-dish and just shakes his head. "Okay, Russell, let's see if you can do better." He jerks his chin toward the other server helping Addie. Was kind of hoping nobody noticed the way she looked at me. But I nod, clear my throat, smooth my hair, and stand up. She's over at the salad bar now, wiping up the pieces of lettuce and bacon bits and crap that tried to escape their bowls.

"Hey," I say and smile.

She looks up, looks away, smiles at the vats of dressing and mutters a "Hey" back.

"What's your name?"

The girl, a tall brunette with braided hair, laughs once. "Not Addie."

I hold out a hand. "Hi, Not Addie, I'm Ian. Nice to meet you."

She laughs again but for real. "Very funny." She turns to look at me full on. "Okay. My name's Jessica. But you can call me Jess."

"Nice. You still have to call me Ian." I move a step closer. "I've only got three letters, but I guess you could call me E."

She flashes me a wicked smile. "So what's the bet?"

I blink innocently. "What bet?"

With a smirk, she wipes up a salad dressing spill. "Oh, come on. I know there's a bet. What do you have to do?"

Busted. With a sigh, I come clean. "Get your phone number. It would really help if I got yours before he gets Addie's." I toss my head in Zac's direction.

"Done." She takes a pen out of the pocket of the apron tied around her hips, grabs my hand, scrawls a number across my arm.

I raise my arms in a *score* gesture, and the guys at the table go wild. "Thanks, Jess."

"You're welcome. You can also call me. That number's real." She flicks her cloth at me, grins, and walks into the kitchen.

I return to the table, a pro among mere minor leaguers. And we stuff ourselves with pizza, breadsticks, and soda. Halfway through the meal somebody smacks the back of my head.

"Hey, little man. Staying out of trouble?"

I whip around, ready to freaking strangle my sister, while the entire table hoots with laughter. She just ruined my life with that damn nickname. "Go away, Val."

Matt's eyebrows go up, and he says something to the guy next to him who answers, "Sister." Matt's smile widens. "Pull up a chair. Hang with us."

Valerie gives us her best *Yeah, right* expression. "Uh. No."

Thank God.

"Go away, Val," I repeat.

Zac holds up his hand. "Ian. You should be nice to your sister. She's beautiful, funny, and just watching out for you." I stare at Zac, but he's not looking at me. He's looking at my sister. There's a gleam in his eye—the same gleam that tells me he thinks she's hot.

My mouth falls open. Oh my God, Zac doesn't just think she's hot. He's trying to charm my sister. She smiles at him—a real smile, not one of those irritating smirks she saves up for me.

"That's right. Listen to your friend, Ian."

Jesus, I'm in a parallel universe.

Zac stands up. "Here. Sit and eat with us. I can get another chair." He flashes the smile, and I shove my pizza away.

Valerie holds up her hands and shakes her head. "Can't. Just meeting some friends and we're off. I saw Ian and had to say hi." She leans over, plants a noisy kiss on my cheek, and I want to tear the long hair from her head strand by strand.

"Got one for me?" Zac holds out his arms. Valerie walks right into them and kisses his cheek. Jesus. I can't believe she fell for that ploy. I shake my head and see Addie watching the drama with a sad, shocked look on her face.

"Zac." I clear my throat. "Addie's watching."

The grin flees, and Zac steps away from my sister, reclaiming his seat. "Good to see you, Valerie. Say hi to your parents."

"Sure thing. Later, little man." She winks at me.

I swear I will get her for this. I don't know how, and I don't know when. But I *will* get her.

Everybody watches Val walk to another table, where her friends are waiting—Cassie and Gina. I've met them a few times. They're pretty cool and don't treat me like a pimple on the ass the way Val does.

"Dude. Your sister is smokin'," Jeremy says with a whistle.

"And off limits." I remind everybody at the table.

Including Zac. Or maybe especially Zac.

We eat like zoo animals, talk trash about the team that placed second, and avoid all talk of Grace Collier. When the bill arrives, Kyle grabs it. "Son of a bitch."

"What?"

"He did it. He fucking did it." Kyle shows us the bill.

Addie's phone number is written across the top. I grin as I pocket my winnings. Maybe with Addie's number handy, Zac will stay away from my sister.

Chapter 9
Grace

Monday morning.

Again.

The days just run into each other—water down a sewer.

I drag myself out of bed. I'm in no hurry to get to school to serve my self-imposed sentence. In no hurry to see Ian. I thought it was bad seeing that look on my friends' faces. And on my parents'.

But seeing it on Ian's? Oh, God, it was like a fist to my stomach. He was there! He saw me, took me to the hospital when I woke up, bleeding and sick. How could he believe that was consensual? The answer dances inside my brain, but I refuse to let it lead. I know he's Zac's friend and teammate. I know they have their little guy code, that whole *bros before hos* thing. I know it and yet—

I stop the thought spiral that's only going to bring me to the bottom of a box of tissues and straighten my shoulders, hold up my head. I will not cower. I won't back off. And I damn well won't let Ian Russell know how much he hurt me.

I pull crap from my closet. A T-shirt, comfortable yoga pants—

both are black—and stare at my favorite pair of black boots. I wish I could wear them, but not sure they can resist the heavy-duty cleaning supplies I have to use. The Bride is always offering to take me shopping at places that sell twinsets and flowy skirts because my dad hates how I dress and she wants to show him how cool she's being to me. Kristie doesn't know this, but I might have liked those things if she wasn't in the frame. My dad can't keep it zipped, so now she's family. That doesn't mean I have to like it or her.

Instead of the wrist gauntlets I love, I fasten a studded cuff. I apply some anti-frizz serum to my hair—not that it does any good—but at least my hair doesn't sound like I'm sanding down a hunk of wood. I leave it loose and do my makeup in my usual way. I stare at the mirror and feel better about looking how I usually look. Ten minutes later with food and my borrowed camera tucked into my bag, I'm ready to rock.

"Mom?" I find her in the basement, feeding clothes into the dryer. "Can you take me to school?"

She glances at me and then her watch. "Yeah, I was just about to leave for work." She makes no comment on my clothes.

"No run today?"

She grins fiercely. "Already did four miles."

Jeez. She always wants me to run with her, but I strongly believe if God had intended man—or woman—to jog, he'd have scaled way back on breast size and sent some of that padding to the soles of our feet. Just sayin'.

We hop in the car and head to the school. The radio's pumping out the hard rock I like and Mom hates. "What time should I pick you up?"

"We're done at four."

Mom winces. "I work until five. Can you get a ride from a friend?"

"Sure, if I had any." I roll my eyes. Lindsay and Miranda still haven't talked to me.

"Still mad?"

With a sigh, I cross my arms. "I'm not mad. They are."

She turns into the parking lot, pressing her lips together. "Did you try apologizing?"

I turn my head just far enough to glare at her. "I was assaulted, Mom. You think *I* should apologize?"

She blows out a loud sigh and shakes her head. "No, of course not. But you did get drunk and flirted with the boy Miranda likes right under her nose. You should apologize at least for that because God knows you could use a friend."

"No, Mom. I got drunk and shot down the boy Miranda likes. Only he didn't stay down, did he?" I shove through the door before the car stops and slam it to cut her off.

I stalk down the main corridor that's blessedly cool, though the weather outdoors is sunny and warm, my face tight and my hands clenched. Ian's already here. He glances my way when he hears my footsteps. There's a second, a flash of interest in his eyes when he sees me. And then it's like he suddenly remembers he's not supposed to be interested in me.

"Hey," he says with a chin jerk.

I don't bother replying. I stow my bag at the bottom of the utility cart and whip a pair of rubber gloves out of the box, snap them on. Ian's watching me, but I don't look at him. I don't need to. I know exactly how his hair falls into his dark eyes and how he sucks in a cheek when he's thinking hard about something. I know he's got a tiny scar on his left hand with straight edges—likely from a knife or other sharp tool. I know that if I stand directly in front of him, close enough to touch, his lips would be perfectly aligned to my forehead. Oh, God, what would those lips feel like if he kissed me there?

I slam the door to the locker I just scrubbed, imagining Ian's face caught inside.

"Bad day?"

He speaks! I deliberately straighten my shoulders and slowly stand to face him. In sneakers, I am exactly tall enough for the forehead kiss scenario, and I clench, willing it out of my head. "It's a day. It's not good. It's not bad. It's just another day of locker cleaning."

His lips curl in a smirk, and he holds up both hands, surrender-style. "Okay, okay. Don't bite my head off. I was just making conversation."

"Oh, conversation, is that it? Really?" I shoot out a hip, put my hand on it, and wave the other for him to continue. "How does that go again?"

"Um, I say something, and then you say something back."

"Right, right. Not like Saturday, when you just shut down, shut up, and turned your back on me. Hate to break the news to you, but I'm not going anywhere. Fucking deal with it."

Instead of rolling his eyes, flipping me off, or just walking away, Ian does something I never expected.

He smiles.

And it's a real smile, not one of those cocky grins every member of the lacrosse team learns on their first day of practice. A real smile that reveals perfectly straight teeth, though one is a few shades darker than the others. I wonder why.

I'm so blinded by the smile that I almost don't notice the step closer he takes. He's in front of me—I mean *right* in front of me—and I have to wrestle my gaze off his mouth, which is now only a few inches away from my forehead. I'm seconds away from sobbing. Or bursting into flames, I'm not sure. Ian hunches down, so we're eye level, and I can breathe again.

"I deserved that, didn't I? Look, I messed up, and I'm sorry. It's… well, yeah." He takes a step back, rakes a hand through his hair, trying to find his words. "Zac's my friend, Grace. I'm sorry."

"Sorry he's your friend?"

He makes a sound of annoyance. "No. Sorry I hurt your feelings."

I stand up straighter. "Me and my feelings are fine."

"So's the rest of you."

Did he just really say that? It was low, almost a whisper, and I'm pretty sure he did. I stare at him, jaw dangling, waiting for something, anything, just a little bit more, but he just nods once and reaches for a pair of gloves.

The question-and-answer portion of our day is apparently over.

We work on groups of six lockers each. Spray each, let the cleanser work through whatever muck and mire ninth-graders have spread inside them, and try not to breathe. When we hit the sixth locker, we go back to the first, scrub it out. Repeat. Repeat...and repeat. I look down the long corridor lined with lockers and wonder if this week will ever end.

By the time I've scrubbed my twentieth locker—I am totally counting—Ian's dragging.

I'm not.

I keep scrubbing and spraying and spraying and scrubbing. Good for me. After another twenty lockers I look up, but Ian's striding down the hall, long legs eating up the yards without a single squeak on the waxed linoleum. A moment later I hear the door to the boys' room squeak open, then bang closed.

I press my lips together and think about it for three seconds and then head for the athletic field with my bag. If Ian says anything about my absence, I'll lie and say I went out to grab food. As soon as I push open the door, my stomach ties itself into a knot. I force my feet to move ahead, repeating the path I took Saturday so nobody catches me.

But one glance at the field and I groan out loud. This is never going to work. Coach Brill has the boys doing skill-builders—drills the players do in pairs. Way too many of them are sitting or standing on the sidelines, watching. There's a heavy weight spinning inside me, a sickness that leaves a sour taste on the back of my tongue. I have a mission. I can't fail. It's all I have left, and I can't fail.

While I stand there with my thumb in my mouth, trying to figure out what to do, Zac McMahon turns and nearly catches me, but I duck behind a shrub before he can. I watch for another minute and finally give it up. Cursing, I hurry back inside the school and into my corridor, where the fumes of disinfectant are practically visible.

Ian's still not there. The sounds of my feet slapping the floor echo in the empty building, and a sick, twisted part of me warns me with a cackle that I'd better get used to it since nobody wants to hang with me anymore.

I pass the boys' room and then halt. What if Ian's head is hurting again today? He could be in trouble. Passed out from the fumes. I push the door open slowly, relaxing when I hear his voice.

I hear the beep indicating he just ended a cell phone call and know I'm about to get caught if I don't do something big to divert attention. I pound my fist on the door, trying to make it look like I only now just opened it. "Ian, you okay?"

"Fine." He joins me at the door. His face is colorless, and his eyes are flat. When I don't move out of his way, he waves his hands. "What? If you gotta go, you're in the wrong place."

"Just wondered if your headache came back. You don't look so hot."

He grins, clutches his chest, and staggers. "Hit me where it hurts."

"Seriously. You're pale and sluggish."

His grin slides away and he pushes past me. "I said I'm fine."

I watch him head back to our section of lockers, only a little distracted by the sight of Ian's butt in jeans. I don't know if it was the phone call or his headache is back or if his hamster died, but I do know this. Ian is anything but fine, and there's not a damn thing I can do about it.

———————

I quietly rejoin Ian, and soon we have our rhythm going again. Spray, spray, wait, wait, scrub, scrub, move. When he gets too close to me, there's this scent that's almost buried under the disinfectant but not quite. When it sneaks through, it makes me want to close my eyes and sigh. I don't know why. Maybe it's all that messy brown hair or his wide dark eyes. But there's something about Ian Russell that makes me think of chocolate. Smooth, rich, melt-on-your-tongue chocolate.

And every time I think about closing my eyes and sighing, Zac's face swims into focus. And instead of Ian's chocolate scent, I smell Zac's. It's sweaty and sour, and vomit burns at the back of my throat.

I slam a locker in frustration, feel Ian's eyes bore into me.

"So what's with the getup?"

I go still. *Getup?* With a loud sigh, I turn, stare him down. "Got a problem with the way I look?"

Melted chocolate eyes travel up and down my body, and he slowly shakes his head. "Not with the way you look, just the way you dress."

"Let me guess. My skirt too short for you?"

Ian's eyes go wide, and then he laughs. A real laugh, a from-the-belly laugh. I force the scowl to remain on my face because I don't understand this. Is he laughing *at* me or *with* me, and is there even a difference?

"No complaints from me on short skirts," he says, the smile crinkling the corners of his eyes. "I'm just saying you don't need the costume. You already look good."

I don't know what he thinks he's doing, but I'm not falling for it. "Thanks, but I'm not trying to impress you. This is how I dress."

The smile freezes, then slowly melts away. "My mistake."

Our heads whip around when the door slams on the level below us. The thwack of flip-flops climbing the steps announces visitors—female visitors. I suck in a deep breath because I already know who it is before they're in sight.

Miranda and Lindsay.

My ex–best friends.

Miranda struts down the hall, sleek blond hair flowing down her back like poured gold, makeup perfect. She's wearing Laurel Point HS sweats with the waistband folded down to show off her navel piercing and a skimpy tank top that reveals bright aqua bra straps. Lindsay trails behind her, tucking soft brown hair behind her ears over and over in a gesture that says, "I'm so sweet," and I try not to gag. I didn't do a thing to either of them, but they hate me. Miranda hates me directly, but Lindsay's hatred is more *indirect*.

No less deadly though.

I brace for combat, but the girls walk right by me and up to Ian.

"Hey, Ian," Miranda purrs. "Heard you got stuck with sanitation detail. Hope you don't pick up anything," she adds with a sneer in my direction.

I spray another locker, noting Lindsay's hanging back.

"Hey." He nods once but doesn't laugh at her insult. Points for him.

"So listen. We're all meeting at my place tonight after lacrosse camp ends. You in?"

He shrugs. "I guess."

"Awesome! See you later." Miranda flips her hair around just as I spray another locker.

She whirls on me, flings her hands up to hair and shrieks. "You did that on purpose. You got cleanser in my hair."

I force my face not to wince at the shrill note her voice hits. "Uh, no. You got your hair in my cleanser. You really should be more careful. You never know what might happen," I shoot back. Miranda nearly goes thermonuclear.

"You bitch!" She advances, and I drop my rags and spray bottle, ready to defend myself if she so much as scratches me with a French-tipped nail. I try not to sigh when she goes for the shove instead.

Weak.

With my feet planted, I can't be moved, so she sort of bounces off me. Naturally that's my fault too.

"Whore!" She comes at me again, tries to grab my hair. I dodge and move out of reach.

"Go home, Miranda. I don't have time for you."

Lindsay finally emerges from her paralytic stupor and tries to control Miranda. "Come on, Mir. Let's just go. It's not worth it." She does that hair-tuck thing again.

Miranda's wild-eyed rage fades a little. "You're right. It's not. She's not worth it. Skank." She wrinkles her nose at me, and I can't resist another jab.

"Who should I send the car repair bill to, Miranda? You or Lindsay?"

Miranda reacts predictably, struggles out of Lindsay's arms, and comes at me, claws extended. I try to remember everything I learned from my dad. Plant my feet, angle my body, protect my face. Okay. I can do this. When she reaches me, I catch the first flailing arm, twist it behind her back, and pin her face-first against a locker. If I've done this right, I'm not really hurting her, just restraining her. I lean in, speak directly into her ear.

"Now, you listen to me. I didn't ask for this. I'm sorry you think I stole Zac, but you were there, Mir. You know what happened, and you know I'm not lying. If you can't deal, that's your problem, not mine, so stay out of my face, and I'll stay out of yours." Still holding her arm behind her back, I shove her toward Lindsay.

Lindsay's staring at me in horror. Ian's staring at me in what looks like awe, and Miranda's staring at me with hate in her eyes.

That's the one that gets me. I turn away, grab my cleanser, and pretend none of this cuts me.

"No. No. Let's just go." Lindsay's guiding Miranda, but Miranda's still rubbing the arm I twisted.

"You bitch! You got everything you deserved. Even your own father knows it."

I flinch at that. I don't know if it's the words or the venom that laced them or the fact that they fell out of my best friend's mouth, but I swear I'm bleeding. I raise my head. I won't run. I won't let her see the blood.

"Okay, okay, that's enough. Get out of here, Miranda. We have work to do." Ian takes her by the shoulders, turns her around, walks with her partway down the hall.

"Ian, she's a slut. How can you stand to be near her? You might catch an STD."

"I'll be fine. Just go."

Mercifully they listen to him. Flip-flops slapping the floor, they shoot me glares over their shoulders, shouting out the words I hear in my sleep. "Whore!"

"Slut!"

"Skank!"

I am immune now.

I watch until they're gone. Until the steel door clangs shut. Until Ian picks up his bottle of cleanser and hands it to me.

Another locker waits for me.

Chapter 10

Ian

"Yo, man, heard you had front row seats to a catfight before." Jeremy's grin is diabolical. "Man, I wish I'd seen it."

I shift in my seat, reach for another onion ring. We're sitting at the front of a Burger King, four guys sweaty from lacrosse practice and me sweaty from manual labor.

"Shit, man, you smell like Orange Crush." Matt makes a face and leans away from me. I throw a wadded-up napkin at him.

"Yeah, well, trust me, smelling like oranges is better than what that shit smells like fresh out of the can."

"I think it's sexy." Zac wiggles his eyebrows, and beside him, Kyle laughs. I flip them both off and pop another ring into my mouth.

"Seriously, man, what the hell happened? Did Collier really whip out a switchblade?"

The Coke in my hand jerks, sloshing against the plastic lid. "What? No! Where the hell did you hear that?"

"Well, what did happen?"

Four pairs of eyes swing my way, and I just grin, sip my Coke, and let them twist until Matt kicks me under the table. "Okay, okay. Look, it was nothing. Miranda got all up in Grace's grill, and Grace got her in a chicken-wing hold."

The table erupts in sounds of awe until Zac cuts everybody off with a fist pounded on the table. "Grace likes it rough." He grins. I don't know why, but that makes my teeth clench.

"What's she starting trouble for?"

Grace didn't start anything. Miranda did. But gotta admit it. Grace likes to challenge you, to get you to hear her, to get you to—

"Russell!" My chair gets kicked again, and I jolt back to here and now.

"Sorry, what?"

"I said, what happened next?"

"Oh. Uh, Grace told Miranda she didn't steal Zac away from her."

This time the table erupts in a synchronized "Ooooo!" Zac's eyebrows wing up. "Wait, Miranda's got a thing for me? Well, this is interesting."

This is not news. "Like you didn't notice." Kyle rolls his eyes.

Zac lifts a shoulder. "Miranda flirts with damn near anything with a Y chromosome."

"Not me, and I have a Y chromosome," Jeremy says.

"No, you don't," Matt retorts, earning a fry tossed at his face.

A cell phone chirps, and Zac tugs his out of his pocket, scans a text message. "Speak of the devil," he says with an evil grin. "Miranda wants to know if we want to party at her house now. You guys in?"

I roll my eyes. I will never understand girls. Miranda said there was a party at her place tonight but doesn't actually invite anybody? What the hell?

Kyle, Matt, and Jeremy are all nodding their heads. The look on her face while she screamed insults at Grace earlier today swims into focus, and I would rather submit to another of my dad's flip-calendar lectures than spend time with Miranda Hollis.

"Russell, you in or what?"

"Yeah, I guess."

———————

Thirty minutes later we're hanging in the finished basement of the Hollis house, a big house with red shutters within walking distance of school. The room is a huge L-shaped man cave. There's a fifty-inch flat screen TV bolted to one wall, fancy surround sound system in a rack next to it, a soft brown L-shaped couch facing it. Behind the part of the couch that's not against the wall, there's a pool table—a real pool table. Behind that, a dartboard hangs on a wall lined in cork, facing a framed picture of Kramer from *Seinfeld* on the opposite wall. A bar with two stools is tucked into the short end of the L. In a corner near a treadmill and an elliptical machine, there's a square table with a chessboard top, game pieces already set up in case somebody feels up to a game.

I don't.

The room smells like new carpet and mildew and a hint of bleach. I look around and figure the door near the bar is where the washer and dryer must be. Matt and Kyle flop onto the couch, trip the recliner mechanism, and kick back. Zac and Jeremy grab pool cues. Lindsay's standing awkwardly near the bar, where Miranda's setting up ice and cans of cola.

"No beer?"

"My parents are home," Miranda says. She smiles coyly at Zac and throws a cautious glance up the stairs because naturally they could hear us.

"Lame, Hollis."

The smile evaporates.

"Miranda, heard Collier kicked your ass today!" Jeremy taunts and then sets up his opening break. The clack of balls echoes in the large room.

"She wishes." Miranda's face goes hard. She pops the top on a can of Coke, sips lightly, and dabs at her gloss-covered lips. She showered and dressed for the occasion. She's wearing a miniskirt with dark tights my sister, Val, would love. Her belly ring is showing, and Zac's eyes keep zeroing in on it. "She came after me, sprayed that locker cleaner in my face."

I angle my head and stare at her with wide eyes. Is she freakin' serious? "Uh. No. She didn't. You got in her face and whipped your hair into the locker she'd already sprayed down."

Miranda sends me a look that screams, "What the hell are you doing?" but I ignore it.

She turns back to Zac and pouts. "She's such a bitch."

"Aww." Zac runs a hand down Miranda's poor, mistreated hair, and she practically drops at his feet. Zac catches my eye, gives me the signal. He wants to move on Miranda. That's fine. But he wants me to move on Lindsay.

That's not so fine.

Lindsay's a sweet, quiet girl, the type to push glasses up her nose as she peers at you over the top. I glance at her, standing alone like that's actually her intent and purpose.

I grab a can of cola and head for the sofa. I'm not in the mood for pool or darts, and Miranda's whiny voice is grating on me. I grab the remote control to the big-ass TV on the wall and flip it on without permission. I scroll through the channel guide and settle on *UFC Unleashed* on Spike and kick back with my Coke.

"Ugh!" Miranda pulls a face. "How can you guys watch this?"

"Russell." Zac's tone holds a warning note.

"What? MMA is awesome." I defend my programming choice. "Got any popcorn or something?"

I know I'm being a dick, but I don't care. I stare at Miranda's perfect makeup and wonder how much she dropped on the latest color collection from Sephora. My sisters have spent entire paychecks there for the promise of hiding some flaw only they can see. But Miranda's shiny lips and smudgy eyes—no, I think the right term is smoky or whatever—don't hide the streak of mean that runs in her like a second aorta.

I turn back to the big-ass screen and watch the challenger execute a perfect Superman move. My mind flashes back to Grace pinning Miranda's arm behind her back. Oh, yeah. I can totally picture Grace in the Octagon. I glance at Miranda, imagine Grace smearing the lip gloss off that face. She'd kick ass. She'd *wreck* her.

Totally.

I grin at the image and swallow more Coke, and Miranda tosses a bag of chips on the table in front of me. I don't bother thanking her. I munch and sip while Jeremy sinks stripes. Zac looks bored. Miranda looks pissed, and Lindsay's still standing off to the side like she just fell out of the sky into that exact spot. I take pity on her, lean over, and talk to Matt.

"Dude, say something to Lindsay, will you? Zac needs a wingman, and I'm not into it."

Matt glances over at her and curses under his breath. "Aw, hell." He pins on a smile and calls out. "Hey, Lindsay! Sit here and watch this dude get pummeled."

Lindsay manages to look grateful and disgusted at the same time. Hell of a skill. But she moves to sit between Matt and me. That leaves Zac free to move on Miranda.

I watch the guy on TV tap out, and then another fight starts… and then another. Matt and Lindsay start making out next to me. His hand's under her shirt, and she keeps making little *mhmm* sounds. Miranda's sitting on top of the bar, arms and legs wrapped around Zac, his mouth busy on hers. Jeremy's leaning on a pool cue, watching like it's Pay-Per-View, hoping he'll get a glimpse of a tit.

I need to leave before I puke. I head for the stairs, smack Kyle on my way, jerk my head to the door, but he shakes his head. His eyes are glued to Matt and Lindsay, who went horizontal as soon as I gave them space. Kyle inches closer, and when he closes his hand over one of Lindsay's tits, I can't stand it. I have to leave.

Now.

Outside in the cold darkness I can breathe again. I start walking, hear something, whip around to find out what, but the street's deserted. Imagination's working overtime, I guess. I take another step, and this time I see a shadow running from the side of Miranda's house.

"Hey!"

The shadow freezes for a moment, then whips around, long hair flying. I walk toward the shadow, but after two steps it flees.

It's Grace. I know it is.

———

By the time I get home—I had to walk—it's almost 11:00 p.m., and I'm wiped out. I want a shower and food and bed. Just as I turn up the front walk, a car pulls up to the curb.

"Hey, little man!"

Perfect, I groan but turn to wait for my sister. "Hey."

Valerie tilts her head and studies me. "Bad night?" Because she actually sounds curious instead of judgmental, I nod.

"Wanna talk about it?"

Hell, no.

Well, maybe. I really want to know if all girls are like Lindsay and Miranda. But Val's a girl. If she's like that, I do *not* want to know.

"Um."

"Come on." Val pats the side of the car. "Pull up a bumper."

I think about it for a second, finally shrug, and lean beside her against the Honda Accord my dad got her when she started college.

"Let me ask you something." I shove my hands into the pockets of my jeans, wishing I had a script or something to work from. "Why do girls make out with guys they're not going out with?"

Val sucks in a deep breath. "Somebody made out with you?"

"No, no. Not me. My friends. We were in this girl's basement. Five of us. Two girls."

"Ah." Val nods.

"Ah?" What? Is this actually a thing? "What does that mean?"

"It means some girls are desperate. Sounds like you found two."

"Desperate? No. I mean, I don't think so. Do you know Miranda Hollis or Lindsay Warren?"

When Val shakes her head, I continue, "Well, they're in my grade. They're both pretty. Actually Miranda's hot. She could be with anybody she wants. So why—"

"Who was she sucking face with?"

I grimace. I'm pretty sure I throw up a little. "Jesus, Val."

"Who, Ian?"

"With Zac."

She nods like she already knew the answer.

"Let me guess. Zac isn't her boyfriend, is he?"

"No."

"There you go. Miranda's hoping he will be."

I shake my head. "He won't be."

Val nudges me with her shoulder. "Do you have a thing for this Miranda chick?"

"No. Definitely not."

"Okay, so no jealousy. So why do you care?"

I don't care.

Do I?

Shit, I have no idea what's up with me.

"Okay, look. We're in Miranda's basement. Me, Zac, Jeremy, Matt, Kyle, and Lindsay. Lindsay's all shy and standing by herself, so I tell Matt to talk to her. Next thing I know, they're making out on the couch next to me, and Zac and Miranda are going at it across the room. Jeremy's standing in a puddle of drool seconds away from a little manual labor—"

"Yeah, I get it, Ian."

"Sorry. I figure it's time to give them some alone time, you know? So I get up, tap Kyle to leave with me. Instead, he, um...well, joins in."

"Let me guess. She lets him."

"Exactly! Why would anybody do that? Lindsay's not dating either of them. I don't think they even like each other that much. I mean, they used to be friends with Grace Collier, and now they say she's a slut. But then they do shit like this. Why?"

"I see."

I wait for Valerie to tell me what she sees, but she just stands there, staring down the street at nothing in particular. "Is Lindsay your friend?" she asks abruptly, and I shrug.

"She's okay. We're not hangout buds or anything."

"And what's the story with the other two?"

The day's floor show replays in my head. "Same deal."

"There you go."

I bite off a curse. "Val, it's been a long and strange day. Do the math for me."

"Okay, follow the bouncing ball here. Miranda's got a thing for your pal, Zac. Lindsay's her pal, right? So Miranda decides on a little home turf advantage and tells Lindsay, 'Do not mess this up for me,' and like a good little sidekick, Lindsay doesn't."

It takes me a second or two to process this, and then my jaw drops. "Are you telling me Lindsay let Kyle *and* Matt paw at her because Miranda told her to?" I stare at her for a long moment. "That's, Jesus, that's—"

Val spreads her hands. "Desperate, like I said. Some girls will do anything to get a guy to like her, and others will do anything just to have friends."

"Girls are stupid."

"Yeah. We are."

Val laughs once. But her eyes can't quite meet mine, and my stomach does a slow roll, then drops to my feet. I straighten up to face her. "You? No way."

She nods. "Never noticed my friend Cara never comes around anymore?"

"Cara. Cara, that's the cheerleader wannabe?" I remember her. Blond hair, Oompa-Loompa tan, irritating cackle. "What happened?"

"She had a thing for a football player, wanted me to be her wingman."

I think this through and figure out what I need to do. "Val?"

"Yeah."

"Who do I need to kill?"

She laughs. "Thanks for the offer, little man. But your mad assassin skills are not required. I, um, chickened out. Cara got pissed, never spoke to me again."

"Good, that's, uh, good." The relief that courses through my body feels so good I almost moan, but luckily my stomach growls at that moment.

"Yeah, it's awesome. Come on. I'll make you a sandwich."

God, yes! Val slings her bag over her shoulder and heads to the door. "Val, wait." I walk to her, hoping she won't deck me for this. "You didn't chicken out. You were brave."

When her mouth falls open, I sling an arm around her neck and rub my knuckles over her scalp. "Now where's my damn sandwich?"

———

Tuesday morning dawns, and I drag my ass out of bed without help from annoying sisters or parents. First thing I do is check my phone for messages. I scroll through the list and shake my head. Looks like the party was just getting started when I left. Zac sent a few pictures of Miranda minus her shirt.

Not bad, but still…eww.

Jeremy sent a few of Lindsay sprawled between Kyle and Matt.

And him.

Ugh.

I stand, scratch, and start pulling clothes from my floor pile, trying to guess what the hell is wrong with Lindsay. I don't know her that well. I've only had maybe three classes with her. She doesn't talk much. Always thought she was kind of sweet and innocent.

Guess I was wrong.

I finish brushing my teeth and grab my gear, find my dad ready and waiting for me.

"Still can't find the damn camera."

I turn and stare at him, entertain the idea of awarding him best out-of-context statement of the day, but figure it's just not worth the extra time on my sentence. I climb in the car and wait for him to join me. "What camera? The video camera?"

"No, no! The plain old everyday camera you put film in." He heads down the street, stops at the red light.

"What the hell is film? Kidding, kidding." I put up my hands when he shoots me a glare before he hangs a right turn on red. "I haven't seen a film camera since I posed for my team portrait when the season started, and I'm not even sure that one used film."

"Didn't we have a decent Canon with the flashy thing?"

"Before my time, Dad."

"No way. I'm pretty sure I took pictures of you when you were born."

"Seventeen years ago."

He sighs. "Damn."

"You know there's a camera in your phone, right?"

"Yeah, not good enough."

I shrug. "What about a disposable one?"

"No, I need a real camera. I have to take pictures of jobs for the website. Big, glossy, glittery pictures."

I unlock my phone, go online, and find a few real cameras. "eBay's got a few for a couple of hundred. You could just buy one."

I'm trying to be helpful. But he sighs, and I curse mentally. Here it comes. In three, two, one.

"I could just buy one, but I only need it for one job. I don't want to toss a couple hundred bucks into the trash. I could use that money to repair the dent you put in the car. You can't just buy whatever you want when you want it. That's the fastest way to dig yourself into debt, Ian."

I put up my hands, surrender with a sigh when he stops for a light. This just prolonged the drive for five more painful minutes.

"So how many lockers have you cleaned?"

I make up a number. "About a hundred. We've got it down to a science."

Thankfully Dad pulls into the school lot, and there's no time to cross-examine me. "Thanks for the ride. See you later."

"Four o'clock, right?"

"Yeah. Later."

A whistle blows on the athletic field as my dad's car pulls out of the parking lot. I turn, watch my team run drills for a minute, wishing I could be out there with them. Damn. Forgot to ask Dad when my doctor's appointment is. I'm still watching when a car door slams. I glance to my right, see Grace near a beige Sentra, and forget how to swallow. She's wearing jeans today with a torn black T-shirt. The rips don't reveal any skin because she's got a tank top on underneath, and I want to throw down a penalty flag for denying me that glimpse. Her hair's loose, the way she wore it yesterday. The studded bracelets, Cleopatra eye makeup, and nearly black lips are back.

She stands there, staring at me staring at her, and finally sneers. "Give me your phone."

Wait, what? I finally remember what muscles are needed to swallow and gulp hard. "What?"

"Gimme your fucking phone," she repeats, nearly snarling, stalking up to me like I'm prey about to be slaughtered. Like an idiot, I tug the phone out of my pocket and hand it to her. She aims, holds up her middle finger, and snaps a picture of herself.

"There. Pictures last longer."

She tosses the phone at me, strides into the school. I can't help it. I laugh.

Once we're all rubber-gloved and ready to start the spray-and-scrub routine, I glance over at her. "So that was pretty intense yesterday. Where did you learn to fight?"

She shoots me a look but doesn't answer.

"Come on. Someone must have taught you that move. Who was it?"

Still no reply. Pissed now, I walk toward her, slam the locker door. She leaps back like I electrocuted her.

"Simple question, Collier. If you could fight like that, why didn't you fight Zac?"

She sucks in a breath. "None of your fucking business, Russell."

"Fine!"

"Fine," she agrees and sticks her arm in another locker, her eyes glued to me.

"It was cool, the way you handled them." I quickly hold up both hands when she opens her mouth to attack. "Just sayin'."

She closes her mouth without saying anything, but she keeps looking at me, a frown intensifying those bright eyes.

"I thought they were friends of yours." I head back to my group of lockers, lay a stream of cleanser down.

"Were. Past tense."

I am just about to say something sarcastic about her finally talking back to me when I see the way her eyes fill. Whoa. Grace Collier crying? I wasn't sure her species had tear ducts. I stand there like a freakin' moron, trying to decide if I should apologize or shut up or ask her more questions or fake a dizzy spell, only Grace doesn't feel like waiting for me to get a clue.

"They're on *his* side."

The way she all but spits the word out leaves no doubt she means Zac. I shift my weight from one leg to the other and back again. I can't do this. I can't discuss a pal with the girl who accused him of raping her. So I do the only thing a guy in my position can do.

I turn my back on her and take out my iPod. But even the buds stuck in my ears can't hide Grace's wet sniffle.

PATTY BLOUNT

We work for hours—in tandem but not *together*. I hurt her feelings. I can tell because something hangs in the air, something heavy and sour and growing. I don't know how to stop it, how to fix things. I can't talk to Grace about Zac. And I can't *not* talk to Grace. While I'm letting all this crap circle in my head, the earth shifts up, then down, then up again, and I slide to the floor, trying hard to hold onto my breakfast.

I keep my eyes closed. It helps.

"Ian? What's wrong?" Grace is right next to me, but I'm terrified to open my eyes.

"Dizzy. So fucking dizzy."

I hear her tear paper towels off the roll on our cart. A few seconds later a cold wet towel gently covers my forehead. God, that feels good. Her hand moves to the back of my head. That feels even better. She lifts my head, slides something soft under it. It takes me a second to identify the paper towel roll.

"You're pale again, like sheet white, just like the other day. Do you have a blood sugar problem or something?"

"Concussion."

"Oh. I was wondering why you weren't playing with the team. Where's your phone? I'm calling your parents."

"Hell, no." My eyes pop open. Big mistake. The corridor is still rotating around Grace.

"Gimme the phone, Russell." I feel a hand near the pocket of my jeans and come way too close to a complete system shutdown.

I shove her hands away. "Butt out, Collier. I'm fine." When I open

106

my eyes again, I'm relieved the world seems to be level again. I sit up slowly, knocking the wet towel into my lap. I put my back against a locker and rub my queasy stomach. "You got any food in that bag?" I jerk my chin at the backpack she always carries.

Silver eyes laser-focused on me, she unzips a pocket, pulls out a couple of plastic-wrapped sandwiches. "Ham or turkey?"

I shrug. "Whatever you don't want, I'll eat."

She immediately holds out the ham sandwich, and I wonder why she bothered to make the sandwich if she doesn't like ham. Then I decide I don't care and just take the sandwich, desperate to settle my nausea. I unwrap it, take a bite. She joins me slowly like she did the other day. "Look, about before. I'm, uh, well, I apologize for making you cry."

Her head snaps up. "I don't cry. Not anymore."

I make a face. "Whatever. I'm still sorry. Also, thank you. That's twice you've taken care of me. You should be a nurse."

She huffs out a breath. At first I think she's mad, but it's a laugh. I think I see teeth. "No, I want to be a journalist."

"Cool." I nod and then sigh. "I have no clue what I want to do. Really pisses off my dad."

"What do you like?"

I shrug. "Besides lacrosse? Building stuff. I have a lot of models at home. Thought it might be cool to build real stuff, you know? But—" I trail off with a shrug and run the damp towel over my face.

"What?"

"Nothing." I'm not smart enough to be an engineer. My scholarship hopes are pinned on lacrosse. "My dad wants me to work with him."

"Doing?"

"He has a tile business."

"And you don't want to lay floors for a living."

"No, that's not what he does. He plans. He sketches out entire designs according to spec, then makes the tile. Somebody else lays them."

"Still not seeing the problem here." She takes the towel out of my hands, pushes my head down, and lays it across the back of my neck.

"Forget it. It's a long, boring story." I take another bite of the sandwich. "Good. This is really good. Thanks."

"No problem."

She shifts on the floor next to me, frowns at her own sandwich, and finally blurts out, "I should thank you too."

"Yes, you should." I like being thanked. "Wait, for what?"

"You know. For yesterday." She still won't meet my eyes.

"Don't waste any tears on them. What they said to you yesterday? Not cool." When her shoulders hunch up, I decide not to repeat the insults. Instead, I pull out my phone and show her the picture message I got from Jeremy, the one of the Lindsay sandwich. "If it acts like a slut, it must be a—"

"Don't." She tosses my phone back and covers her ears. "Don't say that word."

The word the entire school's been calling her. "Right. Sorry." I finish the rest of her sandwich. Wordlessly she hands me the bottle of water she opened for my cold compress and sits in silence, shaking her head.

"What?"

"That picture. It's pretty disgusting. And it's not Lindsay."

"Yeah, it is. I was there." I gulp down half the bottle.

She looks at me sharply. "Did you take it?"

"No. But I was there. I saw it. She was into it."

Grace shakes her head and waves her hand at my phone. "No, I know it's really Lindsay. I'm saying that's not who she is. She's nice. She's not—" She bites her lip, so I finish the sentence for her.

"Easy?"

I thought the same thing. But then she let everybody put hands on her. That's why I left. "You were there last night. At Miranda's house. I saw you." The hand holding her sandwich freezes on the way to her mouth. But she doesn't confirm or deny. "Why?"

She takes another tiny bite, chews it for ages, and flips her hair over her shoulder. "I don't know. Glutton for punishment, I guess."

That is such bull, but I don't call her on it. She used to be friends with those girls. If things were different, if certain things hadn't happened, she would have been in that basement last night. A picture of her stretched out on that sofa, Jeremy leering at her, forms in my mind. Who would she have made out with? How many? The sandwich twists in my gut, and I crush what's left into a ball, pitch it into the bin on our utility cart.

"Um, I need to thank you for something else," she says as if the words taste bad. "For helping me that night."

Right. That night. I suck in a deep breath and blow it out slowly. I can't talk about this with her. But jeez, how can I just stop talking to her now? She fed me, put a cold compress on me, and even tucked a paper towel pillow under my head. While I decide what the proper protocol is for telling the girl who provided first aid that you can't talk to her because your pal says she's a lying bitch who tried to end his college scholarship dreams, Grace suddenly turns to face me directly.

"Why did you?"

I blink, still a bit fuzzy from that dizzy spell. "What?"

"Why'd you help me? That night?"

My eyes bulge. "Was I supposed to just leave you there?"

"Everybody else did," she retorts.

"Yeah. Well, it was dark. It was cold. You were obviously—" I bite my tongue, not sure what to say. She was unconscious and half-naked and…and—

I really want to punch Zac.

"Obviously what?"

"Not capable of driving." Yeah. That's safe.

She plays with her hands—right one rubs left, left one rubs right. "I was bleeding."

I nod. "First time."

Grace jerks back, and the color just drains from her face. A pulse beats erratically at her temple, and I can actually hear her gulp. She moves away from me, watches me from the corner of her eyes. I don't get it, but my words don't just upset her. They *scare* her.

Chapter 11
Grace

Ian's giving me this weird stare, and it's creeping me out. "What?" I challenge him, but he doesn't flinch. Finally he blinks and opens his mouth to say something but reconsiders. "What?" I demand again.

"Okay, look. Today's Tuesday. We have to get through the rest of the week. I can't talk about Zac with you, so let's both agree…no Zac talk for the rest of the week. Deal?"

"Can't or won't?" she challenges me.

"Either. Both. Doesn't matter. Let's just take him off the table."

Nobody talks about Zac? I can live with that. I know Ian doesn't believe me. That comment about fighting Zac off proves it. But he's compromising. I guess I can too. He holds out a hand, and I grasp it, shake once. This is the first time I've touched anybody except my mom since that night, and it's not scary. In fact, it's kind of nice.

"Still dizzy?"

"No, I'm good. We should get back to work before Bob puts us on his report." He slowly rolls to his feet, holds out a hand to me. I take it, stand up, and nod my thanks.

There's an awkward moment when we stand there, holding hands but not really, wondering what we should do next. My cell buzzes. I pull it out of my pocket, glance at the screen, and curse.

"What happened?" Ian frowns.

"My mom can't pick me up today. Have to walk home."

"Sucks. Can you drive?"

"Yeah, but I don't have my own car."

"Same. My dad's been picking me up. I, uh, dented the car last week. Grounded."

He hides his eyes, and I figure there's a lot more to that story he doesn't want to talk about, so I don't nag. "Yeah. My car was trashed, so my mom said no car until college." I roll my eyes. "Makes it hard to find a job."

"Trashed?"

"Yeah. Somebody took the battery, carved up the paint."

"Damn. So what kind of job are you looking for?"

"Whatever I can get to make money. My brother's birthday is at the end of the month."

"You got a brother? Cool. I have two sisters," he admits it like it's a crime.

"Two half brothers. My dad and his new wife. My parents split when I was like…nine."

"That bites," he says. Sucks, bites—what's up with all this vampire language? I angle my head, imagine him with fangs or a cape with a really high collar. With the dark hair and intense eyes, he could totally pull it off.

"What?" he demands. "Mayo on my face?" He swipes a knuckle over his lips, and I suddenly remember that's the first thing about Ian Russell that made me look at him twice. He has nice lips. I mean, really nice lips. They curve up just a little bit, like maybe he's always just a little bit happy. Even when he was sprawled on the floor, gripping his spinning head, he looked a little bit happy.

I'd kill to feel just a little bit happy.

"Nothing," I shake my head and smirk. "Just imagining you as a vampire."

He groans and clutches his head. "No! Not you too!" Then he levels me with a look of exaggerated pity. "Okay. So which one is it? My sisters can't decide who's hotter, Damon or Stefan."

I shrug.

"Not the Salvatores? Really? Hmm. There's no way you're into sparkles, so how about Sheriff Northman? Uh, Spike? Wait, wait, I got it—Barnabas Collins?"

I shake my head, but the last one pulls a reluctant laugh from me.

He snaps on his rubber gloves and sprays yet another locker but doesn't take his eyes off me. "Do that again."

"What?"

"Smile," he says, totally serious. "Looks good on you."

I stand there, wide-eyed. Was that an actual compliment? Time hangs in the air, and it's here, right here. A little bit of happy. I smile again, and he grins back, then tosses me the cleanser. "Quit slackin'."

I laugh, and he bumps me with his hip. I spray the next six lockers.

He grabs the cart, pushes it closer, and starts scrubbing the first locker. I like that we're working together instead of just next to each other. I know he's Zac's friend, but he's not Zac.

"Ugh! What the hell?" Ian removes his arm from the locker, the paper towel sticky and shredding apart.

I peer inside the locker, spot a lump of what looks like it used to be a Rice Krispies Treat fused to the back of the shelf. I grab the putty knife off the cart. "Here, try this."

"Oh, disgusting." Ian wrinkles his face and starts prying.

"I used to love these."

He covers his mouth. "Stop! No, no, no! I can't even look at it."

"Wimp." Laughing, I elbow him out of my way, pry the hardened marshmallow and cereal off the locker, then scrape off the smaller chunks.

"Wimp, my ass." He bends, picks up a few of the pieces, and when his lips curl into an evil grin, I gasp.

"You wouldn't."

"I would." He holds up a chunk of petrified cereal and slowly steps toward me. I back up but can't pry my gaze away from the humor dancing in his eyes.

"We should drop this off at Mr. Tebitt's classroom. Could keep the biology lab happy for days."

His grin widens. "We could, but it wouldn't be as much fun as…this." He grabs a fistful of my shirt and drops the chunk down the front.

I hiss like a cat, do a deranged dance to find and get that shit as far away from me as possible. "Jesus! You idiot!" But I'm laughing as I scream and hiss and dance. "I am so taking you down." I finally locate the offending little crumb at the waistband of my pants and flick it at his face.

He ducks.

Damn it.

I look at the can of cleanser, slowly bring it up, and take aim.

"No—" He raises his hands, and I smile wide. "No, no, no, let's be reasonable. You do that, and I'm gonna smell like a Creamsicle on steroids and won't get laid until college."

I spray him dead in the heart.

He drops his hands and cocks his head to the side as the circle of foam seeps into his shirt. "Oh, that's cold, Collier. Ice cold." He wrinkles his nose and coughs once, then twice. "Shit's strong." He gasps and falls back against the locker, coughing hard. I drop the spray can, lunge for him before he falls.

"Ian! Oh my God, Ian, I'm sorry. Are you okay? Ian. Ian!"

He slides down to the floor, eyelids fluttering. I reach for my phone, but it's not in my pocket. Did I toss it in my bag? Where the hell's my bag? Ian has a phone. Where is it? I pat his pockets, but I can't find it. Panic swells when I notice Ian's not moving. I tap his face.

"Better when you patted my thighs."

It takes me a second, and then I'm cursing and smacking him for playing me. But he catches my flailing hands.

"Never gave much thought to acting, but damn, I got mad skills."

"You son—"

"Oh, come on. I got you good. Admit it."

"As if."

"Admit it, and I'll let you go."

"Oh, you'll let me go so I don't hurt you."

He tugs me closer. "How are you gonna hurt me when I've got your hands trapped?"

I go completely still. *Ian Russell is holding my hands.* Ian Russell is holding my hands. And there's no pressure in my chest, and I haven't warped back in time to the moment when I *knew* I couldn't stop Zac from taking what he wanted from me. Jesus, a boy is touching me, and it's kind of okay. And for maybe the first time in forty days, I laugh.

"What's so funny?" He looks at me sideways.

"Glad you asked." I grin. Since he's on the floor and I'm not, all it takes is a simple shift of my weight, and a second later I've broken out of his hold and have him pinned.

"Impressive. Ow. Very impressive. Ow. I'll applaud once you let me go."

"Stop crying."

"I will when you let me go."

I should probably let him go.

But I don't.

My heart's racing from the power trip of taking Ian down, or maybe it's just because I'm so close to him and thought this was over for me. His muscles go lax. He stops struggling, and I don't let go. I want to freeze this moment and keep it—keep him—forever. Slowly he leans in closer and closer, and I still don't let go. His eyes drop to my mouth, and his tongue darts out to lick his lips. I think he wants to kiss me, and damn it, I want him to—I want him to so badly I almost cry, so I don't let go. Closer, closer, and his eyes shut, and his head tilts. And I don't let go. His lips touch mine, and he kisses me like it matters—like *I* matter—and oh my God, it's amazing. He's amazing, and I don't let go. And then the steel door on the floor below us screeches open, and Ian goes tense, his eyes darting to the stairs at the far end of the hall. And it hits me.

Ian doesn't want anyone to see him with the school slut.

So I break our *No Zac* agreement. "You wanna know why I didn't fight off Zac? Because I was unconscious."

Ian's eyes snap to mine and then away, but it's too late. I already saw the disgust in them.

This is when I let him go.

———

Humiliation burns the back of my eyes, and I force my face into a mask to hide it. I shove away from Ian, grab my bag, and hurry to the girls' bathroom before whoever opened the door shows their faces. I splash water on my burning face and pace in front of the row of sinks. I am so monumentally stupid! What was I thinking, kissing Ian Russell? He'll post it to Facebook and tell the entire team—the school—that I'm exactly what Zac says I am. Lindsay and Miranda will carve insults into my skin this time instead of my car.

Muffled voices and loud laughter leak through the wall shared with the boys' bathroom next door. I can tell one is Ian's, but the other voice is unclear. What if it's Zac? There's a surge of panic, but I swallow it, catching sight of myself in the row of mirrors. My lips tingle, but they look the same. Everything about me looks the same—a crusty coating to hide the scars and grudges that churn inside me.

I hear another laugh and recognize that cackle. That's Jeremy Linz, one of Zac's little worms. He's the kind of guy who just blindly follows his lord and master without question. I'm not sure Jeremy is capable of original thinking. I used to wonder why Zac is even friends with him, but I get it now.

Zac doesn't want friends. He wants disciples, and Ian is one of them. My hands curl into fists, and I pound a door to an empty stall. The door bounces, echoing in the empty room, so I do it again. I nearly do it a third time but then remember kicking a locker is how I got stuck spending a week with Ian Russell in the first place. I could end up scrubbing toilets! Even a petrified Rice Krispies Treat beats scrubbing out toilets. I grip one of the sinks and stare at myself. What the hell is Ian's game? Did Zac put him up to this? Kiss the slut, tell the whole school—oh, God.

The whole school.

What if Ian has pictures? I never saw his phone, but what if he set it up in a locker? He could post them, and things will get worse than they are right now. The harassment, the hate, the taunts, and the threats—it'll just keep coming. Mom already deleted my Facebook account and with it, all the connections I've ever formed. Not that they matter when so many of them joined in when the threats started.

You shouldn't have gotten so drunk! You asked for it!

You don't even remember what happened, and you're ruining someone's life. Get over yourself!

You deserved it!

I hate them all. I don't need any of them.

I roll my shoulders and grab my bag, quietly sneak from the bathroom down the stairs to the exit so I can make it to the athletic field before anyone notices I'm gone. A whistle blows, and I hear light applause. The team is still on the field. I guess Jeremy decided to ditch. Stick close to the tree line. Blend in. Stay low. I can only make it as far as the scoreboard this way. The rest of the field is open—parking lot, bleachers, running track. I unzip my bag, remove the camera, and use the zoom lens to find Zac.

He's in the net, standing with his hands on his hips, looking bored. My body instantly reacts to the sight of him—muscles tense, adrenaline surges, legs coil to get ready to run. It takes every ounce of energy I have to stay there.

It's overcast, and there's a zing of ozone in the air that tickles my nose. But I think I can grab some shots before the storm hits. I leave the flash off and snap shots of Zac flipping off one of the players, laughing at a teammate's spectacular trip, and diving for the ball. The long-range zoom lens grabs some detailed images, but none of them are the one I need. The next play gets rough—sticks fly, and tempers flare—and I feel it in my gut. This is when Zac shows who he really is. Come on, come on! Zac shoves a guy out of his crease, and I keep my finger on the shutter button throughout the entire altercation. It's got to be here. I can't know for sure until I upload the images to my computer, but I feel it. I got the shot. I'm smiling, actually smiling as I slowly pick my way back through the trees. There's got to be one decent shot I can use there.

I pause while Jeremy jogs from the exit back to the field, and I blow out a sigh. Thank God I won't need to run into him. He hits the turf, and that's my cue to cross the parking lot, quietly open the door just wide enough to slip through, and return to the girls' bathroom. I wash my hands and make sure there are no leaves or twigs stuck to me, breathe in, breathe out, force all the tension out of my muscles. Wonder if I can sneak upstairs to an empty classroom and shoot from a window? All this sneaking around crap is giving me chest pains. The first crack of thunder rumbles in the distance, and I tense right back up. The team will quit practice now. What if Zac or Jeremy come looking for Ian?

Once again I hear the murmur of a deep voice through the common wall. Jesus! Are they inside already? But the tone is off. It's not arrogant and bragging like Zac's. It's soft and soothing. It's Ian's.

I open the door and stand in the hall between the two bathrooms.

"Yeah… I wanted to get an estimate. Creased side panel on a Camry. Yeah….uh-huh. I see…thanks."

There's a loud "Fuck!" followed by the clash of a lav door getting kicked. Shit! He can't find me here, eavesdropping. I scoot down the hall, and after a few seconds I hear Ian's steps behind me.

"Grace."

I stop, turn, cross my arms, and shoot him my most fierce glare. "What?"

He winces, and I have to give him points for it. At least he's capable of remorse—unlike his pal, Zac. "Look." He rakes hair off his face, and his hand shakes. "I'm, uh, sorry for before. That was seriously uncool."

I forget how pissed off I am and let curiosity take over. "What exactly was uncool? Kissing me or the horror you showed at almost getting caught kissing me?" I wave my hands in the air.

"Actually, both."

What? I'm stunned and just stare at him, jaw dangling.

"I…um, well, you were so close to me, and you're so pretty. I guess I kind of forgot we're not seeing each other, and I just went for it. That was wrong, and I'm sorry." He stammers and shuffles. "The door opened. Figured it was probably Miranda and Lindsay coming back for seconds and didn't want them giving you a hard time because of me, so I pulled back."

Whoa, back the truck up. This was all about *me*, not him? He's shitting me. Nobody's this decent. I examine his face for clues to what he's really thinking, but I can't find any. His expression matches his words. Holy crap, he's sincere, and I am not this lucky, so what the hell do I do?

"Okay. I guess I'll just…be over there." He gives me a perplexed look and heads back to the cart, and I still can't believe what I just heard. My lips want to smile, and then I figure out why.

Ian Russell thinks I'm pretty. Oh, God, I am pathetic.

———————

By 4:00 p.m., the rain is coming down in sheets. I text my mother, but she can't be here until five. I can't stay here at the school alone, not if the lacrosse team is in the locker room. I could walk if I'd been lucky enough to find an umbrella in somebody's locker, but I wasn't. No surprise there. I tie my hair back, draw my hood up and resign myself to a cold and wet trek. I walk fast, almost run. I need to be off the main street before the lacrosse team's cars start speeding by. If they see me—

I shiver.

They can't see me. It's that simple.

Just as I jog across the street, I hear it. A car pulls up alongside me. A window powers down. A cold dread numbs my legs, and I'm running through quicksand and sinking fast, the panic attack pressure that's become so familiar already building in my core. A figure steps from the passenger side, and I brace. Please don't let it be Zac. Please, please not him. Please don't let it be Miranda or Lindsay. The figure is huddled into a hoodie and is obviously male. Oh, God, no. My hands curl into fists. Hair on my neck stands up, and I beg my muscles to move.

"Grace?"

It's Ian. I skid to a stop, breath coming in loud gasps, my relief so enormous that I almost cry.

"Come on. We'll give you a ride."

We? Oh, God.

"My dad and me, Grace. No one else," he adds when I hesitate.

Good. Okay. That's good. I can do this.

"You're wet, and you're shivering. We can drive you home."

I look down at my clothes. I'm soaked through. I nod and follow him back to the car. The white Camry. I swear, there's this tiny ray of sunshine beaming through the rain that illuminates the car, and all I can think is *safe*. I follow him to the passenger side. He holds the back door open for me. I climb in, my bag on my lap, and draw my arms around my legs, watching the little bobblehead figure of some football player stuck on the dashboard nod at me. Ian climbs into the front seat and flips on the heater. "Dad, this is Grace."

"Hi, Grace."

The man behind the wheel looks just like Ian. Same brown eyes, same smile, same hair, though there's a bit of gray in his. He's dressed in khakis and a golf shirt with a light jacket. He looks at me and frowns, tugs a handkerchief from his pocket, and hands it to me.

"Here you go."

When I reach out to take the square of fabric, our eyes meet, and I freeze. It's there in the same brown eyes Ian inherited—a mix of sympathy and discomfort.

He knows.

It takes everything I've got to hold my head up, and it's not enough. I hide my eyes behind the handkerchief, wipe my dripping face, horrified by the black stains I leave on it. Damn it. Scowling in the backseat,

I almost miss it when Mr. Russell rants about not being able to find his camera.

"Searched the whole house for it. I *know* we have one."

I wait for Ian to mention I'm the school newspaper photographer and that I have a camera right here in my backpack, but he says nothing. I think about that for a minute—how being forced to scrub lockers with me for a week must be putting a serious kink in Ian's life and how me mentioning the camera in my bag at this moment would complicate it even more. "Mr. Russell, I take pictures for the school paper. Anything I can help you with?"

In the mirror his eyes pop. "You're a photographer? This is great!"

"Um, Dad, I—"

"Ian, you couldn't tell me your partner's a photographer? All that time, searching for a lost camera. Whoa, why do you smell like oranges?" Mr. Russell turns back to me. "Grace, how much would you charge to take some pictures for me? Tell her, Ian."

"Dad, I really don't think Grace—"

"You haven't even told her yet. Grace, I need to update my website and marketing materials. I just finished a few jobs that came out really amazing. I need someone to take pictures of them that don't look like they were shot with a cell phone, you know? I'd pay you for the time."

I swear I can *hear* Ian's gut slowly twisting. "Actually I could use some extra money to buy my brother's birthday gift. How much are you offering?"

"I don't know. Ten bucks a picture sound good to you?"

"Great."

"Perfect. You're hired."

"What do I have to do?"

"I'll show you when we get home. Can you come to our place, or do you have to be back by a certain time?"

I think about that for a minute. Mom won't be home from work until six, and my dad calls me only on Fridays. Ian is oddly quiet in the front seat. Half his face is reflected in the side-view mirror, and he looks…worried. Uneasy. I debate with myself for a minute and agree. "Yeah, I guess I can."

In the front seat Ian makes an odd croaking sound. The idea of spending more time with Ian away from the school and away from Zac appeals to me. Guess I'm not that bright. I stuff the camera back in my bag, zip it up tight, and settle back while we ride to the Russell house, my fingers tapping out a beat in time with the windshield wipers.

It doesn't take long. Turns out Ian Russell lives only about four streets away from me. Wow. All the time I was crushing on him, and he lives in my own backyard. My lips twitch at the irony, and suddenly I want to cry. As soon as the car stops in the driveway, I shove out of it and zip by Ian, while his dad chatters on about the job.

"Won't take long. I'll give you the addresses of each job site, call the owners, tell them not to freak out when they see this girl with a camera, and that's all there is to it. When can you start?"

"Oh, um, well."

"Dad. Let's take this a step at a time, okay?"

Mr. Russell rolls dark eyes. "Ian, it's not rocket science."

He unlocks the front door, calls out a greeting to whoever is home—Ian's mother maybe. "Come on in, Grace."

I follow him inside, aware that Ian is hanging back, watching me with that same frown of worry I noticed in the car. After a moment he moves past me, climbs the stairs to the second floor, and disappears.

"Um. Yeah. Sorry about that. He doesn't quite know what to do with you."

Yeah, right.

"Come on. Let's see if we can find you some dry clothes." He turns to the staircase and shouts, "Valerie! Claudia! You home?"

There's a creak in the ceiling over my head. A door opens, and a girl appears at the top of the stairs, wearing yoga pants, a sweatshirt, and no socks. Her hair is pulled up in a messy bun, and she's wearing black glasses over green eyes. But despite the differences, I can still see Ian in her.

"Yeah, Dad?"

"Oh, hey, Val. This is Grace, one of Ian's friends. You got any clothes she can borrow?"

"Sure, come on up."

I head up the stairs, squirming under my skin, but Valerie is already pulling out drawers and tossing stuff on her bed.

"So you're the famous Grace Collier, huh?"

The polite smile I wear freezes in place, and I halt just inside her room. She stares at me for a long moment. "I'm sorry. For what happened to you."

My jaw tightens. "You didn't do it."

"True, but from what Ian says, there are lots of people who didn't do it but haven't exactly made it easy on you."

From what Ian says? I don't know what to say to that, so I stay silent.

"These should fit you. Come on. Bathroom's this way."

I take the pile of clothes she hands me and follow her to the bathroom across the hall. She nods once and leaves me alone. I lock the door, strip down, and dry myself with a towel folded neatly on the sink. The mirror is a horror show. I grab some tissues and wipe at the makeup that's running down my face in goth-black rivers and finally just wash my face, conceding defeat. The clothes are practically identical to what Valerie was wearing—yoga pants, sweatshirt, tank top. I pull a brush from my bag, drag it through the nest that's become of my hair, and scoop it up into an elastic band.

I feel naked, but at least I'm dry again.

I pull open the door and nearly collide with Ian, who also changed his clothes. In a fresh pair of jeans and a black T-shirt under a plaid shirt, he looks great and smells even better now that the orange scent is gone. He still looks like he'd rather submit to a root canal than be anywhere near me, so I smirk and can't resist needling him. "I kind of like you orange-scented."

A slow grin spreads across his face and turns evil when he takes a step toward me. I'm not frightened because it's Ian, but I realize—too late—that he's carrying his dirty clothes under one arm. "Yeah? Well, here. Take all you want."

He rubs his shirt into my face, and I shove him back a step, laughing and cursing.

"Ian."

Valerie is back, and Ian and I separate, still laughing.

"Thanks for the clothes." I smile at her.

"No problem." She rolls her eyes and laughs.

We head back downstairs, find Mr. Russell sitting behind a desk in a home office behind the garage. "Oh, good. There you are. Nice and dry?"

"Yeah, thanks."

"Have a seat. Ian, you too."

There's a small leather sofa under the window, facing a cool glass desk. I sit, and Ian sinks down beside me. Mr. Russell scoots over on his desk chair, hands me a sheet of paper.

"Here you go. Those are the addresses of my best projects. The first one? I want to feature that one on the cover of the new brochure and the website." He swivels around, taps a few keys on the laptop on his desk. "Here's the design for the project. This is a pool where I designed the fish at the bottom. I'm hoping you can take shots with special filters, make the sun glint off something bright, stuff like that." A few more taps, and a new design appears. "And this one's a kitchen backsplash."

"Dad, um—"

But Mr. Russell's too excited to hear him, so Ian mouths, "Sorry," over his head while his dad chatters on. "And the others I'll use for the new online gallery I'm planning. Three of the six are pretty close by, and the other two are kind of a long drive. But I was thinking maybe Ian and you could ride out there on Sunday, if you don't have plans."

Works for me. My mom's not trusting me with the car anytime soon, so I'd need him to drive me to all these sites. "Fine by me. Okay with you?" I turn to Ian, and he's staring at his cell phone, a frown puckering his brow.

"Hey. Ian." Mr. Russell snaps his fingers. "Grace asked you a question."

"What? Oh, sorry."

"Is all this okay with you? I mean, if you have issues being seen with me—"

"Of course he doesn't, right, Ian?"

Ian smiles and takes the list from me. "We can go right now if you want. The first one's just a few blocks from here."

"Now? It's pouring out." I point out the obvious.

"Well, you've already melted." He grins, indicating my face, which is now free of all makeup.

"I don't care about my makeup. I care about the camera."

"Oh. Right. Okay, tomorrow. After we finish. Dad, will you let me take the car?"

"For the purposes of taking pictures, yes. Nothing else, Ian. You're still grounded."

"Okay, Dad." Ian rolls his eyes and stands up. A second later, it dawns on me that I should probably leave, so I stand up too.

"Thanks, Mr. Russell. I really appreciate this. I'll email you a link to the pictures I take so you can pick your favorites."

"This is great. Thanks, Grace. I can't wait to see what you do."

"Thanks for the ride."

"Oh! The ride. Right." Mr. Russell slaps his head. "Here, Ian. Drive Grace to her house." He slips keys from his pocket and tosses them.

Ian snatches them out of the air with one hand, and for a few seconds I panic.

Me.

Alone in a car.

With Ian Russell.

My lungs stall out, and I figure another one of those panic attacks is about to deck me. But then logic comes to my rescue. I've scrubbed lockers alone with Ian Russell since Saturday, and he hasn't attacked me.

I'm safe with him. I'm safe with him. I'm safe with him.

"Grace, you okay?"

I nod and hurry outside where I can breathe. *I'm safe with him, I'm safe with him.* The panic fades when my body finally listens to my head. Outside at the curb, Ian clicks the remote to unlock the doors and quickly slides behind the wheel. I sit beside him and wonder if maybe I should sit in the backseat so no one sees him with me. A second later I think, *Fuck that.* I'm not the guilty party here. I won't hide.

130

"Okay. Out with it. You hate the idea, don't you?" I say when I can't take the silence anymore.

"Driving you home? Yeah, it's as hard for me as it obviously is for you."

I let that go. "No, smart-ass. I mean me taking these pictures for your dad."

"No, it's fine." He drives in silence for a long moment.

Crap, I knew he wasn't cool with this. I consider him. I could just shrug and tell him it's too damn bad and he'll have to deal. But then I remember this is Ian, the same boy who carefully replaced a sick girl's locker contents instead of trashing everything, the same boy who worried about me. He's not a jerk, despite his choice of friends, so I guess I can cut him a break.

"Look. I used to like you. Before Zac, I mean. So don't worry about it. I'll make other arrangements since I already told your dad I'd do this."

He sucks in air, blows it out hard. Abruptly he pulls the car to the curb, throws it into park, and turns to face me. "Grace, I'm not trying to be a dick about this, but don't you—I don't know—just get tired of all this shit? I mean, you just about fainted at the thought of getting into the car with me. Then there's Miranda and Lindsay cursing you out, vandalizing your car, everybody shunning you at school, and the video Zac posted—" He breaks off, frowning at the steering wheel to spare me the brutal truth. The video was incriminating. I've seen it. Jesus, who am I kidding? It's porn, and I'm the star.

"I guess I just don't understand why you don't put up your hands and say *uncle?*"

"Because it's not true!" I scream. "None of it's true. I said no, Ian. And he didn't listen."

Ian presses his lips into a tight line and shakes his head. "We're doing it again." When I frown at him, he fills in the blank. "Talking about Zac. We agreed—no more."

Right. I nod, hold up my hands. "You're right." And then I paint a cheerful smile. "New topic. What do you like besides lacrosse?"

He laughs once. "Oh, man. I like long walks on the beach—"

I slap his arm, and he laughs. I really love when Ian laughs. "Okay, okay, sorry. What do I like? Let's see. I don't know. I like hanging out with friends. I like video games. I like movies."

"What kind of movies? Comedies or action stuff like *Iron Man?*"

"Both, I guess."

I nod. "Me too. What's your favorite?"

He rolls his head up and back. "Man, you ask some tough questions. I don't have one favorite. I love the *Lord of the Rings* movies. Oh, and the *Spider-Man* reboot. *The Hangover* movies make me laugh every time I watch them, and I've watched them like four or five times now."

"Wow."

He grins. "What about you?"

"Um." What about me? What do I like? I don't like anything lately, and with a sharp pain in my chest, I remember that's Zac's fault. So I stick to safe ground. Before the rape. *BTR.* "Well, I love taking pictures, but I guess you knew that already." I shrug. "I like those movies too. And yeah, I don't have just one favorite. I like hanging out with my little brothers."

Ian laughs. "That's because they don't live with you. Trust me, siblings are always up your ass, in your stuff, framing you for stuff you never did. It gets old fast."

I laugh. "You have a point. I visit them on their territory, and when I go home, the chaos stays there."

He nods and then looks away. "Um, so I—well, what you said before—that you, uh…you know, liked me."

Oh, God. Kill me now.

He picks at something on the steering wheel. "I liked you too. Before Zac, I mean." He blows out a loud sigh and laughs once. "It took me two months to get up the guts to ask you out, but he got there first."

My eyes pop. "Two months? What did you think I was going to do, stab you?"

He turns those intense dark eyes on me and grins halfway. "You have no idea how terrifying it is to ask a girl out. Does she like you too? Is she gonna laugh at you, make you the topic of conversation at lunch with her giggling girlfriends? Immediately rush to Facebook and change her relationship status? It's so much pressure."

By the time he finishes with a groan, I'm laughing so hard I can't breathe. But Ian stops laughing to watch me. "What?" I rub my face. "Do I still have raccoon eyes?"

He shakes his head. "No, you don't have any makeup left." His hand cups my cheek, turns my face from side to side. "Look better without it. Especially when you laugh."

We sit like this for an eternity, his thumb skating along the curve of my cheek, my knees jumping up and down against the dash. Why am I shaking? It's not fear because I'm not afraid of Ian. I think it's anticipation…or maybe just plain hope. And that's when it hits me. *He's* the one who's afraid. I stare into those dark, mysterious eyes, memorize the shape of his jaw and his lips, wish I had the courage to just reach out and touch them, touch him, while his hand on my face sends little shocks up and down my spine. I suddenly blurt, "What about now? Do you still like me?"

As the words drop off my tongue, I wish I could suck them back in. His eyes harden. He drops his hand from my face, and he says nothing, just puts the car back into drive and a few minutes later pulls up in front of my house. I wish I could be shocked he knows where I live, but ever since I accused Zac of rape, I figure my address is probably on a map by now—*Laurel Point Losers* or something.

He waits for me to get out, but I just stare out the windshield, watch the rain fall. "My mom wants me to sign up for the semester abroad program. She says it'll be good for me to *get away from all this*." I roll my eyes because really how likely is that? "And my dad, he's been trying to get me to go shopping with his wife because there's some rule written down someplace that says women who wear pearls and fluffy pink sweater sets with coordinating lipstick and nail polish are respectable—even when they aren't—and don't get the batteries stolen right out of their cars." I turn, look him dead in the eye to finish it out. "I won't give up, and I won't run away. And I won't change how I look even if you do think I look better this way because I'm not the problem here! Everybody says it's my fault because I got drunk, and you know what? That doesn't count! Everyone was drinking that night. There's only one thing that counts, but nobody wants to hear it."

The look on his face is anger and frustration and disbelief, and I get it. I totally get that I will never convince Ian Russell I was raped. Sighing loudly, I add one more thing. "Look, I really need the money so I can repair the damage to my mom's car and buy my brother's birthday present. I can do all this work by myself, so you don't have to see me or be seen with me or whatever it is about me that bugs you."

I grab my bag, my pile of wet clothes, open the door, and put him out of his misery. "Giving up is easy, not right. If doing the right thing were easy, nobody would ever do stuff they know is wrong, like kiss their daughter's dance instructor or rape an unconscious girl who already said no."

He snaps his face up to mine, eyes saucer-wide, but I hop out and close the door before he says anything that makes me change my mind about cutting him that break.

Chapter 12

Ian

Wednesday morning dawns way too soon for me. If I slept more than a couple of hours, that's being generous. Everything Grace said, every word, every flash of those weird bright eyes of hers replayed in my mind on an infinite loop. Zac said she was totally into it, into him, and he shared the pictures to prove it. I've known him a long time. I can tell when he's lying and I don't think he is. The thing is, though, I don't think Grace is lying either.

That's not the worst of it. There's all that stuff she said about doing what's right instead of what's easy. She looked right at me—I mean directly into my eyes—and I swear I could hear her thinking, *I know you know, you dick, so why don't you just admit it?*

Even that's not the worst part. No, the worst part is I kissed her. I fucking kissed Grace Collier, the girl who cried rape. And I almost did it again.

God, this is useless! I toss the covers aside, get out of bed, rub my eyes, and head for the shower. I can't risk driving her all over the county to take pictures of my dad's projects. I can't be close to her. I can't date the girl trying to ruin Zac's life. I finish dressing, but it's still too early to leave, so I flop back down on my bed and stare at the walls.

A cobweb dangles from one of them. I haul myself back up, grab a towel, and wipe it. What the hell. May as well clean up the rest of the room while I'm at it. I toss dirty clothes into the hamper, put the ones that don't stink like either oranges or me back into my dresser, and organize my desk. By the time I'm done, it's time to leave.

"Ian! You ready, it's—" My dad opens the door, sticks his head inside, and forgets his sentence. "You cleaned your room?" He frowns, puts a hand on my forehead. "You sick or something?"

I shrug off his hand. "I'm fine. Did you make my appointment yet?"

"Yeah, it's Friday."

"Cool. Thanks." I grab my jacket, phone, and wallet. "Let's go."

"Okay, what's up with you? You don't clean your room without being threatened, so what's going on?"

"Couldn't sleep. I woke up early, needed something to do."

"Your head hurting you?"

"Yeah—no! Not the concussion. It's this whole thing with Zac and Grace."

He waves a hand. "Why don't you ask your other friends what they saw? Maybe that will help."

I shrug and nod. "Yeah. Maybe."

"Breakfast is ready. Don't be long."

He shuts my door and I stare at it, wondering what the hell just happened. This kinder, gentler Dad confuses me.

Ask my other friends, he said. I actually haven't talked to anybody. Jeremy, Matt, and Kyle were all there. So were Lindsay, Miranda, and Sarah Griffin. I haven't asked any of them what they saw. Is there any point? The guys will all stick by Zac. Lindsay and Miranda dumped Grace, so they obviously believe Zac's side of the story. The only question mark is Sarah. I should talk to her, see if she believes the current theory. Grace and Miranda fought, and Grace wanted to get even with her, so she hooked up with Zac.

I shake my head. No stupid fight with somebody could put the fear I see in Grace's eyes like yesterday when Dad tossed me the car keys. During midterms, Mr. Tebitt misworded a question on a bio test. Everybody else sat and whined about how unfair it was, but Grace was the one who challenged him. She actually went up to him and said there were *two* correct answers to that question and everybody who chose either answer should get credit. He told her to sit down and then threatened to send her to Mr. Jordan's office, but Grace never backed off. I would have flunked that test if Grace hadn't gotten all of us credit for the bad question. Before yesterday I would have sworn to God there's no way Grace Collier is afraid of anything.

But she *is*.

I curse and fling the towel to my bed. Another day with Grace. How the hell do I face her after all the shit I said yesterday?

How the hell do I deal when I still like her?

————

Half an hour later I'm snapping on latex gloves, and Grace is nowhere in sight. I unseal a new can of the industrial orange cleanser and start spraying lockers, trying hard not breathe. A glance up the corridor at all the lockers we've cleaned so far makes me feel good.

Until I look down the corridor at all the lockers still to go.

We're never going to finish them all. The directions on the can say not to leave the foam sitting on any surface for more than thirty minutes. I shrug and figure it can't hurt. I use the master key to open all the lockers from here to the boy's bathroom at the end of the second floor hall and start spraying. With luck, the Eau d'Creamsicle scent won't be so overpowering by the time I get back down here with the brush and towels. Back where I started, I wipe out the foam as quickly as I can and move to the next locker. It doesn't take longer than two minutes or so. Thirty minutes later I'm back at the final locker.

Still no Grace.

Just as well. What the hell do I say to her? *I think you're nuts for not giving up this whole rape story?* Yeah, that'll fly. Suddenly Lindsay pops into my head. Maybe this whole thing started because Miranda wanted Grace to wingman for her the way Lindsay did the other night? Maybe Grace chickened out. Maybe—

Aw, hell, there's no way Grace Collier is too chicken to do anything. That girl is the definition of badass. The way she fights? The way she pinned me? I still can't believe she didn't put Zac down.

I was unconscious.

Her words circle my brain, and I don't know what to think. Girls lie. I've seen stories in the news. But would Grace lie about this?

The steel door downstairs squeaks open and then shuts with a clang.

The click of heels grabs my attention, and my heart rate kicks up a notch. I know this sound. Grace is wearing her ass-kicking boots, the boots that she's always wearing in my dreams.

Yeah. I dream about Grace Collier. So what?

"You're late," I say to piss her off. But I get only silence in reply.

Great. We're back to ignoring each other. But when I look her way, she's not pretending I don't exist. No, she's standing there, jaw dangling, and eyes round.

"What?"

"You cleaned all these lockers? By yourself?"

"Oh. Yeah. I just sprayed all of them, spent about half an hour scrubbing them out. It gives the Agent Orange a chance to dissipate."

Her lips twitch, and there's a sound I think may have been a laugh. Can't be sure.

"Yeah, I guess this crap could kill a jungle or two." She hooks her backpack onto the cart, grabs a pair of gloves, and dives in.

"So where were you?"

"Had to walk. My mom still won't let me take the car, and she had to go to work early."

She walked with those boots on? Jesus. "Sucks. Hey, why didn't you call me? We'd have given you a ride."

Eyebrows climb up her forehead. "A, I don't have your cell number. I have your dad's. Plus you made it pretty clear yesterday that riding with you isn't a good idea."

I stick my head in a locker, pretend there's something in there that requires extra scrubbing, and mutter an apology, but when Grace strides down the hall, I lean out to watch, my eyes stuck on her ass as it sways.

_____

My stomach lets out a loud grumble sometime close to one o'clock. Grace looks over at me with a smirk. She's wearing head-to-toe black. Her eyes are done in that weird Cleopatra makeup she loves, but her lips are bare.

I can't stop staring at them.

"Yeah. Lunchtime. Did you bring yours?"

She shrugs. "Yeah. Sandwiches again."

My wallet's got what, thirty or forty bucks inside? I tug it out to check. "Sit tight. I'm heading across the street. I'll bring you back something."

She shrugs and goes back to scrubbing. I head out. As soon as the door bangs closed behind me, I breathe easier. There's a cool breeze blowing that feels incredible after I inhaled all those orange fumes, so I stand at the door and just watch the lacrosse team for a while. Coach Brill is getting in Kyle's face, waving his arms around like a traffic cop, and I laugh. Kyle probably missed a shot. Happens sometimes. No big deal.

I jog across the parking lot and head out to the main road. Across the street and down about half a mile, there's a pizza store. By the time I get there, my stomach is turning itself inside out. I scarf down three slices in the store, then order two more for Grace.

Figure I owe her since she fed me all week.

A horn startles me. The driver is a girl, checking me out. I straighten my shoulders and grin back. *Thanks, baby.* I head back up the drive that leads from the main road to the school. It's long and kind of windy and lined by thick trees, and there's Grace following that tree line over to the athletic field. She takes out that big-ass camera and aims it right at Zac. She hasn't noticed me, and even though we're separated by the width of the parking lot, there's no missing the tension in her body, in her face.

What in the actual hell is going on? Why is she out here sneaking pictures of Zac if she's so damn afraid of him? Do I call her on it? Do I pretend I didn't see her? Do I tell Zac? Fuck, I don't know. Back inside the school I put the bag carrying her two slices on top of the utility cart. I snap on new gloves and turn toward a locker, kicking something on the floor that goes pinging off the opposite wall. I check it out, discover it's a steel stud—probably one of a few million on Grace's boots. I shove it into my pocket and get back to work. Five minutes go by, then ten. I hear the toilet flush in the girls' bathroom and whip around. How did she get back inside the school without me hearing the heavy steel door?

She walks over to me, so I point to the bag. "Bought you pizza."

"Thanks." That's it. One word. She opens the bag, slides out the paper plates holding the slices, sinks to the floor against a locker, and takes a bite that's anything but dainty. Last year I took Kimmie Phillips to dinner, and she ate half a slice with a knife and a fork, so this is pretty damn impressive. "How's your head today?" she asks after a minute.

With a shrug, I tell her, "Okay, I guess. No dizzy spells today."

"So how did you get hurt?"

"This time? I got checked by a really big player."

"How many concussions have you had?" She frowns at me over her plate.

"This is my second."

"Isn't that really dangerous?"

"Yeah. That's why I'm benched. Have to be tested and cleared by my doctor."

"So you'll get to play in the play-offs? You must be happy." She cracks the seal on a bottle of water, chugs. "Oh. Almost forgot. This is for your sister. Her clothes. Cleaned, dried, folded." She shows me a plastic bag on the bottom shelf of the utility cart that I didn't notice before. "Tell her thanks."

"Yeah. No problem."

This is how we waste the rest of the day. Small talk and manners so fucking polite it hurts. She never mentions Zac or the photo op or what I said yesterday in the car. She never mentions any of it, but it's all there, hanging in the air like the goddamn orange crap we're forced to use. And while I'm wondering which one will succeed in choking me first, the door opens with a loud screech, and a moment later Zac strides down the hall.

Chapter 13
Grace

As soon as the door clangs, I leap to my feet and tense up. That's my default reaction to everybody I see these days. But when Zac appears at the end of the corridor, my body doesn't just tense. It almost self-destructs. Breath and spit clog my throat. My heart lurches and then kicks into high gear against my ribs. My hands curl into fists, but my legs are off-line, disconnected. And it's this Herculean task to remain standing. I want to run. I want to hide. I want to throw up. I want to scream. I want to punch and kick and gouge.

I just watch. What the hell is wrong with me?

He gets closer and closer still, and I'm still watching, paralyzed by the knowledge. *I know what you did. You fooled everyone else, but you don't fool me.*

"Well, well, isn't this cozy?" Zac stops a few feet away, smirking at the rags and the cleanser and the lockers. My hands clench on the cleanser. I'll aim it right in his eyes if he steps toward me. "Let's go, Russell. You've been at this long enough."

Ian shakes his head, I think. "Can't, bro. Here until four."

Zac rolls his eyes. "Come on, man. That's not even an hour. So what if you ditch early? Who's gonna squeal? Not the collie, right, girl?" He's trying to bait me, but I don't say a word.

We stare each other down, neither of us showing our hand. Suddenly Zac feints and shouts, "Boo!"

I jerk and drop my can of cleanser, my only defense. Damn it. Goddamn it, I can't let him see I'm afraid. Beside me, Ian picks up the rolling can, puts it back on the cart, and Zac laughs, big loud obnoxious sounds that echo off the lockers.

I want to press my hands to my ears, but I can't let him see my fear.

He takes another step closer, and I finally remember how to move. I snap up a hand. "Far enough."

His eyes narrow, and he angles his head. "That sounds like a threat, Collier. Did that sound like a threat to you, Russell?"

"Zac, man, leave it alone. Just go. I'll meet you later."

"No, no, I think the collie just threatened me." He takes another step toward me. "What are you gonna do now? Tell the whole school I invaded your personal space?"

More obnoxious laughing that grinds my teeth and reddens my vision. Deep inside my body, heat is building. White hot and bubbling, it's nearly ready to blow, but I hold it down, hold it back. I'm not ready yet. This hot fury is the only thing that's keeping me from curling into a ball with my thumb in my mouth. I will not let him see my fear. I will not.

I find my voice, and thank God it doesn't crack or tremble. "We're here until four, Zac. You trying to get Ian into trouble too?"

A spark of anger lights his eyes. "Ian's a big boy, Collier. He doesn't need a slut like you looking out for him."

My knees are shaking, but I don't back down. "I'm only a slut because you got everybody in this school fooled, McMahon. I know what you really are."

He paces back and forth, clutching his hands together, and I know I'm getting under his skin. "You'd better shut your mouth, whore, before I—"

"Before you what, McMahon? Think carefully because I'm not drunk or unconscious this time." I can't feel my legs, but I force them into a fight stance because I am not backing down now.

"Okay, okay, cool it, Zac. Just go. I'll meet you in an hour." Ian steps between us, and inside I'm cheering because this means even he's convinced I'm not a quivering mass of Jell-O.

Zac glares at me for a long moment and then nods once. "Fine. But this isn't over. I hear you calling me a rapist again, I'm coming for you, Collier."

Oh, shit. Oh, fuck. Oh, God. "Bring it, McMahon."

Ian tosses an arm around Zac's shoulders, leads him down the corridor, murmuring platitudes under his breath.

"Dick."

"Bitch," Zac tosses over his shoulder.

I'm cheering, flipping a few mental cartwheels because I didn't back down. I'm openly watching them and not even bothering to pretend to clean lockers. I am not taking my eyes off Zac McMahon for a minute.

"Enough!" Ian shoves Zac into the lockers. "Will you cool it already?"

"Dude, you did *not* just do that." He shoves Ian back.

"I did, and I'll do it again if you don't take your head out of your ass. Anything happens to her, if she gets so much as a broken nail, who do you think everyone is gonna blame? Huh, smart guy?"

I watch Zac's shoulders sag. "Yeah. Okay."

"Why are you here? You know I'm scrubbing until four. Did you come just to bust balls?"

Zac glares at me while he answers Ian. "Come on, Russell. It's like three thirty. Who cares if you bounce early?"

A moment later he breaks eye contact and ducks his head, lowers his voice. I can only hear a word here and there like *fault* and *future* and *proof.* Ian looks upset. The color's gone from his face, and his body is tight. Zac's shaking his head violently and says *no* again and again. I may not be able to hear exactly what they're saying, but whatever it is, Ian's nervous about it.

A few minutes later Ian strides back down the corridor toward me, and I wish I didn't feel safe and happy about that. Ian watches me, a frown wrinkling his forehead. "It's okay. I'm gonna leave now."

I look away. "I'm fine. He doesn't scare me. He's only dangerous when I'm unconscious."

Ian opens his mouth to say something but doesn't. He grabs his stuff, then turns back.

"Grace, I wouldn't laugh at you for being scared."

"I said I'm not scared." I leap to my feet, grab my can of cleanser, and finish the last group of lockers alone.

I run to the door as it clangs shut, watch Ian hop in Zac's car with some other guys from the lacrosse team, and sigh heavily. I finish scrubbing out the last run of lockers for the day and text Mom at four o'clock. She can't leave her office for a while yet, so I can either hang here or start walking. I go back to the cart, wheel it to the corner, and grab my gear. I check the first address Mr. Russell wrote down and realize it's not far from here. I may as well get started.

Ten minutes later I'm standing in the most beautiful backyard I've ever seen. The homeowner, a woman named Cathy, is beyond proud. She's pointing out all the highlights of the design as I take out the camera, remove the cap, and set up for some shots. I take a wide-angle shot of a gorgeous pool. Tiles made out of irregularly shaped blocks of slate surround the pool and work their way up into a waterfall. It looks like a lake instead of a pool. By the house, a stone patio complete with barbecue grill, fridge, and bar rises out of the rock that surrounds it. I scroll through all the shots I've taken and figure Mr. Russell will be thrilled with the haul. I thank Cathy and head out.

Another address is just half a mile from here, so I head in that direction. It's getting cold now that the sun is setting, and my boots are killing me. I push through the pain, and just as I turn down the street where the second property is located, I hear a squeal of tires and whip around.

"Hey, slut!" someone's voice shouts. I whip around in time to see a silver object sailing toward my head. My hands automatically come up to protect myself, and I drop to a crouch. The object—a soda can—lands in the grass a few feet away. The car speeds off with laughter—girls' laughter—trailing behind. I didn't recognize the car, so it wasn't Lindsay or Miranda. I didn't get a good look at the driver or passengers. Hell, I'm not even sure what kind of car it was. I'll just sit right here on the cold, damp ground until I can breathe normally again. Until the ache in my chest eases a little. Until the fear makes room for rage because I really like the rage. It takes about twenty minutes, but finally I knock on the door to the second property Mr. Russell wants me to shoot.

The door's answered by a guy named Don Harding, a short, thinks-he's-a-player guy wearing a T-shirt that's too tight to be anything but sad. He looks me up and down, smirks a Zac kind of smirk, and invites me in. In my head warning bells sound, sirens wail, and forces are mobilizing for a full-scale attack. Don, the homeowner, looks at me like I'm nuts while I try to convince myself this is safe. But it's not safe, and I know it. He knows it, and he's daring me to do it anyway.

"You live here alone?"

"My wife won't be home for a while yet, sweet thing. You could come in for a while." Another smirk. Yeah, this is definitely not a good idea.

"When's your wife home?"

"Six-thirty or so."

"I'll come back then, Mr. Harding."

"Call me Don, honey."

How about no? "I'll come back." With a bodyguard and maybe a weapon.

I head down the walk, so happy not to be trapped in a room with this creep.

"Aw, come on. We're both here now. Why you gotta be like this?"

Me? Oh, you douche. I whip around, not surprised to find that he followed me down the walk. "You wanna know why I have to be like this? Because you're a slimy asshole—that's why. I came here to do a job, but you have to act like a dick and then say it's me. It's *my* fault. It's *my* problem."

He holds up his hands in surrender. "Jeez, I was just—"

"Oh, you were just what? *Playing around?*" I wave my hands. "Oh, oh, you were *joking* and didn't mean anything? News flash, *Don*, I don't find guys like you even a little bit funny. I'm here to take pictures of your new kitchen. Period. I'll come back when your wife is home, so pray I don't tell her what you tried to do." To add more weight to my bluff, I whip my phone out of my pocket and wiggle it in front of his face.

I turn to leave.

"Aw, baby, come on—"

I flip directions, stride right up to him so that we're standing toe-to-toe, and grab a fistful of his T-shirt. "My name isn't *honey*...or *baby*...or *sweet thing*. I am not here to amuse you until your wife gets home. Last chance—are you gonna get out of my way, or do I have to mess you up?"

"Okay! Okay! You on your period or something?"

My vision tunnels, and I want to tie this guy's tongue in a knot. Before I can do something I'll have to be bailed out for, I turn on my heel and leave. Don Harding's new kitchen is not going to make it into Mr. Russell's new brochures, and I really don't give a shit.

When I reach the corner, it hits me I'm not scared anymore. Guess I'm too mad to be scared. I call Mr. Russell, tell him word for word what just happened, and apologize.

"Grace, what did Ian do when Mr. Harding got fresh with you?"

"Oh, he's not here."

"I see."

Crap. I think I just got Ian in big trouble. "He got a ride home from one of his friends. I decided to visit the properties near the school after he left."

"I see."

"Mr. Russell, please. It's not his fault, really. Zac was causing trouble, so Ian got him away from me."

"Well, that's something. Where are you now?"

"Um, walking to the Millers' house up on College Drive."

"I'll meet you there."

He ends the call before I can protest. It takes no more than ten minutes to find the third address on Mr. Russell's list. When I turn up the walk and knock on the door, the homeowner holds up his finger. "Yeah, she's here right now. Okay. Bye."

He ends the call and asks, "Are you Grace?" When I nod, he opens the door wide. "Come on in. That was Steve Russell on the phone."

I hesitate. "Are you Mr. Miller?" The man is tall, with a ton of gray hair streaking the sides of his head. He's wearing a pair of wire-rim glasses and has a tiny gut hanging over the waistline of his Dockers. When he smiles, he seems friendly, not slimy.

"Yeah, Brett Miller. My wife is outside with our kids." He holds out a hand to me, but I still hesitate. After a moment he lowers his hand and loses his smile. "Grace, Steve told me what just happened."

I shut my eyes with a groan.

"It's okay. Why don't you walk around the house to the yard, and I'll stay in the kitchen, okay?"

I look at him sideways. "Really?"

"Really." He grins again.

I nod and walk around the house. Mrs. Miller is pushing a toddler on a swing set. An older boy is running around with a soccer ball. A door slides open, and Mr. Miller calls out. Mrs. Miller picks up the baby and heads indoors. A few minutes later the little boy follows. The yard is like a park with tons of perfectly clipped grass and curvy flower beds. Mr. Russell designed custom tiles that resemble scales for a large fish at the bottom of the pool. I don't know why the pool is uncovered in April, but I'm glad it is. The sun's at the perfect angle to show off those colors. There's something about framing the perfect shot, something soothing, maybe even cathartic. It's like your whole world gets reduced to just light and shadow, to whatever fits in the viewfinder. Mr. Russell does beautiful work. The pictures I'm taking will make people want to touch this fish, see if those scales are real.

With a happy sigh, I carefully pack the camera away and turn to wave at the Millers, watching from their kitchen. I wind my way around the house and find Mr. Russell leaning against the white Camry. "How'd it go?"

"Mr. Russell? What are you doing here?"

"Making sure nobody else gives you any trouble."

I blink. My dad told me the same thing once. It was after my first day of kindergarten. I walked out of the huge steel doors and found him leaning against our car. I ran over to him, and he scooped me up into his arms and asked me if anybody was mean to me. Nobody was until a few weeks later when a little witch named Samantha got me sent to the principal's office. Strange how after Zac assaults me and everybody's mean to me, now his response is "What do you expect me to do when you—"

He never finished that sentence. I guess he knew he didn't really need to.

I swallow hard. "Thanks, Mr. Russell. Really."

"So can I see what you've got so far?"

"Yeah. Sure." I unpack the camera, switch to scroll, and hand it to him.

"Grace, these are amazing. Thank you so much. Wait, what's this?"

I snatch the camera from him when he scrolls too far and sees one of the Zac shots I'd taken. "Nothing. I should go. It's getting dark."

"I'll drop you off."

"No! I can walk."

Mr. Russell's eyes, so much like Ian's, go hot for a moment. Then he sighs. "Grace, I know you don't know me, but I promise you this— you're safe with me. I am so, so sorry about what happened to you."

My throat closes, and I nod once, then take off. He drives slowly behind me as I walk all the way home. I hate that he knows what happened. I hate that he thinks I'm afraid of him, that I can't handle myself.

I hate that he's right.

Chapter 14

Ian

Zac and I cross the deserted parking lot to his Mustang. A stiff breeze rustles the leaves finally growing on the trees that line the school property, and I shove my hands into the pockets of my hoodie. I shut the car door, and we sit in silence for a long moment, fury sweating out of every pore on Zac's body. I shift in my seat, pick my way over barbed wire words and explosive accusations. One false move and I'm the enemy, and I don't want that.

"You get that I didn't ask to work with Grace, right? It was either this or miss the tournament."

"Yeah."

"So what are you pissed off about?"

His jaw twitches, and I know he's clenching his teeth. "I'm pissed because you defended her, man! The girl who's telling everybody I'm a psycho rapist."

"Did you see the way she reacted to you up there?" I wave a hand toward the school. "You scared her. On purpose. Seriously uncool, man."

He starts the car and just stares out the windshield. He pulls the cap off his head, scrubs a hand over his hair once, twice, three times. "Okay. Maybe I did. I just don't get her, bro! I mean, the first time's never that great for the girl, big deal. Why is she being such a bitch?"

I stare at him, but he's serious. "Zac, the thing is…she's not saying it to get back at you. She really thinks you raped her." He whips his head around, stares through me with hurt in his eyes, and before he can defend himself, I hold up a hand. "She's afraid."

"Afraid?" He looks at me sideways. "Bullshit. She threatened me, Russell. You heard her!"

"It's an act," I wave away his protest. "You strutting down that hall just now? Come on, Zac! You knew she'd be there. You rubbed her face in it."

Zac's workout flush drains out of his face, and he shuts his eyes with a groan. "Okay, but come on, man."

"She said she broke up with you. She told you no."

"Yeah, she did. But the night of the party she was different, so I just, you know, went for it." He lifts his hands, palms up.

A blood vessel in my head throbs. "What really happened?" I already heard the version he fed Jeremy and the other guys on the team and saw the visual aids.

He presses his lips together, puts the car in gear, and exits the lot. I figure he's not going to tell me anything. He doesn't talk until we stop for a red light near the pizza store where I picked up lunch. "Me, Kyle, Matt, Jeremy—we got there after they did. Miranda, Lindsay, and Grace. I think Sarah was there too. They were already tanked.

Grace and Miranda were dancing." His lip curls. "*Together*, dude. It was so hot."

The light turns green, and he drives down Main Street, pulls into the Burger King on the south side, and parks. "She was wearing a short skirt with those boots, the ones she's wearing today. Her hair's all loose, and she smelled amazing. Why did she do all that, Russell? Why did she do the hair and the makeup and the outfit and the perfume if she wanted me to keep away?"

That's a really good question. I don't have an answer for it either.

"There were six-packs all over the clearing. Grace had a bottle of whiskey. She kept looking over her shoulder at me, so after I had a few beers, I started dancing too. That's why we were all there, right? To get a little wasted, have a good time?"

I look down at my hands. They're clenched tight. He's right. That's what these parties are all about. Get wasted. Get lucky.

"Miranda got pissed. Grace never stops bitching about her stepmother or something—I don't know. She and Grace mixed it up a little, and Grace stormed off. I followed her, you know, to do the sensitive, supportive friend thing. Whatever works, right? Come on, Russell. I've seen you do the same thing."

He's right. I have. And it works. "Yeah, I'd have followed her too." The words leave a sour taste in my mouth.

"So she's all upset, and I'm trying to comfort her, you know? I kiss her once, and she pulls away, says she's not into it. Whatever. That's cool. But she keeps talking about how Miranda's selfish and never has time for her and only wants to talk about *her* issues. Grace says she has issues too but nobody ever wants to talk about hers. I take her hand, lead her to that hunk of wood—you know, that old railroad tie? We sit down. I put my arm around her. She doesn't move it off. I touch her knee, and she doesn't complain. She's almost crying now about her dad and her stepmother and Miranda and you—"

What? "Me?"

"Yeah, you. Collier's got a thing for you, bro."

I know that now, but why would that make her *cry*? "And you still moved on her?"

Zac shrugs. "Sure. You weren't together officially, so what's the big deal?"

I open the door, climb out of Zac's car so I don't knock his teeth out. I never moved on Grace because he asked her out first. Douche.

"Hold up, bro. You wanted to know what happened, so at least hear the whole story."

Shit. I don't want to hear anymore. I lean against the rear bumper and cross my arms.

"You know what? I wish you'd been there. You should have been there, bro, and maybe none of this would have happened!"

I shove my hands in my pockets and look away.

"She was all weepy, Russell. You should have been the shoulder she cried on, but you weren't there. I was. Was I supposed to just leave her like that? I never saw her that way before. Grace is always tough and pissy, you know? So I figure…here's my shot. Don't blow it! I lean over to kiss, her but she turns her head away, so I kiss her neck." He touches a spot just below his ear. "I thought she liked that. She moaned a little, stretched out on the ground flat on her back. You tell me that's not a sign."

Damn it, I can't.

"She wanted it. She gave me all the signs. So I moved next to her, kissed her some more. She was shaking. The ground's barely thawed, and she was probably cold, so I stepped things up. You know, to get her hot. She didn't stop me. She didn't push me away. She didn't say anything, except for the moans. So I kept going. When I got her top off, I took out my phone."

I was unconscious. Grace's voice echoes in my head, and I want to choke my best friend right now. "She passed out, Zac."

"No! Goddamn it, Russell. She was moaning. Tell me how that's rape because I don't get it. I didn't hold her down! She had plenty of time to run, to push me away, to go back to her friends, but she didn't."

I hold up my hands. "What about *after*, Zac?" He blinks at me, and I curse. "Come on, man. *After.* When you all scattered because you thought the cops were coming. You *left her* there."

"She wanted to find her clothes! Said she'd catch up to me later." He shakes his head and flings up both hands. "Oh, come on, Russell! If you were there, you'd have done the same thing. Admit it."

His words worm through my brain, tangling with Grace's. I think about Lindsay letting my friends put their hands on her and how disgusting that was, and suddenly my brain shoots to Erin Specht and the night I lost my virginity. It's the same scene, the same goddamn scene. Only that time I was totally into it instead of disgusted. Fuck! I shove off the car's bumper and stalk into the restaurant. I'm done. I'm done with this conversation. I'm done with Grace. I'm done with the whole goddamn drama.

"Yo! What's up?" Jeremy holds up a hand, and I high-five him on my way to order food. A few minutes later I'm scarfing down a couple of burgers and doing my best to shove Zac's words the hell out of my head.

The guys are breaking Kyle's balls over his haircut. The Mohawk spikes are gone. All he's got left is a flat strip over the top of his head. I don't feel like playing. I scan the restaurant. There are a few flat-screens bolted to walls, sound turned down. One's set to the news. Another's set to ESPN. My phone vibrates. It's my dad. For a second I seriously think about hurling it through one of the TVs. What could I possibly have done this time—or maybe *not* done—to piss off my dad? The food I just swallowed decays, and my stomach clenches. I'm on my feet but don't remember standing, and Zac is right next to me. "Ian, chill. Let's go get trashed, okay?"

Yeah. Yeah, okay. Make it stop, make it go away. I can't deal with my dad right now. I look at my friend and nod my thanks.

Half an hour later Zac and I are sitting in his living room, kicked back with a couple of beers. His parents are upstairs. Zac claims it's cool. Whatever. I chug some more beer and then blurt, "Zac, I gotta tell my dad the truth."

He looks at me from the recliner across the room and then shakes his head. "Bad idea, man."

"I was buzzed. I drove the car and almost hit somebody."

"But you didn't. Telling him the truth is only gonna get you in more trouble."

I put the beer down. It suddenly tastes like acid.

"Come on, Russell. Think about it. Brill will kick you off the team, and you can kiss scholarships good-bye. You'll be laying tile next to your dad until he keels over, and then you'll keep doing it until *you* keel over because it's all you can do. If that's the life you want, then tell him." He shrugs.

Shit. I'm losing it. I fold over my middle and rock. "I was lucky, Zac. All I hit was somebody's mailbox. What if I'd hit that guy walking his dog? Or some kid on his bike?"

"So what? Look, you can't fuck up your whole future for a bunch of what-ifs. You had what, two beers? You weren't drunk. Do you want to spend your the rest of your life listening to your dad tell you your grout lines suck or watching the tiles bake in some oven?"

I stare at him in horror.

"Didn't think so." He stares at me for a minute and then rolls his eyes. "Look, man. I get it. The what-ifs keep rattling around up there." He taps his temple. "You're looking at this all wrong. Don't keep saying what-if. Say, 'Okay, I learned I'm a lightweight and next time won't drive after two beers.' Case closed. I'm hungry. You hungry?"

I can't even hear the word without wanting to puke.

"Mom!" He shouts up the stairs. "Can I get a sandwich or something?"

I hear the ceiling creak and panic. Jesus, do I hide the beer or what? Zac's still got his in his hand and doesn't seem concerned when his mother appears at the bottom of the stairs, wearing a robe.

"Hi, Ian. You boys want some spaghetti and meatballs? I can reheat it."

Zac looks at me, shrugs, and says, "Yeah, that works."

"How was practice today? Did you boys have fun?"

Zac looks annoyed. "Mom, food?"

"Right, coming right up." She hurries into the kitchen.

He rolls his eyes at me, then drains what's left of his beer. The refrigerator door opens. Then the microwave beeps, and the sounds are normal. Comforting. I kill the rest of the night pouring more beer over the acid churning in my gut while Zac scarfs down a plate of pasta. I don't stop until I can't feel anything. It's after midnight when Zac drags me out of his car, almost carries me to my door and dumps me on the couch in our living room. I fall asleep the second the door closes, dreaming of boys on bicycles and old men walking dogs and girls with bright eyes.

A bright light pierces my head like a laser, and I groan.

"Get up, Ian."

Hell, no. Getting up means moving, and I can't do that. There's a truck parked on top of me. My tongue feels like it spent the night licking every postage stamp ever printed. And I'm not sure, but I think there's a construction crew jack-hammering the base of my brain.

"Ian! Ian, what the hell is wrong with you! Get up. You're already late."

Late. Late for what? Whatever it is won't mind if I just stay here and die.

"Ian, damn it, get off this sofa. Now."

Sofa? It moves while I try to remember why I'm sleeping downstairs. Or maybe it's the clash of tectonic plates. My head spins, and my stomach vibrates for a second, executes a complete 360, and lands somewhere in my esophagus, and believe me, the postage-stamp taste is ten times better than what I'm tasting now. I drag myself to my feet, manage the twenty-story climb to the bathroom, and try not to lose my spleen along with every meal I ate over the last two or three years of my life.

"Jesus, Ian, are you hungover? I can't believe you!"

Oh, crap. I'm a prisoner in my own body, and my dad's gonna rattle the bars on my cage. Hell, he'll probably take the whole day off, make a holiday of it. I peel myself off the bathroom floor, fall into the tub, still dressed, and shower away the puke that's sticking to parts of me. Fifteen minutes later after I manage to escape from my wet clothes, I'm vertical—no easy feat—but the headache is no better. I wrap a towel around my lower half, happy to find the bathroom deserted. My room is also empty, though there's a cup of steaming black coffee and bottle of pain reliever on the table next to my bed.

I swallow a few pills and sip the coffee and say a short prayer of thanks that neither of them are returned to sender. I find some jeans, manage to pull them on without losing consciousness. The sound of a throat clearing makes me jolt. My dad's sitting at my desk, watching.

Waiting to pounce.

I prepare myself, go through the checklist. No talking back. No eye-rolling. No heavy sighs. I'm ready. Bring it.

"Feel any better?"

Slowly I nod and brace for impact.

"Mom's making you some toast. Go down when you feel up to it, then go back to bed."

I scan his body. There are no outward signs of alien or droid take-over, so I nod again. Dad shakes his head with a sad little smile and leaves me alone. Fifteen minutes later I think it's safe for me to attempt walking. I head downstairs, find my mom in the kitchen.

"Hey, Mom."

She spins, her ponytail whipping the air. "Ian, you scared us both to death."

"Sorry."

"Sit down. Eat some toast."

I sink to a chair at the table, grab a slice of toast from the plate, and nibble. My stomach doesn't protest, so I nibble some more.

Mom sits next to me. "Ian, what were you thinking? You've just had a concussion, and you drink yourself into a stupor on top of it?"

Whoa, my parents have obviously switched bodies. I groan and drop the toast. "Mom, I'm sorry. I got a little drunk. I didn't drive, and I didn't run over anybody—" I clamp my lips together and grip my head tight.

"Well, that's something at least." She sips a cup of coffee, and I look for mine. Only I left it upstairs. Over the rim, she examines me. She's ready for work, hair tied back in a neat tail, comfortable shoes on, slacks, and sweater. Her uniform. Same thing every day, same damn thing. I stare at her and wonder, *Is this what it'll be like for me?* Graduate high school, spend four more years getting a degree for a shot at some job that I'll count the days to escape from? Is this my future, the one Zac is so sure I'll ruin if I admit I dinged the car because I was drinking?

Mom pushes the coffee cup aside and leans over to grab my hands. "Ian, I know something's wrong. Tell me. Please?"

My eyes snap to hers. Is it written across my forehead? How the hell does she know? I open my mouth, shut it. I can't. I just can't.

I grab my gear and leave.

Outside it's cold, colder than the last few days have been. The bite in the air does wonders to clear up my head. School is less than half a mile's walk, but the closer I get, the slower my steps are. I stop for more coffee and a bagel. I waste time scanning a newspaper somebody left behind. Grace is probably wondering where I am. She might even be worried about me a little, the way she did when I got dizzy.

I shift in my seat, feel the steel stud in my pocket like a goddamn thorn in my side. Damn it, I feel torn with Zac on one side and Grace on the other, and I hate it, hate feeling like the knot on their tug-of-war rope. After everything that happened yesterday, everything that Zac told me, did for me, I can't believe he's what Grace says he is.

There's no way I can look Grace in the eye and tell her that. So I do what I do best.

Take the chickenshit route.

Chapter 15
Grace

"Grace, you ready yet?" Mom calls. I grab my camera bag and jog down the stairs. Her mouth falls open. "Wow. You look so pretty. What's the occasion?"

I face the mirror hanging on the hall wall and make sure my hair's still smooth. I wrestled with it for an hour last night, blowing out my curls until my hair looked like a shiny curtain. I'm wearing jeans and a plain T-shirt. All my leather and spikes are upstairs. I don't have to wear armor every day. I can be—you know—*soft*, I guess.

I slip my feet into comfortable flats instead of my studded boots and head for the kitchen to make a few sandwiches.

"Mom, where's the roast beef?" I rummage through the drawer with cold cuts.

"Since when do you eat roast beef?" She nudges me out of the way, finds the roast beef hidden under a package of Swiss cheese.

I slap some mayo on a few hard rolls, layer on cheese, roast beef, and turkey, and then wrap the sandwiches in plastic.

"Okay, I'm ready."

"Grace, seriously. What's the deal?"

"No deal, Mom."

"Okay." She smiles. "Good for you."

Fifteen minutes later she's driving off while I head into the school. Damn it. Ian's not here yet. I stow my bag, push the utility cart to where we left off yesterday, and snap on a fresh pair of gloves. Shivering, I glance around. Yep, definitely alone, but I swear I can still smell Zac standing right here, where Ian shoved him into a locker.

That was way unexpected. But seriously appreciated. I hope Ian knows that. I get how hard that must have been, going up against a friend. Lindsay won't do it, even though I know she hates what Miranda's turning her into. I glance at my phone. Ian's late. Hope he didn't have another dizzy spell. Oh, crap! I hope I didn't get him into big trouble with his dad last night.

A noise way down the hall has me whipping around with a gasp, but nobody's there. Frozen in place, entire body clenched, I finally notice an overhead light just popped, but I can't relax. My fingers are numb. My heart's galloping, and sweat beads line the back of my neck. I do not have time for this now, goddamn it. I am stronger than this. I grab the cart, wheel it to the lockers by the stairwell. I spray a bunch of lockers and scrub them out, looking over my shoulder after every one.

The door downstairs is still closed. But the numbness is spreading, and my chest is getting heavy.

Where the hell is Ian? I should call his dad. No, wait. If he's ditching,

I'll get him in trouble. But what if he's passed out somewhere? I can't breathe. I grab my phone, call my mother, put it on speaker.

"Hey, Grace."

"Mom. Help."

"What? What's wrong? What happened?"

"Can't breathe, Mom."

"Okay, hold on. I'm pulling over. Okay, get your water."

Water? Right. My bag. It's not on my shoulder. The cart. I put my bag on the cart. I crawl over, unzip the bag, find a bottle of water, and chug.

"Get a towel, put some water on your neck…like I showed you."

Yes. Towels. I tear off a few from the paper towel roll, pour some water over it, drape it under my hair.

"Okay, breathe."

"Can't."

"You can, honey. You are."

"I'm alone, Mom. All alone."

"No, Grace. Never. I'm right here."

"When is this gonna stop?" I whisper and rub my chest, and she sighs.

"I don't know, Grace. Maybe if you didn't have to see him every day. Like in Europe. You could meet new friends, friends who don't know you, don't know what happened. You can start over, honey."

I shut my eyes, let my head fall back, and imagine climbing the Spanish Steps in Rome or exploring the Louvre in Paris. I could hang with my hosts or go out and meet new people, people who don't know I'm a slut, people with fancy accents and…and manners and courtesy and—

No.

No. I wipe the cold sweat off my neck and know it won't be any better across the world than it is here. I have to face this. If I run, Zac wins, and he's already won enough games.

The knots in my intestines unkink, and I can breathe again.

"Grace, you okay?" Mom asks after my gasping breaths slow down.

"Yeah," I say and scrub my hands over my face. "Yeah," I repeat with more certainty. "Better now. Thanks, Mom. Love you."

"Love you too, Gracie. Call me later, okay?"

"Yep."

I tuck the phone back in my pocket and climb to feet I can barely feel. But they hold me, and that's enough for the moment. I glance out the window that overlooks the parking lot and watch the lacrosse team. Even from this distance, I can pick out Zac just by the way he stands— hands on his hips, head up.

I return to my row of lockers. Behind me is the stairwell. I can't miss hearing the door downstairs open. Reassured, I scrub locker after locker by myself until my stomach rumbles and then stop for lunch.

Still no Ian. I hope he's okay.

I sit in the window, watch Coach Brill hand out water bottles and the boys flop to the turf. I'm exposed. Entirely visible to anybody who looks up here. But nobody is, so I take the camera from my bag and check out the zoom.

Damn it, not close enough to catch facial expressions. Okay. Time for a little espionage.

Instantly my chest tightens, and my knees shake. But I have to do this. I have to get that picture so everyone will see. I pull on my hoodie, grab my bag, and sneak closer to the field. By the time I reach my favorite tree, the team's break is over, and everyone's back on the field in position, waiting for the whistle. I hold up the camera, check the view, and it's perfect. I can see the beads of sweat roll down faces. I aim, shoot picture after picture.

"You going to Miranda's after practice?" Kyle shouts to Zac, who shrugs.

"Maybe. If nothing better comes up."

"We should head to the woods, forget Miranda's."

"That's better. We'll hang, wait for Russell to finish his housekeeping."

"Text him. He's not here today."

"He's not?" Zac turns to face Kyle and lets a ball slip by him.

The whistle blows. Coach Brill shouts at Zac to get it together, but Zac ignores him.

"Too hungover," Kyle confirms.

The look, the exact expression I've been trying to shoot, crosses his face when he turns to stare up at the second-floor window exactly where I should be. I press the shutter button, my hands shaking, and pray I get it. With this, I can show everybody the truth about Zac McMahon.

"McMahon, are you here to play or work on your tan?"

"Sorry, Coach."

"Bring it in, guys!" The whistle blows, and I start the perimeter trek back to the school. I sneak along the trees to the parking lot, dart between parked cars, stick to the shadow of the building, and slip through the heavy steel door. I rush up the stairs to the second floor and skid to a stop.

Ian's sitting on the floor, back against the lockers. "Where you been, bright eyes?" he asks—for what reason, I have no idea because the ice in his voice tells me he already knows.

Chapter 16

Ian

Whoa.

Grace looks hot. Smokin' hot. My mouth waters at the sight of her. Her hair's down and smooth, and my fingers itch to touch it. She's wearing no makeup—no Cleopatra eyes, none of that goth lipstick. Her cheeks are red—probably from that black op she just executed. Even her clothes are different. Doesn't notice me until she's a few feet away. Doesn't know—or maybe hopes I don't notice—she's wearing a shit-eating grin when she runs up those stairs.

It disappears when she finds me here. She shuts it all down, tosses hair over her shoulder, and lifts her eyebrows. "You still work here?"

New look, same attitude. Yeah. Definitely should have stayed home and gone back to bed because, because…aw, hell. She almost had me with that *I like you, do you like me* routine, but I know what she's really doing with her fancy camera. She's just another Zac conquest, another in a string of them who can't stand knowing she's just another hump-and-dump.

I stand up, walk to the utility cart, grab a can of cleanser, and toss it at her. She tries to catch it, fumbles. That's when I snatch the bag off her arm and fish out that big-ass camera.

"Hey!" She grabs for it, but I dodge her hands. Does she think I didn't notice that she disappears every day? Does she think nobody sees her sneaking around the lacrosse field? I power on the camera, scroll through the images stored on the card.

"Ian, please. That's a five-thousand-dollar camera somebody donated to the school paper. It's not mine."

"Yeah. I know. What I don't know is why you're filling up a memory card with pictures of the guy you *claim* raped you."

I'm baiting her, but she's not biting. Instead, her shoulders fall. "You wouldn't understand."

Got that right. "Oh, I get it, Grace. You let Zac do you, then got pissed when he didn't stick. What's not to understand?"

She flinches like I kicked her in the stomach but recovers fast, ready to brawl. "And where were *you* today?"

"Hungover. Zac and I had a party last night. And a nice long talk. You know what he told me?" I scroll through more pictures. "Oh, look! Here's one of Zac leaving Miranda's party. And one of Zac blocking a shot. And another one of Zac. And another. And another." I shove the camera at her. "He told me you got so trashed that night you could hardly stand up straight. He said you and Miranda had a fight and you left. He said he was worried about you. Followed you like any friend would. Said you let him kiss you, take off your shirt, and do you." Another flinch, but I'm in too deep to back off now. "He said you never told him no."

She looks at me, bright eyes wounded but dry. No tears from Cunning Collier. This whole sweet-faced girl thing? Yeah, no. Not buying it anymore. "You believed him?" she finally asks, her voice wobbling, but I'm immune now.

I shoot her a look. "I've seen his pictures, and now I've seen yours, so yeah. I believe him."

"Then you're an ass." The wobble is gone, and *poof!* she morphs back to Kick-ass Grace, lips sneering. "I went to that party for *you*, you jerk. I got dressed up because I wanted you to notice me, not him. I broke up with him after two days, Ian. Two. Know why?"

She gives me no chance to tell her I don't give a shit and just plows on ahead.

"Because he's not *nice*, Ian. The first time I noticed it, I thought it was me. Maybe I misunderstood, so I gave him another chance. But it *wasn't* me. He just doesn't care about anybody but himself, and you guys, you don't care about his character as long as he's good in the net."

I huff out a laugh at that, circling her while she scrolls through the pictures to make sure I didn't delete any. If she knew anything about our team, she'd know how totally untrue that is. Coach Brill is all about building honor and character and respect. Says he'd rather lose the whole season honorably than win a single game by playing dirty. He benches players for things like—well, like cursing at him. Zac made sure I got home safe last night. When Jeremy and Matt and I all needed math help, Zac was the one who tutored us after Coach Brill said we couldn't play until we passed.

"When I told him I wouldn't go out with him again, you know what he said? He got pissed off, cursed me out, said there were half a dozen chicks hotter than me lining up to…to do him." She sneers, and I figure what Zac had really said was a hell of a lot more descriptive.

It's also true. A guy who can bang anybody he wants—anywhere, anytime—doesn't need to force a girl.

"Here's what I didn't know about Zac McMahon. He's a sore loser, Ian. The biggest sore loser there is." She meets my gaze without blinking. "I was drunk and pissed off, and I thought he was being nice and trying to comfort me because of how we left things. But I was wrong. God, I was so wrong. He was plotting revenge. He had to prove to me that he never loses. *This* look, *this* expression—it's the last thing I remember." She jabs a finger at the camera, turns it so I can see the image.

All I see is Zac in the zone.

"I've seen this face before. You have too. On the lacrosse field every time he gets a penalty."

I'm shaking my head, but I can't look away from the image on the camera. Even frozen in bits and bytes, the sneer on Zac's lips, the way his jaw is clenched, the way his eyes fixate on his enemy—it's feral, the way a lion stalks prey.

"Now I see it every time I shut my eyes."

A chill crawls down my back, and I shove the camera away. "Proves nothing." I pace a few step away.

"It proves *everything*," she snaps back. "Why do you defend him?

You know I'm right. Remember the game against Holtsville High School? He put one of their attackers in the hospital, Ian."

Shaking my head, I pace back. "It was a clean hit. That kid turned at the last minute."

She throws up her hands. "Fine. You believe what you want. I'm done." She shoves the camera in her bag, hikes the bag over her shoulder, heads for the door. "I cleaned all morning alone. You can clean all afternoon." She stalks to the stairs and turns back for one last shot. "I thought you were different."

That one draws blood, and I turn my back so she won't see. The door slams downstairs, and I move to the window, watching her stalk across the lot like the pavement offends her and must now die. She crosses the bus lane, and that's when Jeremy and Kyle catch up to her. My gaze whips to the field. The team's on a break. Coach Brill's got out the clipboard. He can't see Jeremy and Kyle through the circle of guys watching him map out a play.

Zac's swilling water, Matt's rolling his shoulders to work out kinks. Nobody notices one big guy and one not-so-big guy flank one girl. Nobody sees Kyle touch her or her wriggle away. Nobody sees Jeremy pump his fist in a rude gesture that would get his fucking ass kicked if he did it in front of one of my sisters. Nobody sees. Nobody hears. And I can't help thinking of a stupid riddle—if a girl's attacked in the forest and no one's around to see it or hear it, did it really happen? Even from here I can see the terror in her bright eyes that she tries so damn hard to hide behind tough talk and too much makeup.

I see.

Muttering curses, I slide on the rail down the main stairs, shove open the door, and catch up to Kyle and Jeremy just as Grace plants her knee in Jeremy's gut. He doubles over, gasping for air. I grab one of my friends in each hand and muscle them off. "Get the hell away from her."

Jeremy whips around. "Russell, she—"

"Save it, Linz. I saw the way you hassled her. You're lucky Coach Brill didn't see, or you'd both be off the team. Get your asses inside and take a piss or whatever you're supposed to be doing before he notices." I let go of them, and they back off, glaring, and head inside the school.

I pick up Grace's camera bag and hand it to her. She takes the bag, studies me for a long moment with a deep frown like I'm some question on a pop quiz she can't figure out, and finally takes off. I watch her until she's out of sight.

Somehow it makes me feel better.

By the time I get back inside, Jeremy and Kyle are spitting mad at me. "Dude, what the fuck was that?" Jeremy gets up in my grill, so I lean into his.

"That was me stopping you from being an asshole." I shove him back a step, then turn on Kyle. "Are you brain dead or something? Did you really think she'd let you two get away with that? You're lucky she didn't go straight to Coach Brill."

"And tell him what? We were just talking."

Rolling my eyes, I slap Jeremy in the head. "Just talking. You always talk with your right hand?"

"Jeez, relax. It was a joke—"

"It wasn't just talk, and it wasn't just a joke. You circled her. You surrounded her. You put hands on her, and then you said shit to scare her. Why?"

Jeremy's eyebrows jump. "Why?"

"Yeah. Why?"

He looks at Kyle, but Kyle scrunches up his face and looks at Jeremy. "Um—"

"Kyle, if anybody tried that with Val or Claudia, what do you think I would do?"

He scrubs his head, but his Mohawk isn't there anymore, so he drops his hand and looks away. "Go bat-shit crazy on their ass."

"Damn right."

"Dude, I would never act like that around your sister," Jeremy assures me.

"Then why would you do it around Grace?"

They exchange glances that tell me they think I've been sniffing orange cleanser for too long. Probably right.

"Because Grace is a—"

I snap up a hand. "Grace is a girl. That's it. You want to slap on any other names, knock yourself out. But don't ever forget she's a girl first, and we don't treat girls like that. Feel me?"

Jeremy's hands come up, surrender-style. "Yeah, yeah, okay."

Tension thickens as the three of us stare down. I'm waiting for one of them to say it, to ask the obvious question, but both of them are too pissed off at me to say it and expose me as the hypocrite I am.

Since when?

While they return to the field, shooting me glares over their shoulders, I pick up the can of cleanser and scrub lockers so hard they'd bleed if they were my friends' skin.

Chapter 17
Grace

I run from the school like the entire lacrosse team is chasing me. I look over my shoulder for the twelfth time, but Jeremy and Kyle aren't there. Neither is Zac.

And neither is Ian.

I've never seen him like that—so cold and hateful. A shiver skates up my spine, and I pick up my pace. He knows what I've been doing with the school's camera. I wonder when he'll spill it to Zac. Zac will probably have me arrested for stalking or harassment or something. Oh my God, how is this happening? Pressure builds in my chest, rises like molten rock under a volcano. I didn't do anything wrong! Why do I always get punished? I rub the pain in my chest that's been growing steadily for the past two weeks from all the people hacking at it with rusty blades. I wish I were home. I wish I could just blink or snap my fingers and be off the streets, where every sound is a threat.

A cold wind blows, and I burrow deeper into my jacket. I don't know when I made the choice to come to my dad's house—he's still at work—but here I am, standing in front of it. The lush green lawn, the sculptured flower beds where the spring flowers are already in bloom, the basketball hoop over the garage—it all makes me want to vomit all over the perfectly paved driveway. I don't belong here. I know this, but here I am anyway.

"Grace?"

I spin around, and my mouth falls open. There's my dad in Dockers and T-shirt, rake in his hands.

I don't know why he's home in the middle of the day, but I'm glad, so fucking glad. All that pressure, all that emotion boils up and out of me in a single sob. "Daddy."

A second later I'm folded up in his arms, crying for what? Everything, I guess. I reached the breaking point. I can't do it anymore. I can't be tough anymore.

"Honey, what happened?"

I shake my head, unable to form words even if I could find the right ones.

"Come on. Come inside." With an arm around my shoulder, he guides me up the walk, but I hang back.

"It's okay, Grace. Come inside. It's cold."

In minutes he's got me tucked under a blanket on the sofa in the family room, a box of tissues on the table in front of me. Kody's LEGO blocks are spread all over the floor next to Keith's video game. Pictures of the boys adorn the walls, the shelves. Pictures of Dad with Kristie perch on the end table.

There are none of me. I'm invisible—unless you want sex. Then I'm low-hanging fruit.

"You ready to talk now?" He brushes the hair from my eyes, smiles for a second.

When he smiles, I can see why my mom and Kristie fell for him. Like I fell for Ian. "Guys are jerks."

The smile drips off his face. "Which guys?"

"All of them."

He laughs once. "Yeah. But which guys specifically?"

I take a deep breath and tell him everything. "Zac's friends hassled me today. The team's doing lacrosse camp this week. I kicked one because he said stuff to me and touched me. Well, he tried to anyway."

"Good girl. The way I taught you?"

Nodding, I grab another tissue. "Right in the solar plexus. I remembered at the last minute that he was probably wearing a cup so I just, you know, recalculated." I smother a grin. "He turned as red as his hair."

His arm, still draped around my shoulders, squeezes in approval.

"Dad, I don't get this whole slut thing. Don't sluts like sex and sleeping with everything that breathes? If I were really like that, I should be the most popular girl in school, not the least."

He shifts his hand to my hair, pets me. "Is that what you want?"

"No, no, I just want them to leave me alone. I don't get why they need to surround me and call me names and threaten me, you know?"

"How did they threaten you?" The hard edge in his voice is kind of nice. It makes me feel…safe. For the first time in weeks, I feel… almost good.

"Zac's friends. Jeremy Linz and Kyle Moran. They circled me like vultures, took turns trying to cop a feel. Every time I batted one away, the other moved in. Kyle said girls like me aren't worth dating. Then Jeremy said he thinks I'd look good with his—" Oh, God, this is my dad, and I can't say it. I can't say those words to him. So I show him.

He makes a choking sound and sits up straighter.

"Why do guys think this is okay?"

He's quiet for a long moment, staring down at his hands. They're no longer around my shoulders. Now they're clenched in tight fists. "Gracie, some boys think sex is a contest. A competition. A sport. Girls are just points to collect. And some girls—" Abruptly he slaps his hands to his legs. "Well. That's all you were to Zac."

"Daddy, he—"

He holds up his hand to cut me off.

"What really happened doesn't matter, Grace. It can't be proved. The police won't arrest Zac. The school won't expel him. You can't do anything about him. All you can do is control how you respond." He scans my body and smiles. "I think this is a great start. Dressing like a nice girl—"

My eyes snap to his. Did he really just say that? "Whoa. What the hell does that mean?"

"Well, honey, you wear a lot of leather and spikes and tight clothes, and that just tells boys—"

"Tells them what? 'Here I am, boys, come and get it!'?"

"Uh, I wouldn't put it that way."

"How would you put it?" I toss the blanket off, stand up, and cross my arms. "You think this is my fault. You actually think all of this is my fault, don't you?"

"Damn it, Grace, you made it easy! You were out at night in the woods, drunk, and dressed like…like—"

"Like a slut."

His lips clamp shut.

Oh my God. I stare at him. I have his eyes, his DNA, his blood, and he's ashamed of me. Before I can say anything, before I can breathe, the front door opens, and tiny feet pound into the room. "Daddy!" "Hey, Dad!"

Kody and Keith tackle their dad—

Their dad.

I press my hand to my chest because the pain's back, and it's brought company.

"Hey, Grace!" They tackle me next, and I force out a smile. Kristie walks in, carrying a few grocery bags, and looks from me to Dad. The room temperature drops ten degrees.

"Oh. I didn't know you were stopping by today, Grace."

Stopping by? Oh, I see. I need an invitation to enter my father's house.

"Kirk, I wish you'd told me Grace would be here. I only bought enough for us." Kristie makes a face, that fake *Oh, darn* wince that's really a *Too bad, so sad* gloat, and I want to strangle her with her freakin' fake pearls.

"Yeah, Kristie, I get it. I'm not invited to dinner." Like I could eat.

"Grace, that's not true. It's just—"

"Grace," Dad cuts her off. "Come on. I'll take you home."

Home. Sure, fine, whatever.

In the car Dad clears his throat. "Sorry about that. Kristie likes to plan everything and—"

"I get it, Dad." I don't have a K in my name, so I guess I'm out of the klub. Like I even give a krap.

Mom and I don't live that far from Dad and Kristie. I could have walked, but I guess he needed to feel fatherly or something. We stop for a light, and the dashboard clock says it's not even two o'clock yet. "So why are you home during the day?"

"Oh, I'm on vacation this week."

I swallow down the acid my stomach is shooting up into my throat and just nod. "That's nice. Would have been nicer if I'd known you were on vacation. Maybe we could have done something together."

He squirms. "Kristie and I coordinated our schedules so we could be with the boys this week."

"Oh, the boys."

He shoots me a look and sighs. "Come on, Grace. Give me a break. You're seventeen years old. The boys are little and—"

"And don't need to spend any time with their sister the slut."

"Damn it, Grace. That's not fair. I—"

"Drop me here. I'll walk the rest of the way." The light turns green, and he drives past the school.

"Grace—"

"Look, I get it, Dad, okay? You wanted a do-over," I shout. "I'm sorry I 'dropped by' without waiting for a written invitation. Just drop me here, Dad." He turns off Main Street, abruptly pulls to the curb, and just stares straight ahead while I grab my bag and open the door.

I slam the door and hear the squeal of tires as he pulls a sharp U-turn. I walk the rest of the way home, my temper smoldering like oil-soaked rags near an open flame. I can't believe him. Takes the entire week off and never once says, "Hey, Grace, we're taking the boys here or there. Want to come?" Does he think maybe it's been a totally horrible week for me and that I could use more than a five-minute weekly phone call? Hell, no. I kick the front door, send it bouncing off the wall in our entryway. I stomp all the way upstairs to my room, drop my bag on my bed, and blink the sting out of my eyes.

The house is quiet except for a few creaks and groans. Too quiet.

I snatch the heavy chain belt I never wear anymore because it's— well, heavy—and grip it tightly in both hands. I check my mom's room, behind all the doors, even in the bathtub, but nobody's here.

I'm alone.

The house lets out another creepy sound. Why does it do this only when I'm alone? Why doesn't it moan and creak and sigh when the house is full of people to assure me there's no psycho serial killer hiding in my clos—

Oh, God. I didn't check the closet.

I creep slowly back to my room and whip open the closet door, the chain in my hand snagging some hangers and knocking three pairs of pants off the rod. "Jesus, I'm losing it." I drop into the chair by my desk and scrub my hands through my hair. There's always homework to do, I suppose. Or watch some TV and try to drown out all the spooky sounds with canned laughter. Usually at this time I'd be hanging out with Miranda and Lindsay—around school, shooting pictures, or shopping at the mall.

I reach for my bag, take out the camera, and connect the data transfer cord to my laptop. One by one, the pictures I shot upload from card to hard drive. The progress bar counts down—twelve remaining…eleven remaining…ten. It starts to sound like footsteps—heavy cleats dropping on each step leading to the second floor…to my room. There are twelve steps—one for each image.

The house moans, and I whip around in my chair with my heart rate lurching into overdrive, but nobody's here. Six more images remaining. I grab my chain and head downstairs. From the kitchen, I fill my arms with cans from the pantry, stack them in front of the door, and make sure all the locks are engaged. A knife would probably be better than this belt, so I slip one out of the butcher block, hold it out in front of me like a sword. By the time I get back to my desk, all of the pictures are uploaded. Gulping down the foul taste that coats my tongue whenever I see Zac McMahon, I scan through the images and find it—the one. The picture that's going to get me my life back.

Chapter 18
Ian

Sometime around two o'clock tires screech outside. I toss my rubber gloves to the cart and head to the window to see what's up. Some guy shoves out of a minivan and marches to the field. I don't know what's going on, but it beats locker detail, so I hurry outside to watch just as the coach reaches him.

"Sir, can I help you?"

"Jeremy and Kyle. Which ones are Jeremy and Kyle?"

"Please leave the field, or I'll have to call security," Coach Brill warns the angry man.

"Yeah, you do that. I want to talk to Jeremy and Kyle right now."

Oh, shit. I know who this is.

Coach Brill steps forward. "Sir, this is a closed practice session. I'm going to say it again. Leave, or I'll call security."

"I'm not leaving until I talk to Jeremy and Kyle." The man struts around, glaring at everybody. When I see his face, my mouth tightens. Bright eyes. Just like Grace's.

"Russell! What did you do?" Jeremy shouts.

I hold up my hands. "Not me, dude."

The man whips around, points to me. "Who are you?"

"Ian Russell."

"Do you know Jeremy and Kyle?"

Coach Brill, scrolling through his contacts list, shakes his head, so I stay quiet. The man paces around the field, trying to read names on jerseys.

"Not leaving here until somebody tells me which one is—" He changes direction, hones right in on Jeremy, whose red hair sticks out from under his helmet. "You. Redhead. Are you Jeremy, you little punk?"

The man's eyes, so much like Grace's, narrow to slits behind wire-rim glasses, and his face goes red. He lunges, and a bunch of us surge between them. "Whoa, back off, man!"

Coach Brill is on the phone with 911 now. Zac is watching from a few yards back, saying nothing. Kyle looks like he just crapped his shorts, and Jeremy is paralyzed.

Mr. Collier struggles against the guys holding him off Jeremy. "You go near my daughter again, and I will knock you out, you hear me?"

A rumble ripples from guy to guy as they figure out who the angry man must be. Then the stances shift. The guys take off their helmets, lean on sticks, move a little bit closer to Zac. Pleasant smiles are pinned on faces, but muscles are coiled, ready to brawl. It's a show. It's a goddamn production. I'm on the fringe, and part of me knows I should close in. Isn't that where I belong? By Zac's side?

Coach Brill approaches Mr. Collier slowly, hands out, like he's a rabid dog. "The police are on the way. I don't know what this is about, but if you don't want to be arrested, you should leave now."

"This is about my daughter. You keep these animals the hell away from her while she's here. You're the adult. Anything happens to her, I will come after you."

"Sir, I don't know who you or your daughter are, but I can promise you this—my boys will not leave this field without my direct supervision. You have my word."

Mr. Collier stares hard at Coach Brill and finally nods. "I hope you teach them some respect for young girls. One of them already did enough to hurt her." He glares directly at Zac, but I shift and squirm because it feels like he's talking to me.

"Who's your daughter?"

"Grace Collier."

Somebody says it. Somebody actually has the balls to mutter, "Slut!"

Mr. Collier whips around. "See? This is what I'm talking about!" He flings out an arm in the general vicinity of the insult.

Coach Brill straightens his shoulders. "Who said it? Who said that?"

The guys shuffle their feet, kick the dirt. Coach steps closer. "I heard it. I want to know who said it. And I want to know right now, or this team will sit out the tournament."

Sounds of disgust and outrage swell over the team. "What? You can't do that!"

"You really want to test me?" Brill dares them. "Who won the tournament in '07?"

All of us stare at him in shock. In 2007, our school didn't play in the All Long Island Tournament. There was an incident with four seniors and a freshman that year—an incident some call *hazing*, but others call it what it was—homophobia. Coach Brill is *not* bluffing, and we know it. Slowly heads turn, and elbows nudge. Finally a throat clears. "Um. Coach? It was me."

Matt steps forward.

It wasn't him. Matt's taking one for the team, and I think the coach knows it. Coach Brill crosses his arms, frowns at Matt. "Get your gear. Go home."

"But Coach!"

"Get your gear. Go home. You're suspended."

Matt shifts his weight, glares at Kyle. He grabs his stick and his helmet and leaves the field.

Mr. Collier faces Coach Brill, his anger defused. "Thank you."

"What is it you think Jeremy and Kyle did?" Coach takes a step closer.

"They cornered her today. Touched her, called her names." He turns his sneer on Jeremy. "That one told her she'd look good with his dick in her mouth."

Coach Brill's eyes almost explode out of his face. "Linz!"

Jeremy jerks like he's been shot. "Coach?"

"Is this true?"

"No, sir! Kyle and I, all we did was go into the school to use the bathroom, but Grace said we weren't allowed. We told her that was bullshit. That's all that happened." He looks at Kyle, who nods on cue.

In unison, they both look at me, begging me silently to keep their secret so they don't get benched. Coach looks embarrassed. But Mr. Collier looks frustrated and helpless, and my patience snaps. This is Zac's fault—all of this is Zac's fault. He shouldn't have touched Grace. She liked me. Damn it, she liked *me*. But he just stands there like the god he thinks he is while the rest of us pay *his* dues. I've had enough. I can fix this. I know what happened. I open my mouth, ready to spill what I know, and…and nothing comes out. Not even air.

Because I'm lazy and will never amount to anything and always looking for the easy way out and am just a big fat disappointment. I grind my teeth together and look away.

"Mr. Collier, I've done all I can do."

Grace's father nods. "Keep a tighter leash on these boys. I don't want any more trouble. Grace has been through enough." He shoots one more look at Zac and leaves the field.

The minivan drives away. I glance back at Jeremy and Kyle. They're huddled with Zac now. Our eyes meet, and I can tell he knows what Jeremy and Kyle really did. He nods once. It's a nod of approval, not of gratitude. I turn my back, put distance between us.

I have more lockers to clean.

Chapter 19

Grace

Metal clashes against metal, and I practically faint from fear.

"Grace Elizabeth Collier, what on God's green earth is all this?"

Crap. I shut my eyes and rest my head on my desk for a moment until my heart restarts. Then I go down to meet her. "Hey, Mom."

"Hey." She drops the foot she's rubbing between both hands and limps toward the stairs, where I stand. "Wanna tell me what's going on here?"

I lift my shoulders. "The house groaned."

"Groaned?"

I nod. "It was…scary."

She stares at me for a long moment and then just opens her arms. "Come here."

I drop down the last two steps and fling myself into her arms, and for the first time since I got home, I relax. After a few moments of just pretending I'm little and will never meet the monsters I imagine under my bed in real life, I pull away. "Thanks, Mom."

She smiles. "You want to clean this up while I start dinner?"

Five minutes later all the cans are back on the pantry shelf and Mom's swirling some oil into a pan. "Grace, where's the butcher knife?" She opens the silverware drawer and the dishwasher.

Uh-oh. "Um."

She turns to me, gives me the side-eye. "Where is it, Grace?"

"My room," I say with my eyes on the floor because I can't look at her. With a sigh, she heads upstairs, so I follow. In my room she reaches for the handle of the knife, half under my math notebook, and wakes my laptop where my picture of Zac is maximized.

"Grace, what the hell is this?"

With a sigh, I drop to my bed. "A picture of Zac."

"I can see that. What I can't see is why he'd be on your computer after what he did to you."

"It's kind of a long story."

Mom sits beside me, puts the knife down, and crosses her arms. "I have time."

I fiddle with my hair, clear my throat. "Okay. Well, everybody believes Zac is like…perfect, you know? But he's not. It's a disguise. A mask he puts on." I shut my eyes and cover my face for a second. "But I know what he's like behind the mask…when he thinks no one's looking."

The breath stalls in my lungs, but I power through the pain. "I thought if I could show them what he's really like, maybe people would leave me alone."

"And this shot shows what he's really like?"

"Yeah. I took this seconds after he found out I was by myself in the school today."

Mom's back snaps up straight. "What? What happened to your partner?"

I shrug. "He didn't show."

With her lips pressed tightly together, Mom shakes her head. "No, no, that's not acceptable. If you're left by yourself in that school, I want you to call me immediately, okay?"

"Mom, I'm fine. I was scared at first, but nothing happened."

"But it could have. Damn it, Grace! This picture—you said you took it after he found out you were alone. I don't like the way he looks, Grace. It's almost…feral."

My imagination starts running away with that thought, and I can feel a panic attack building.

"Grace, Grace, come on. Deep breaths, baby. You're safe."

Mom and Dad used to say things like that when I was a little girl and woke up from nightmares.

I'm not a little girl anymore.

———————

My alarm rings. Sighing, I kill it and slip the phone back in my pocket and lie back on my bed. I've been up for hours. It's Friday.

Forty-three days.

Forty-three days since Zac hurt me.

It's my last day of locker cleaning jail with Ian. I'm kind of surprised we didn't get forced to work this Saturday too, but I'm not kicking the gift horse in his teeth or however that saying goes.

There's a soft tap on my door, and then my mom pokes her head in. "Oh. You're already up?"

"Yeah. Couldn't sleep."

She walks all the way in, wanders to my desk, glances at the photographs of Mr. Russell's job that I printed out last night. The mirror above my desk is bare. She looks for all the pictures of me and my friends that are now gone. But she doesn't say anything about them.

"So I talked to your dad last night. He wanted to see how you're doing."

My entire body stiffens. "Oh, really."

Mom rubs her arms and pretends to shiver. "Whoa. Careful, you could freeze hell with that sneer."

I laugh once, and she sits on my bed, still in her workout clothes, dark hair pulled up in a sweaty ponytail. "So how much did he tell you?"

"Oh, only that you said he thinks you're a slut and all of this is your fault and that none of that's true."

I try to laugh again. "So everything."

"Pretty much." Mom nudges me with her shoulder, smiles like we just won the lottery. "Come on, Grace. You know that's not true. He loves you."

I roll my eyes. "Really, Mom? Doesn't feel that way. Feels like I wasn't good enough. You weren't good enough, so he got a free spin. Oh, look what he won! A new wife, a new house, two new kids—boys this time."

The light fades in my mother's eyes, and so does that silly smile. "Okay, Grace. You want me to tell you I'm not upset and disappointed and…and brokenhearted over everything that's happened? I can't. I'd be lying. It all sucks. Everything!"

My eyes go wide. *Sucks?* This is not a word I've ever heard from my mother's lips before.

"But I'm not going to sit here and cry myself to death over it, and neither are you. Where's your fighting spirit?"

"My what?"

"Your fight. Your spit. Your bad attitude. Where'd you hide it?"

"Mom, I don't feel like snapping on wrist gauntlets and thigh-high boots today." I fling myself onto my bed and drape an arm over my face. With luck, she'll leave me here to sleep until I'm twenty-one.

"Not the costume, honey. The attitude."

I open one eye, sigh, and shut it again. "I think I'm empty."

The mattress shifts. Mom's sitting crossed-legged on my bed, facing me. "You know, Dad and I always figured you'd go to law school. Defend the innocent. Change the world."

I don't know about the world, but I guess I changed Laurel Point High School. "Mom," I say and shake my head. "I know what you're trying to do, but I'm not an activist. I just want to get back what Zac took from me, you know?"

"Grace, I'm so sorry. I am. There's nothing you can do about that. All you can do now is decide whether you want to move away…or stand proud the way you always have. I won't lie and pretend I don't want you to seriously consider that semester abroad. I want you far away from him, Grace. But the more I think about it, the more I get that's for me, not you."

I used to wish I'd gotten Mom's eyes instead of Dad's silverish gray ones. Hers are such a sunny blue. After Dad left, they turned cloudy. But every once in a while something happens to put a little life in them again. Today they're sunny, and I'm so afraid I'll be the one to suck the twinkle out of them. "Mom, I'm so tired."

Her lip trembles, but she smiles. "I know, baby. I know." She folds me into a hug, and a moment later, she starts singing, "I love you. You love me."

"Oh, God, don't."

"We're a happy—"

"Mom, I'm begging you. Not that song."

"What? You used to love that purple dinosaur."

"I was three."

The sun still lights her eyes, and she claps. "Come on. I know what we have to do." She bounces off my bed, grabs my hand.

"What?" Oh, please! Let it not be a 5k run. Anything but that. She leads me downstairs, picks up the remote, and the stereo turns on. She's got it tuned to some classic station that plays tunes from the '80s.

"This is perfect! Dance with me."

It takes me a few minutes to recognize The Romantics. Mom starts jumping in time to the frenetic beat of the group's biggest hit, "What I Like About You." I don't know. Maybe it was their only hit. She grabs me, spins me around our tiny living room, and I'm falling all over my feet because I can't move this fast. But I'm laughing, and she's doing her special belly laugh. And it feels so good because we haven't laughed in so many years, and I've missed it. Oh, God! I've missed it so much. We dance and jump and spin until we can't talk, can't breathe, can't be sad, and collapse in boneless heaps onto the sofa when the song fades and the traffic report plays. We prop our feet up on the coffee table, where there are pictures of the three of us when we were still a family. When we stop panting, Mom lowers the volume and turns to me.

"Grace, what do you want to do?"

The endorphins from our dance workout are pumping freely, and I'm not the least bit sad when I tell her.

"I wanted to crush him, Mom." I clench my fist. "I wanted to hit him where it hurts, get him kicked off the lacrosse team." I open my fist, drop it to my lap. "But that's not going to happen. He's got too many fans. He could rob a bank, and they'd just say the bank deserved it for flaunting all their money. So I'll settle," I say and shrug. "I'd be happy if the rest of the school treated me like a human being again instead of Zac's broken toy."

Mom fans her face. "You're not going to take that semester in Europe, are you?"

"No. I'm not running, Mom."

"That's my girl." She grins, and I frown.

"Okay, I'm really confused. Why did you keep pushing the semester abroad if you didn't want me to go?"

"Grace, I just want you to be happy, whatever it takes. If you want to run and hide, fine. If you want to stand tall and fight, that's fine too."

I suck in a deep breath. "Yeah. Maybe. Europe sounds pretty good to me. It really does. But—"

"But?"

"But it feels exactly like running. Hiding. You deleted my Facebook account, and I get why you did it. But I just think I shouldn't have to shut up or apologize or change the way I dress for anybody." I lift my hair off my damp neck. "But I'm keeping the hair. I kind of like it like this." I toss it over my shoulder and stand. I need to shower off all this sweat and get dressed, but my mom grabs my hand.

"Grace, about your dad. There's something you need to know."

I sit down again, frowning. "What?"

"He…well, he was arrested last night."

"What?" My eyes bulge. "For what?"

Mom rocks her head, won't meet my eyes. "Well, after he drove you home, he was angry and went to your school, accosted a few of the lacrosse players. The coach called the police, but your dad left before they got there, so they went to his house."

I jump up. "Well, come on. Let's go. We have to help him."

"Honey, relax. He's home. He wasn't held. The charges were dropped." She stands, takes me by my shoulders to stop my manic pacing. "Kristie's pissed off, but other than that, everything's fine. I only told you so you'd see Daddy *does* care. He has a hard time with emotions and expressing himself. Believe me, he's furious about what happened to you and even angrier that the police have walked away from the whole thing. But he's mostly angry at himself for not protecting you."

I scoff at that. "Then maybe he shouldn't have left us."

"Grace," Mom says and lifts my chin. "Come on. Be fair. I'm not thrilled he left either, but even if he'd stayed, you'd still dress the way you dress and do the things you do, even if they made him nuts, right?"

No! Okay, maybe, but still. With a sigh of surrender, I shift my weight and say nothing.

"I don't want you to hate him."

"I don't." I only hate Kristie and all her kuteness.

"Okay." She gives me a quick squeeze. "Let's get dressed, and I'll drop you off."

We head upstairs, and I decide to wear the toughest outfit I own. I don't care how many eyebrows I raise.

Chapter 20

Ian

When the light fills my room—still clean, by the way—I'm already up. I didn't sleep well and when I did finally catch a few z's, my dreams were freakin' bizarre. I kept seeing Zac with Grace. Like I was watching them while they—ugh. I don't want to go there. She knew I was there, kept looking at me with those amazing bright eyes begging me for help.

But I just stood there.

Then Zac looked at me and did that nod thing like I was standing there for him because we're friends. Teammates. Like it's my duty.

I rake my hands through my hair with a loud sigh. One more day. Just one more day to get through with her.

I don't think I can do it, and the thing is I don't know *why*. Why does she keep getting under my skin? Why does it piss me off when she lifts that chin and sneers at me? Why was she with Zac at all if she liked *me* so damn much? Why did she let him—

My door opens, and I jump. "Jesus, Dad!"

"Oops, sorry. Didn't mean to scare you. Since you're up already, come down for breakfast with the rest of the family."

"Okay."

"Why are you up? Any more dizziness? Headache?"

"No, I'm fine."

He frowns at me, tries to figure out why I'm lying, but lets it go. "Good. Don't forget. Your follow-up appointment is this afternoon. Three thirty."

Thank God. Then I can get back on the field, where I know what I'm doing.

"Good morning." Mom's not dressed yet. She pads over to me on bare feet, ruffles my hair. "You have your—"

"Yep. Got it. Dad just told me."

"Hey, little man. I'm making eggs. Want in?" Val cracks eggs in a bowl, starts scrambling.

God, yes. "Thanks." I grab the loaf of bread, feed some slices into the toaster. Claudia's pouring coffee. I snatch a cup, hope it will defuzz my brain. She glares at me, dark eyes circled with makeup, almost the way Grace does hers. "What's with all the eyeliner?"

Her mouth falls open. "What do you care?"

"It's a question, Claude! Jeez. Why do girls wear all that stuff? You're prettier without it."

Now Val, Mom, and Dad's mouths fall open like some synchronized dance. I roll my eyes. "What?"

Claudia looks at Mom. Mom pretends to wipe away a tear. "I think…I'm not sure, but that might have been an actual compliment. I'm so proud." Mom throws her arms around me.

I wriggle free, laughing. "Shut up, you guys. I'm just sayin'."

"It was a compliment. You think your sister is pretty. Admit it."

I shoot a look toward my dad, silently beg him for help. He grins and shakes his head. "You're on your own, pal."

Oh, God, I'm in hell. Three women and abandoned by the only other guy in the house? "Cold, Dad." The girls circle me, tease me, and the toast pops. I finally throw my hands up and admit it. "Okay, okay, you're all pretty. Happy now?"

Like somebody flipped a switch, they stop. Mom nods. Claudia grins, and Val plants a noisy kiss on my cheek I wipe off with a dish rag. A few minutes later we're all passing plates of scrambled eggs, bacon, and toast to each other and sipping juice and coffee. It's kind of nice to have extra time in the morning and—

"Little man, pass me the napkins."

And we're done. I drop my palm to the table. "Val, will you stop calling me that? I'm taller than all of you."

"You are not." Claudia rolls her heavily lined eyes.

"Dad. Stand up." I stand, put my back to his.

"Holy hell, when did that happen?" Val wonders.

Mom wipes another fake tear. "My baby's not a baby anymore."

Oh, God. That's it. I'm done. "Dad. We should go."

"Should we?"

"We should totally go right now so I'm not late."

With one final sip of coffee, Dad's up and kissing each of the girls good-bye. "Wash that crap off your face. Your brother's right."

I run for the door, Claudia's wail of "Daaaaaaaad!" the last thing I hear.

In the car I blow out a heavy sigh.

"So what the hell was that?" Dad jerks a thumb toward the house.

I lift my shoulders. "I just don't think she needs all that eyeliner to get noticed, you know?"

"Agreed, but why did you notice? You never have before."

Crap, crap, crap. He's good. Set me right up.

"Ian, you have a thing for Grace. Is that what this is about?"

"What? Me?" I wave my hand with a laugh, then hiss in pain when it smacks the closed window. "No. Definitely not."

"Oh, really. You sure about that?" His raised eyebrows tell me he's not buying it. There is no *thing*. Okay, so she's seriously hot in an in-your-face kind of way. And yeah, she's kind of funny. And smart, definitely—at least when it comes to her mouth.

Her mouth. God, her mouth tasted good. And her scent. I could bury my face in her hair and smell all those lilacs for the rest of my life. Only I can't because Zac moved on her first.

"Yes. No! Just, ah hell, just forget it." I swing the door open and stalk into the school. The heavy steel door practically bounces off the wall. I jog up the stairs and skid to a stop.

Grace is already here, and there's nothing—no spark, no interest—because I do not have a thing for her. Okay, so her legs look good in those curve-hugging pants, ending in mile-high boots. Nice enough, if you're into the rock star look. And yeah, that little sliver of skin that cuts up the head-to-toe black and the leather wristbands that lace up her arms are both hot. And maybe the talon bracelet she wears wrapped around her left bicep makes her look like a warrior, and all that sleek hair shining in the sunlight makes my hands itch to touch it. Big deal. The face without its typical heavy makeup that lets those bright eyes of hers shine. Only they're not shining today—

Oh, fuck.

Everything I was worried about, everything that confused me, just every damn *thing* in general that's been circling and buzzing around my brain, keeping me up at night—it all just stops to stare. Stare until looking just isn't enough. "Jesus, Grace, I'm sorry," I blurt out. "So sorry."

I wait, wait for her to smile, wait for her to nod, wait for her to freakin' say something.

She doesn't.

Instead, she whips around and kicks a locker door.

Chapter 21
Grace

Ian climbs out of his dad's white Camry, looking seriously pissed off, and I take an involuntary step away from the second-floor window where I'm watching him. But then I remember, *This is Ian*. Ian, who wouldn't throw away all the stuff in a sick girl's locker. Ian, who defended me from my friends…and his, sort of. I thought he was better than all the other guys.

I thought he was decent.

Until yesterday, when he flipped out because of that picture.

Now I know better. Now I know he's just a boy, and boys are scum.

The door downstairs slams open and closed, and I flee before he catches me, hand pressed to my galloping heart. Is that why he's mad? Did I get him in trouble with Jeremy and Kyle? I bite my lip and then shrug it off. If I did, too damn bad. Those guys are slime. What if I got him in trouble with his dad? I fling up my arms and curse. Why is every little thing so goddamn hard? Why do I even care so much? He was nice for a few days, but yesterday he was cruel enough to pick at all my scabs and leave me bleeding. I should just join a convent or something. Swear off men, take a vow of chastity. As his feet pound the stairs, my blood heats up, and my stomach flutters. And I know I will never keep that vow.

He stops abruptly at the top of the stairs and just looks at me, a dozen emotions rushing across his face. He curls his hand into a fist because it's trembling. I don't know how I know that bugs him, but I do. His mouth works, but he's unable to form any words. He shifts his weight under my scrutiny.

Who are you? I want to scream. I want to grab him by the shirt, shake him, and—

"Jesus, Grace, I'm sorry. So sorry."

What? I stare at him for a second more. Oh my God, who the hell are you? Why do guys have to be so irritating and frustrating and aggravating and—fuck! I can't take anymore and plow my foot into a locker door.

"Grace, are—"

"What is your deal, Russell? Just what the hell is your deal?" I shout, hands on my hips. When he stands there like a statue, I rant and pace around him. "One day you're this sweet guy who…who saves people, and then suddenly you're this…this vicious dirtbag with a tongue that stabs through hearts. I don't get it. Is this more payback? Are you and the entire lacrosse team using me as a fucking team-building exercise? What did I do to you? Tell me! What the hell did I ever do to any of you except—"

"Except what?"

I clamp my lips down and sneak a look at him from under my hair. He's stunned. If I didn't know better, I'd say he was shell-shocked. God, I groan silently, slide down to the floor, and let the last of my anger go. There's no point to any of this. Maybe Mom's right. A semester or two in Europe and I can start over. Be whoever and whatever I want.

A shoe squeaks on linoleum, and Ian is kneeling next to me. Slowly he puts out a hand. I don't know. Maybe he thinks I bite. I should stop him. But I'm more curious than angry now. His hand touches my hand, a soft, hot brush of skin and then a soft squeeze, and it—oh, Jesus—it completely undoes me. I break down in a flood of tears, and now his arms are around me. His lips kiss my forehead.

Damn it, *my forehead*.

It's even hotter than I'd imagined it, and I wish I could turn off my brain's center of confusion.

"Sorry," I hiccup. "I thought I was done with the crying. I don't know what's wrong with me."

"I do," he says after a moment. "You had enough." He finishes with a shrug. "I think maybe I was the straw that broke your camel."

I burst into laughter—loud, wet giggles. "That sounds so…so—"

"Kinky?" He fills in the blank with a grin, and I roll my eyes.

"That works." Then I get serious. "You were horrible yesterday."

"I know. Sorry. Saw you sneaking away from the field with that camera and thought, *Liar*."

I flinch, and his hand tightens around mine.

"Grace, listen to me. I don't know what Zac's thinking."

I try to pull back, but he won't let me go.

"I swear I don't," he adds. "But I know you're not lying. You're not." He squeezes my hand and smiles wide. "Let's go out tonight. Just us—no Zac talk, no Miranda or Lindsay talk. Let me make it up to you. I'm not an ass, I swear."

My other hand flies to my mouth. That ball of dread that curled up and died deep inside me just shrunk to half its size. He's kidding me. He has to be kidding me.

If he's kidding, I will break into a million pieces—I know it.

After I kill him first.

"What about your friends?" I have to ask.

He lowers his eyes and drops my hand. "I don't know, Grace. One step at a time, okay?"

"What changed your mind?"

He shifts to sit next to me, brings his knees to his chest, and frowns. "Maybe it was all that stuff you said about doing things that are easy or right." He lifts a shoulder. "It would be so easy for you to—I don't know—hide. Run away. Pretend." He shakes his head. "But you get in people's faces. You don't back off. Even when you're scared. And you're scared a lot lately, aren't you?"

"Am not."

He leans closer. I hold my breath. "Liar," he whispers.

A second later we both crack up laughing.

It's the best day I've had. Ever.

He climbs to his feet, sways a little.

"Dizzy again?"

"Nah. Got up too fast. I'm good." He heads for the cart, peeling off his jacket. He hangs the jacket on one of the hooks and then pushes the cart to where we left off. He's wearing jeans—nothing new there. But the shirt's different. It's clean, wrinkle-free and fits him. Fits him well enough to make sure I notice he's got a seriously nice body.

Oh, boy, do I notice.

I swallow hard, grab a fresh set of rubber gloves, and we soon have a rhythm going. We work for hours side by side, and the only tension in the air is ours—not Zac's.

"Hey, Grace?"

I look over my shoulder at Ian. He's not scrubbing. He's looking at me with a frown. Immediately the ball of dread swells. "What?"

"What do you want to happen?" While I consider how best to answer that, he keeps going. "With the camera and all of this getting in everyone's faces. What do you want to accomplish?"

I glance at the wall clock and strip off my gloves, slide to the floor, and try to find a way to explain it. "I just want people to believe it happened." I shiver, suddenly cold. "Nobody does, you know. The cops wanted to know if I was Zac's girlfriend, if I was drinking, doing drugs, if I ever I worked as a stripper, if I ever kissed Zac before that night. What the hell does any of that have to do with what happened? Do the laws against sexual assault not apply to strippers? To girlfriends? I don't get that." I wrap my arms around my legs, put my head on my knees, and shut my eyes. "Not even my parents believe me. My dad—all he kept saying is, 'Are you happy now, Theresa? Are you happy now? You let her leave the house looking like this and look what happened!' And my mom—she thinks I should apologize to Miranda for stealing her guy and then go to Europe for a semester or two so I can *forget*."

"Your dad believes you."

I lift my head, frowning.

"He was here yesterday. Wanted to rip Jeremy and Kyle into tiny pieces."

I scrub my hands over my face. "Yeah. I heard about that. He got arrested, but they let him go." I rest my head against the locker behind me. "But that's only about what Jeremy and Kyle did yesterday. He still doesn't get that I was actually raped. He thinks because I went to the woods, drank alcohol, and dressed the way I dress, I should have *expected* this to happen. That I actually *wanted* it to happen. Ugh!" I fist my hands and pound on the lockers behind me.

"Did you?"

I glare at him through narrow eyes. "Are you kidding me?"

He holds up both hands. "Serious question. Why do you dress like this? You want guys to notice you? Stand out from the crowd? To want you?"

"You want to know why I dress like this? Fine. When I was about nine, I used to take dance lessons. I loved it. Loved my lessons, loved my teacher. She used to wear these silky skirts over her leotard. I loved the way they floated around her when she twirled. She was so graceful. And beautiful. She had the smoothest, shiniest blond hair I've ever seen.

213

Her eyes were like the color blue of the car we had back then. I couldn't stop staring at them. She was perfect. Absolutely perfect in every way until the day of my first dance performance when I saw her backstage, wrapped around my father like he'd just saved her from drowning." I sit up, curl my legs under me, and lean forward. "She went after him, Ian. A man she knew was married and had a family. She went after him, got pregnant, and he left us to be with them and—" My voice hitches. "And at their wedding, their fairy-tale wedding where she had the nerve to wear white, he tells me he wants Kristie and me to become great friends because she's such a wonderful woman and he hopes I'll learn from her. Learn what? How to be a cold, calculating home-wrecker?" I hold up both hands. "No. Hell, no. I'd rather wear black clothes and black hair color for the rest of my natural life than let anybody believe for a single second that I am anything like that woman."

He angles his head and peers closely at me. "So what's your real hair color?"

I roll my eyes. "Same as my dad's."

"Like light brown?"

I nod.

"But Kristie's blond?"

"Yeah, so what?"

"So why do you dye your hair if it's not the same color as Kristie's?"

"Oh." I run a hand through it, stare the dark tresses. "Because my mom's always saying how much I look just like him. I hate that I make her sadder than Kristie already did."

"You think she's a slut."

Ian says those words so flatly, so genuinely. It fuels my fury.

"Kristie's president of the slut club and wears cashmere for God's sake! He doesn't get it. Nobody gets it. I was with *friends*. People I know, people I've known for all of high school and even before that. I should have been able to stand there buck naked and be safe. Why didn't anybody help me when I passed out? Isn't that what friends are supposed to do? Why did Zac think because I was unconscious, my body was nothing more than a, than a *slot* for him to use just because he was pissed off and horny?"

Before he can respond, my phone buzzes. I tug it out of my pocket, open an email from Detective Buckley. I read a sentence or two, and after the part that says, *Not enough to convict*, the rest just blurs.

"Problem?" Ian asks, and I shrug.

"You'll be happy to know the police say the picture I sent them doesn't prove anything, so Zac will get away with raping me."

Ian sucks in a sharp breath and turns away. When a minute goes by in silence, I figure he's not so surprised by this news. I press my lips together. Okay. Fine. I square my shoulders, stand up, and get back to work. It takes me a few minutes to realize I never really answered his earlier question.

I glance at him, scrubbing the door of a locker, jaw clenched.

I guess my answer no longer matters.

Chapter 22

Ian

I am such a dick.

I didn't mean to get her all upset, and now I don't know if I should hug her or give her space or pretend I never said anything. I saw her dad's wife that night in the hospital. She looks like a sitcom mom. She was wearing a skirt. My mom only wears skirts to somebody's wedding. And Lindsay, she was wearing just jeans and a T-shirt at Miranda's party, but she let three guys touch her. Jesus, how the hell did everything get so complicated? I don't even know why I asked her about the camera in the first place, and now I'll never get that image of Zac with Grace sick and losing consciousness out of my head. I don't know what to say, what to do, what to think about this—any of it.

So I say nothing. I pick up my cleaning crap and go back to scrubbing lockers and can't stop wondering what color Grace's hair really is.

Like I said. I'm a dick.

I didn't mean to upset her. I'm just trying to understand. So, yeah. I think Zac messed up big-time here. But was it really rape? I can't ask Grace that. She'll tear my tongue out and choke me with it. Why do girls not get that there's a fine line between *looking good* and *asking for it*? Okay, so now I get why she dresses like a heavy metal chick, but the high-heeled boots? The skin-tight clothes? There is no question that Grace is hot and noticeable. Why can't she just—I don't know—wear sweats and not wash her hair if she wants to be the opposite of her dad's wife? It's like the people who leave their doors unlocked and then cry when they're robbed. Why are girls not smart about this? I don't get it, and damn, my head really hurts now.

"Need a break." I mumble over my shoulder and head to the boys' bathroom. I take my time and then splash some water on my face. The phone in my back pocket buzzes, and when I pull it out, I see Zac is getting a bunch of people together to party in the woods tonight. I text him back.

> **Ian:** Can't. Have MD appt to sign off for play. Guarantee parents won't let me out tonight.

> **Zac:** Sucks

I laugh.

And then I think about it. Another cold night drinking colder beer, getting wasted. Watching the guys try to get laid—Jeremy usually fails, and Zac usually succeeds. Watching Miranda prostitute Lindsay so she can be close to a guy who doesn't really want her in the first place. I don't want to go. I don't care about missing it.

I laugh again because I guess I suddenly turned into my dad. I scroll absently through my phone's apps and check the news. The local paper claims a resident reported a vandalized mailbox on Old Brooke Road. Witnesses say a black SUV was seen speeding from the street shortly after midnight. Police are asking anybody with information to call their Crimestoppers hotline.

Christ. Jesus Christ, it wasn't a black SUV. It was a white Camry. It wasn't midnight. It was about 1:00 a.m. I know this because I'm responsible, and I'm lucky, so fucking lucky it was the mailbox and not the guy walking a dog in the street I swerved to avoid.

I lunge for the closest empty stall and hurl into the toilet, trying to convince myself it's the sour smell that's making my eyes burn and nothing else. When I think I've run out of bodily fluids to lose, I flush, lean back on my heels, put my head on the cold porcelain, and try to think up ways to hide this, to make sure my dad never finds out I did the stupidest thing I could have done, to fucking turn back time so it never happened in the first place.

The touch of a hand on my back nearly catapults me into orbit. "Jesus, Grace. This is the *boys'* bathroom."

She ignores my indignation and hands me a bottle of water. I accept it gratefully, swilling some and spitting into the toilet.

"Ian, what's up with you? The headaches, the dizziness, now this—How bad is that concussion?"

Concussion. Okay, concussion. "Find out later. My parents are taking me back to the doctor this afternoon." I move back to the sink, wash my face, avoid eye contact. In the mirror, Grace picks up my forgotten phone, and my blood goes cold.

"You broke this mailbox."

I whip around, eyes popping. "How the hell do you know that?"

She cocks her head, and I want to kick myself in the ass for practically drawing her a freaking diagram. I want to lie. I want to tell her to mind her own business, but those freaky eyes x-ray me so that I have no secrets, no thoughts she can't see. I resist the temptation to pull my phone of out her leather-covered hands and stomp on it. "Yeah, I did, okay? What's the big deal? I didn't kill anybody." My voice scratches and shakes, and I can't figure out why I said that. See? It's those X-ray eyes.

"You tell me. You're the one vomiting over it."

Jesus. I rake both hands through my hair, wishing she'd come looking for me just a few minutes later."

"Obviously it bugs you, Ian," Grace says with a wave toward the toilet. "Did you tell anybody?"

I shake my head. "Just Zac. He's the only one who knows because he was in the car. None of the other guys know."

"Tell me."

I slide to the floor and break it down for her. "Friday night we were down in Holtsville, and we were drinking. I wasn't drunk. I had maybe two beers, tops. Driving back, there was somebody walking in the street. I swerved to avoid hitting him and hit the mailbox and freaked out. So I kept going. I didn't stop because I didn't want a DWI and it was just a mailbox."

I rock back, sit on my heels, but can't meet her eyes. "The next day my dad grounded me for denting the car. No car for one week. I sulked in my room, studied until I got bored." I look up, knowing I'll see disgust in her eyes.

But I don't. She just looks—I don't know—worried, I think.

"I called Zac. I couldn't tell my dad. He was freaked out about the car and still freaked out about the police calling the night you—" I don't finish the sentence. Figure she was there. She doesn't need reminding. "If he finds out I was drinking, this will put him over the edge—I know it. He'll probably send me to military school or something." Fuck, I'm practically whining.

"You need to tell him."

I slide her a look. "No. I really don't."

"You're puking up your guts because you feel guilty. That's not a bad thing. You'll never do it again—that's for sure."

Christ, she sounds just like Zac. The breath leaves my body in a *whoosh* when I think of Grace and Zac sharing anything, even the same thought. I hate this. I fucking hate that she caught me freaking out over something that shouldn't be such a big deal, and now I'm freaking out more because of her—her disapproval? I glare at her. "And what about you?"

"Me?"

"Yeah. What was all that shit you said to Zac? You're afraid of him, so you goad him? Why?"

She stiffens up. "We're not talking about me, Ian. We're talking about you. Come on. You know I'm right."

"Seriously. What is up with you?"

She blows hair out of her face. "Okay, fine. I said that to piss him off. When he's pissed, he shows his true colors. That night? In the woods? Jeremy kept taunting him about me. He had to do something then."

Had to. Right, right, here we go again. Zac says one thing. Grace says the other, and somehow they're both right. I can't focus. I can't deal. I climb back to my feet, grab the phone, and turn for the door. "I need to think. I need some air."

I leave her sitting on the cold tile floor.

———————

Dad and Mom are in the car that afternoon to pick me up for my follow-up appointment.

"How was your day?" Mom asks lamely.

I shrug. "Glad it's over. I may smell like orange cleanser for the rest of my life."

"Did Grace get any more pictures for me?"

I shake my head. "No, I don't think she had time."

Now that we've run out of small talk, I can hear Beyoncé singing about being a boy and just sigh. Even superstars think the entire male sex just sucks, and the even sadder part is I'm starting to agree. I replay everything that happened since the night of the party—everything Grace said, everything Lindsay and Miranda did. Seriously, what the hell is up with them? Maybe the whole female sex is worse than the males, the way they turn on each other, transforming from bat-shit crazy into straight-up vicious over some guy.

Jesus, even sharks aren't that mean.

The song ends, and the news plays. My entire body kinks up. I squeeze my eyes shut, whispering prayers to a God I'm not even sure I believe in anymore.

"Ian, you coming?"

I open my eyes, and we're here. Dad's parked. "Oh, yeah, sorry. Must have fallen asleep."

After a twenty-minute wait we're inside an examination room, me up on the table, Mom on the single chair, and Dad standing beside her, hands shoved into his pockets while he reads some stupid poster hanging on the wall. Dr. Bernard comes in, shakes everybody's hand, and starts looking in my eyes, making me follow his finger.

"Any headaches, dizziness?"

I shrug, refuse to tell him how bad it was. I cannot be benched.

"Yes, he was dizzy enough to fall back to the bed when I woke him up."

Great, thanks, Dad.

"Trouble concentrating?"

"He's been irritable, depressed, and unable to sleep too."

Dr. Bernard asks me to stand and then does drunk tests like making me walk heel to toe in a straight line, touching my finger to my nose, and grasping his fingers with each of my hands. He rotates my head around while I'm standing, and I lose my balance once.

"Ian, your brain isn't recovering as quickly as I'd like to see. This is fairly typical in athletes who have sustained multiple concussions, but I want to be cautious and keep you off the field until we can run more tests."

My heart falls to my feet. "For how long?"

"Until we can repeat your MRI and EEG, but certainly for the rest of this term."

"Dr. Bernard, my school has a shot at the title this term. And I'm playing in the All Long Island Tournament this June. I can't miss these games. I can't let down my team."

The doctor just shakes his head and turns to my parents, ignoring me like it's past my bedtime or some shit.

"This was Ian's second concussion in high school. Concussions can be serious. In Ian's case, repeated concussions are beginning to cause some minor damage."

"Damage? Like actual brain damage?" I interrupt.

Bernard nods. "Yes, Ian. Actual brain damage. Every time you bruise your brain, tiny blood vessels burst and bleed, sometimes scar. The brain is a large network of neurons. Those scars force certain neurons to drop off the network. Network connections are rerouted around off-line neurons. They don't reconnect."

Shit. Holy shit. What does this mean? Am I—he's not saying—I can't be *dying*, can I? Jesus.

"If you continue to play and are hurt again, more damage will occur. Over time it will render you unable to function."

"Muhammad Ali," my dad murmurs.

Bernard nods. "Sustained blows to the head can cause similar closed-head injuries like Ian's concussions."

"Is this permanent?"

"I don't know. Sometimes it takes longer to heal from a concussion when you've had one or two before. With time, I hope we'll see a reversal. First we need to map the damage, assess its significance. Let's get you signed up for another EEG and MRI as soon as possible, and then we'll know."

The three of us follow the doctor to the main desk, shuffling our feet, dazed and confused. A hand claps my shoulder and squeezes, and I jerk. I was numb until that second. I sit in the waiting room while my parents coordinate schedules, and then we're back in the car for the ride home.

"Ian, we don't know anything for sure, so try not to worry, okay?"

I nod and then worry anyway. I can't play. I may not be able to play ever again. There's no shot at an athletic scholarship now, which means community college for me. Yay. Christ, what do I do? What the fuck do I do?

Chapter 23
Grace

The weekend passes quickly. Mom let me take the car to two more of Mr. Russell's job sites, where I took some excellent pictures, uploaded them to a file-sharing site, and got an excited message from him telling me how much he loved them. With some extra money in my pocket, I buy Kody a few Iron Man figures—one with an extra Tony Stark head and one with electronic action. Whatever that is. I finish all my *Taming of the Shrew* reading and the essay that's due this week. On Sunday evening while I'm wrestling to straighten my hair, my cell buzzes, and a grimace replaces my instant pang of excitement that somebody is actually calling me. "Hey, Kristie."

"Hi, Grace. Listen, sweetie, something's happened. There was a glitch in the petting zoo booking system, and they're not coming."

Aww. Kody's going to be so disappointed. "Wow, that sucks. Kody was really looking forward to it."

"I know. I'm not sure what we're doing yet. Probably just doing cake for the family."

The way she says *the family* prickles my ears. "So you're canceling the big party?"

"Well, yeah, since there won't be any entertainment. We'll just do something small. Keep it simple and low-key. I wanted to let you know right away so you could make plans for next weekend."

Plans, of course. Since I have such a busy social life. Well, I'm not letting her off the hook that easy. "No problem. I can walk over to your place after school whatever night you're planning to do the cake. Wouldn't want to miss it."

"Oh. Well, the thing is…we're not sure yet. I'll have to let you know. Plus, it's a school night, and I don't want to get you in trouble with Theresa, so don't worry about it. Kody won't mind if you miss it this year."

"No, I couldn't. You only turn five once, and he is my brother."

"I know you're disappointed. Imagine how we feel. A stupid double-booking mistake and Kody's plans are crushed."

"We could take him to the zoo instead."

"Oh, you know how your dad hates crowds and parking and all that."

This is true. My dad does hate these things.

"Well, I have to run. Just wanted—" There's noise in the background, and I hear my dad's voice. "Well, okay, honey. Thanks for calling. Bye!"

She ends the call before I can say anything. What was that *thanks for calling* stuff? She called me. I want to spike the phone to the floor and crush it into a million pieces, but I manage to hold on to a little self-control. I suppose I can call my dad and ask to come over one day during the week to drop off Kody's present, preferably on a day when

Kristie isn't home. I fall asleep with thoughts of sneaking Nair in her shampoo bottle entertaining me all night.

The next morning I wake almost happy. It's such a weird feeling. I totally suck at life from just about every angle, but yet I feel kind of bouncy.

It's Ian. I know it.

There's this—I don't know—a *cleanness* around me this morning. Like I dusted out all these emotional spiderwebs, and now there's room to play and dance and sing inside me. Okay, my step-monster obviously doesn't want me anywhere near her precious baby boys, and my dad doesn't understand me. And my mom still hopes deep down that I'll run away to Europe, but all that fades away whenever I remember there's one guy who believes me.

One special guy. I dance down the stairs, kiss my mother's cheek.

"Wow, you're in a good mood." She's already dressed for work. "Want to share with the class?"

"Oh, Kristie uninvited me to Kody's birthday party, and I'm plotting payback."

"Excuse me?" Mom whips around, pulls out her best oh-no-she-didn't voice, and I hold up a hand.

"Seriously, I'm good. I'm fighting back, remember?"

She nods and slowly smiles. "Okay. Just, you know, try not to do anything that requires bail, okay?"

We laugh and climb in the car, and a short while later we join the line of cars doing the morning drop-off.

"You'll be okay on the bus today?"

I shake my head. "No, no buses for me. I'll either walk or get a ride with Ian."

With a wave and a last "love you," she's off.

Despite the week off, I am still the hottest topic buzzing around school. I climb the stairs, head for my sparkling clean, orange-scented locker, dodging the whispers and mean comments and the guys trying to grab me. I'm not fast enough to evade one, and when I feel a hand close over my breast and squeeze, I don't stop to think about it. I just react the way my dad taught me, catch the unknown hand in a finger lock, and twist.

Somebody screams out a string of curses. I don't stop to see who.

I make it to my locker and dump all the books I had to take home for the break. My first class is English lit. I roll my shoulders, grab the text, slam my locker, and start the long trek to the third floor. Ian Russell's heading this way, laughing with Jeremy, Kyle, and Matt. When they see me, all four of them come to a full stop in the center of the corridor.

I keep walking.

Jeremy looks scared, and there's a part of me that likes that a whole lot more than I should. Matt is pissed, and that makes no sense. I didn't do anything to him. I try hard not to stare too long at Ian, but it's not possible. His lips are parted, his dark eyes wide, and I know my outfit has done its job.

I'm wearing a leather motorcycle jacket over black pants, black boots. Under the jacket, a slashed T-shirt that *does* reveal some skin, though nothing in any strategic places. Leather wrist gauntlets tied with crisscrossing straps disappear under the jacket's cuffs. My hair is straight and loose, and yeah, I'm wearing black lipstick and black eyeliner.

Deal with it.

Ian's mouth goes thin. I figure he's not happy I've gone back to my costume, as he calls it, but he stands aside. Kyle, Matt, and Jeremy cross their arms, plant themselves in the center of the corridor, forcing people to squeeze by them. Well, Grace Collier does not squeeze by anybody. I shove my way right through their line. Jeremy's kind of a runt, so that's not difficult.

Loud laughter follows me down the hall to the classroom, where I drop my gear, take out a notebook, and get ready to work.

At the front of the class two girls I don't even know talk about me like I'm not there. "Is it Halloween already?" and "Oh my God, did you see her makeup?" As if those are the worst things anybody's said about me. The funny thing is that I've been dressing like this since freshman year and nobody ever raised an eyebrow over it. My friends thought it was cool—back when they were actually my friends. I shake my head and let it roll off.

Nothing can hurt me today.

"When Grumio says in act 1, 'Katherine the curst! A title for a maid of all titles the worst,' he's calling her a shrew, the worst name you could ever call a girl," Mrs. Kirby tells the lit class, and I roll my eyes.

It's not the worst name. Trust me.

"But Petrucchio kind of liked her, would you agree?"

Maybe. I think he just saw dollar signs when he looked at her, not hearts.

"What did you all think of Kate? Was she really the shrew everyone believed her to be?"

"She was a total bitch," someone called out from the back of the room. I twist around, decide it was Allie.

"Guys, would you want to marry Kate?"

The guys all make faces and shake their heads.

"So why was Petrucchio so determined to not only marry her but tame her?"

I zone out when the boys Mrs. Kirby calls on make some lame-ass vague comments that prove they never finished reading the assignment. There's no debate, just a rehash of Mrs. Kirby's remarks…until some brave moron says, "If Kate were my woman, she'd learn respect real fast."

What?

A murmur of "Ooo" ruffles over the class, and Mrs. Kirby grins at Jax, a guy who pretends he's a gangsta. "What would you do differently?"

"I'd put it to her straight up. You want out of your daddy's house, girl, then you gonna do things my way," he adds, waving his hand like a rapper.

Oh my God, seriously? I sigh and shake my head.

"You disagree, Grace?"

Uh-oh. My classmates turn to laugh at me, sneer at me, make lewd gestures at me that somehow Mrs. Kirby fails to notice. I don't answer her, but she's relentless.

"I'd like to hear your thoughts."

I clear my throat. "My thoughts? Okay. I think Kate was centuries ahead of her time. A woman with original thoughts and intelligence. O woe for her poor father!" I fling a hand to my head to add some drama. A few people laugh, but Mrs. Kirby's eyes gleam.

"Why do you say original thinking and intelligence brought woe to her family?"

I look at her sideways. "Come on. Isn't it obvious? She's a girl. She's nothing but property. Her father pimps her out to the highest bidder because that's all girls were good for back then."

"Not much good today either," Jax adds, and the guys roar.

The girls shoot him indignant looks, and a spark flares inside me. Mrs. Kirby opens her mouth to encourage more stupidity, but I don't have the patience to hear it.

"Coward," I volley back. A few of the girls actually cheer. "The only guys who actually believe we're better off in the dark ages when women were just some man's property are the ones afraid of girls. You afraid of girls, Jax?"

He blinks at me and then pins on a confident grin. "I ain't afraid of no girl."

The class cracks up again, but Mrs. Kirby isn't done. "Hold it. Hold it. I think we're on to something here. Grace, continue your point."

I draw in a deep breath. "My point is that Kate didn't want to simply be bred to wed, and that's all her father expected of her. When all those guys started circling her younger sister, her father was so happy to be rid of the pair of them that he actually paid guys to take them off his hands. And the guys, what do they care what the girls are like? They're not only getting paid, but they're getting pretty girls and guaranteed sex. And if the girl didn't even like her husband, that was too bad. She didn't even get to pick him."

"Still not seeing the problem here." Jax shrugs and gets a fist pound from the guy next to him.

"Really? You don't see the problem? What if my father paid you to marry me? I can't stand you, and you definitely don't like me. You don't see a problem there?"

"You'd have to sleep with me because you'd be my wife, all legal and stuff." He grins. "And you'd have to do all those other things a wife does like clean and cook and wash my clothes. I could live with that even if you are a—"

"Jax, that's enough," Mrs. Kirby cuts him off before he can call me something worse than *shrew*, but it's too late. I know what he was going to say. So does the rest of the class. I try not to let the pain show, but it's part of me now.

"You think I'm a slut."

"Grace—"

"No, Mrs. Kirby, it's okay. That's what you were going to say, right, Jax? We all know it."

Jax doesn't reply. He just throws an arm over the back of his desk and grins like he owns the world.

"Why do you think that? I don't remember ever having sex with you, so I'd like to know why you think that."

"Grace, that's enough. We're talking about Shakespeare, not you."

"Fine. Let's talk about Shakespeare." I will deal with Jax the jerk later. "Kate had no choice. No options. No hope. Petrucchio comes along, already won over by the money he's going to get, and then decides he needs to break her spirit the way you train an animal."

"A bird." Mrs. Kirby corrects me.

"Whatever. It's disgusting."

"This play is frequently called misogynistic for the ways in which women are treated. However, other scholars disagree and say the play is a farce, with Shakespeare trying to shed a little light on the way things were at the time. Some even go so far as to say Shakespeare was a feminist."

I consider that for a moment. That explains the ending of the play. When I first read it, I felt let down. Like Kate just gave up. But now? "Mrs. Kirby? The speech Kate gives at the end of the play. The one about the bet? She wasn't serious, was she?"

"I don't know, Grace, was she?"

If he was a feminist, I totally misunderstood the ending. "She just caved in. Said what her husband wanted her to say."

"Yeah, 'cause she learned her place," Jax says and laughs.

"No! No, she wasn't tamed. She wasn't broken. She was still herself, still a smart woman who thinks things through. I think she made a deal with Petrucchio. I think under all the posturing for the busybodies, they actually liked each other. Kate realized she could do a lot worse and was willing to give up the shrew stuff if he'd help her too." When everybody sits there, vacant, I wave a hand. "Come on, isn't it obvious? Kate's still thinking, still scheming. She just found a partner willing to do it with her."

"That's because she's hot. Hot girls always get guys to do whatever they want them to."

"Yeah, and then lie about it later."

"Hey, hey, that's enough." Mrs. Kirby tries to regain control when the class erupts in a loud cheer, but I stand up and face the nasty little witch sitting near the window. Her name's Camryn, and she hasn't said a word to me since high school started. She's petite with a sleek fall of dark hair that sweeps her shoulders, soft eyes, and a nice smile, which I don't see because at the moment because she's too busy sneering at me. First Jax and now her?

Okay, I'm done playing now.

"I didn't lie about anything. Anytime you want to hear the truth, you come find me."

"Grace, sit down and be quiet."

I whip around, face Mrs. Kirby. "I will not be quiet when students in your classroom call me names, Mrs. Kirby." I stare her down. "And get away with it," I add to make her eyebrows climb.

"Camryn, apologize to Grace."

"But I didn't—"

"You called her a liar. Apologize or see Mr. Jordan."

Camryn crosses her arms and stares daggers through me. "Sorry."

"What? I didn't quite hear that—"

"I said I was sorry. Happy now?"

I turn to face Jax. "And?"

He pats his chest and looks at Mrs. Kirby to save him, but she nods.
"You too, Jax."

"Aw, man. Fine, I'm sorry you're a slut."

"Jax!"

"Okay, okay." He clears his throat. "Sorry. But if people don't want
other people to notice how they dress, then maybe they shouldn't dress
to be noticed."

"Jax, this is your final warning."

He holds up both hands, and I stand down, take my seat, laughing inside
at the way Camryn's face is turning an interesting shade of purple. But I'm
not done yet. I told my mom I was done hiding, done staying quiet. I mean
it. "You know, not much has changed since Shakespeare's time. People still
can't be who they are and not have to worry what others think."

"Okay, Grace, you've made your point."

The bell rings, and the sounds of desks scraping the floor and books
slamming fills the room. I've learned to wait for the crowd to thin a
bit before I move. I grab my gear, turn to the door, and freeze. Robyn
Nielson and Khatiri Soni stand in front of me. Robyn's biting her lip. I
cock a hip, cross my arms, and brace. "What?"

Robyn holds up her hands. "Nothing, nothing. Just…that was really great."

My eyebrows shoot into my hairline. "What was?"

She laughs and quickly swallows it, like that laugh had been chained in a dungeon and just broke free. "The way you shot down Jax and Camryn and even Mrs. Kirby."

"You are so fierce," Khatiri adds with this note of awe in her voice.

I blink and finally nod. "Thanks." I grab my stuff and pass them, but Robyn stops me with a hand to my arm.

"We believe you."

My lit text squirts from my hand, thuds to the floor. I want to grab Robyn, twirl her around the classroom the way my mom used to twirl me, and then make her sign a statement that I can photocopy and stuff into every locker I cleaned.

With a smile and a nod, they're gone. The rest of my classmates glare or whisper behind their hands, but I hardly notice because somebody thinks I'm fierce.

Somebody *believes* me.

———————

The third period bell rings, and in the crush of students trying to make it to their next class on time, I see Zac and Ian having a hot argument. Ian makes eye contact but says nothing, so I give them space. I lean against a locker until they separate and then straighten my spine, suck in a deep breath, and approach Ian to ask if we could have lunch together later.

"Not now, Grace." He sidesteps me and keeps walking. Whatever Zac said to him just now really upset him, so I force myself not to take his words personally. His face is pale, too pale, and as he strides away, he grabs his head like he did last week. Crap, I hope he's not having another headache or dizzy spell. I have pain relievers with me. Maybe I can give him some at lunch. Except I don't eat in the cafeteria anymore. I usually pack sandwiches I sneak into the library and nibble on them behind a large textbook.

Maybe this morning's lit class made me ridiculously bold, but I figure I could eat in the cafeteria today, especially if Ian's head is bothering him again. I battle back the dread that keeps trying to talk me out of this idea throughout my entire third-period class. When the lunch bell rings, I pull it together and join the line. I hear the whispers and notice the raised eyebrows but stride through that food line like I own the place, and even though I have sandwiches, I plop two slices of pizza on my tray.

Everybody seems to really like the pizza.

While I pay for the food, Ian comes in, but he doesn't see me. He heads straight for the lacrosse team's table on the far right of the cafeteria over near the trophy case. Zac sits in the center of the long table, Jeremy the disciple to his right. Matt and Kyle are standing guard. When Ian gets close, they seem to close ranks, prevent him from getting near Zac. I hang back. The tension's thick.

"Zac, come on, man." Ian holds out his hands, palms up. His face is way too pale not to be something to worry over.

Zac shoots him a bored look. "The skank table is over there." He jerks his head in my direction, and my stomach falls to the floor with a thud. I didn't realize I'd been spotted. Ian turns and his dark eyes zero right in on me and then shift quickly back to Zac. The other guys sneer, laugh, and then get really serious. I'm standing here, carrying a tray with two meals and a bottle of Tylenol on it in some pathetic attempt to keep the only friend I have, and they know it. They're waiting, *salivating* for what comes next.

"Zac, seriously," Ian tries again, but Zac just angles his head.

"Don't you want to know what the little woman has for you?"

"Probably an STD," Kyle says, and Jeremy bumps his fist.

I give it a few seconds, a few seconds for Ian to step up the way he did last week—first with my former friends and then with his. But he doesn't.

"Ian?" I call him, and the effect is like pouring water on flame. The cafeteria goes silent except for the hiss from the spectators who suddenly notice the floor show served with today's meal.

"No skanks, just men allowed here," Jeremy calls to me.

"Guess you'll have to eat somewhere else," I shoot back.

"Back off, bitch." He tries to look mean, but he can't pull it off.

Ian finally finds his voice. "Chill, Linz. What do you want, Grace? Sense a disturbance in the Force?" He snaps at me, and I flinch when the guys howl behind him. His eyes keep bouncing from me to Zac and back again, and with a dread that grows like a weed, I know. I get it. This is a court, and Ian's on trial. They're making him choose—them or me.

I want to drop the tray and run, flee, buy my plane ticket to Europe, and never come back, but everything I told my mom comes rushing back to kick me in the gut. I said I was done running. I said I wouldn't back down or hide or be quiet. I shift my weight to one side, throw a challenging look Ian's way. *Come on, jerk. Bring it. I won't make this easy for you. Look me in the eye and say it.*

"Ian," I try again, but his name is a hoarse croak.

"Nice outfit." Ian's lips curl into a smirk. "You really like having every guy in the school undress you with his eyes, don't you?"

He ambles closer, examines the tray I'm still holding. "Food for me?"

"Please," I whisper. "Please don't do this."

If he hears me at all, he shows no sign. He picks up a slice and then makes a face of disgust. "You didn't touch this, did you?" He throws it back on the tray but takes the Tylenol, shoves it in his pocket. Behind him, Zac watches and grins. "Wouldn't want to catch anything." The guys erupt in loud cheers for that one. "Get the hell out of here," he murmurs under his breath, and damn it, I can't tell if he's threatening me or warning me. I give it no more than a second of thought.

It doesn't matter the motive. All that matters is the action. And Ian Russell just stabbed me in the back.

I whip around, hair flying, and strut to the trash bins, dump the whole tray. I don't run. I don't cry. I keep my head up when they call me *slut* and *whore*. In the corridor I can still hear them, whooping it up over Ian's testimony.

I guess the verdict is in.

Chapter 24

Ian

She doesn't run.

Even with the jeers and laughter and food hurled at her, she doesn't run. I watch her leave, rub my chest where it keeps burning, and wonder why the hell she had to pick today of all days to stage that tender moment. What the hell was she thinking? Today's the day I have to tell these guys—my brothers—that I can't play the rest of the season. That I may not be able to play ever again. They're cool, so they'll slap my back, shake their heads, tell me it blows, but that'll be it. Life will go on.

Without me.

They'll play in the tournament and celebrate their win while hot girls like Addie and Jess serve them breadsticks and stuffed-crust pizza. Some of them will even get the scholarships and head off to play college lacrosse, and I'll still be here, standing in the same fucking spot with thinning hair and a beer gut. And goddamn it—it's gone, over, all of it, and it never had the chance to happen. I shove my hands into my pockets and turn back to Zac.

"Well, well, well, Russell, you're just full of surprises." Zac stands, muscles through the wall of men. "What the hell is going on?"

"Nothing. We cleaned lockers for a week. My dad hired her to take some pictures, and I'm driving her. That's it."

"Really." He raises his eyebrows. "Did you tell the collie that? 'Cause she looked a bit…uh, surprised." The guys all laugh.

"Took care of it, didn't I?"

Zac nods. "Yeah. Yeah, I guess you did." After another long silence Zac nudges me with his shoulder. "So what happened at the doctor yesterday?"

I sigh. "Long story. You got time?" I jerk my head toward the rear exit.

Zac shrugs and starts walking. When Jeremy stands, he puts out a hand to keep him planted here. The rear exit leads directly outdoors to a parking lot. Zac heads for an empty spot, sits on the concrete stop block, and waves a hand. "This doesn't sound good."

I stay on my feet. "Ah," I say and rake my hands through my hair. "It's…um, not good at all."

"You serious? How *not good* are we talking?" He shifts to look at me straight on.

"There may be some brain damage. Need more tests." A lump suddenly forms in my throat. It's a full minute before I can talk. "Can't play the rest of the term. May have to miss the tournament. May not be able to play ever again."

"Jesus, Ian."

"Yeah."

It's damp and warm out. Too warm. Everything I just said to Grace rumbles in my head like the thunder I hear in the distance. When the sun hides behind clouds, I clear my throat. "Know you don't want to hear this, but I *did* talk to her last week."

Zac knows which *her* I mean. "Aw, hell, Russell, will you give that a fucking rest already?"

I take a deep breath. This is gonna hurt. "You messed that girl up. Big-time."

He surges to his feet, gets in my face. "I messed *her* up? Are you kidding me?"

"Listen. Just listen."

He paces a few steps away, turns back, and waves a hand. "Just say it."

"She was sick, man. Passed out, drunk. In her mind, that's rape."

Zac shoves me back a step. "Fuck you. I know you! If you were there, you would have done the same thing, man. The same thing. Don't you try to tell me otherwise."

I ignore the heat in his eyes because under it I can see the fear and worry. "In her mind," I repeat my earlier words.

"Yeah, I heard that. What the hell do you mean?"

"I mean this is all just a colossal misunderstanding. She thought you were her friend. She doesn't get why you didn't try to help her. Or why you left her lying there. Maybe this goes away if you just apologize, tell her you didn't know she was sick."

He levels me with a laser glare. "Are you high? Getting laid is what those parties are for, Russell. Everybody knows that. Why didn't she stop drinking if she felt so sick? Why didn't she stick by her girlfriends if she didn't want me to touch her? Apologizing is like admitting I did something wrong, and I didn't."

"To her, you did. You're the man, Zac. Be one. Stop instigating shit with the other guys and even the girls. This all blows over if you do."

He rolls his eyes. "And you're psychic now? See into the future?"

"Jesus, is it really so hard for you to see where you went wrong here? Are you that blind? I spent a week with her. Her parents are pissed off. Miranda and Lindsay want to tear her hair out, and most of the school is on your side. Hell, Jeremy and Kyle nearly got their asses kicked *and* kicked off the team. How much more do you need? Everyone supports you! Everyone's got your back! I'm telling you if you just tell Grace what you told me the other night, she'll see it from your point of view too and maybe stop calling you a rapist. That clear now?" I fling myself to the stop block with a grimace.

"Yeah," he says quietly and sits next to me. I turn to look at him. He's leaning over his knees, staring at the ground. "Yeah, it's clear. Thanks."

I nod once.

"I still can't believe she really thinks I'd—" He breaks off, shaking his head.

"I know, man. She's got this thing in her head that you wanted to… like maybe *punish* her for saying no. She's been following you all over the place with a high-powered zoom, trying to get a shot of your game face." I tell him with a sad laugh. "Says it would prove you wanted to hurt her."

"My game face?" Zac stiffens.

"Yeah, she says that's the last thing she remembers."

After a long moment he shakes his head. "I swear, if I live to be a hundred, I will never get girls, bro."

I huff out a laugh. "Same here."

"You still like her, don't you?"

I shift my weight, try to think of something to say. "I do, but we're friends, Zac. I won't move on her."

He laughs. "The disturbance in the Force thing? That was pretty damn funny."

I try to smile, but I can't. It wasn't funny. It was fucking cruel.

"Okay, look, I get it. You're in the middle of all this. I'll tell the guys to lay off."

I nod. "Great."

The bell rings, and Zac gets up. "Social studies."

Zac walks ahead of me back inside the school. Like always, I follow.

————————

Time drags its ass. When the last bell rings, I can't escape fast enough. The clouds finally crack open, and rain falls in a steady drumbeat on the roof of my dad's car. I sit in the student lot for a while, wait for traffic to thin out. I got nowhere special to be. I was supposed to drive Grace to the next job site on my dad's list, but no way she'll hang out with me now.

What the hell was she thinking, showing up in the freakin' cafeteria, dressed like a goth Hells Angel? Playing the Dr. Phil role in this drama is exhausting. Everybody's so wrapped up in who's right and who's lying that nobody sees what it's doing to the guy in the middle. Okay, I get that Zac and Grace won't ever be able to hang out in a big group anymore, but why do I have to take a side? Why does it always piss off the other person whenever I try to stay neutral? Grace looked like she wanted to stick one of her high-heel boots through his jugular before, and Zac—jeez, if I so much as glance in Grace's direction, I'm a traitor. The abrupt surge in temper surprises me, and I smack the steering wheel. I mutter curses and put the car in gear. As I leave the lot, I spot a face I haven't seen in a week and power down the window.

"Hey, Sarah! Need a ride?"

"God, yes! Thank you so much. I missed the bus and don't want to stick around for the late one." Sarah Griffin scoots into my passenger seat, rakes soaked hair off her face, and dries her hands on her jeans. We went out a few times back in tenth grade. She's cute but not obvious about it like some people. When I brake for the traffic light at the exit of the school's lot, she shifts in the seat to face me. "So what the hell was that in the cafeteria before?"

Grinding my teeth, I try to answer without yelling. "Spent the week cleaning lockers, and now Grace thinks we're going steady. Had to set her straight." I drive down Main Street, dodging deep puddles.

"Huh." Sarah laughs once. "Looked like you kicked her puppy or something."

245

Yeah, well, maybe she shouldn't have surprised me like that. "What do you think of her?" I ask after a minute.

Sarah's mouth falls open. "What do *I* think? I don't know. I think she's got some issues to work out."

"Very diplomatic." Laughing, I sneak a glance at her and put my eyes back on the road. "Come on. What do you really think?"

Sarah lowers her eyes, fidgets with her seat belt. "I think she's a pretty damn good actor. Always trying to look so tough. That's gotta suck, you know? I mean, she knows she can't let her guard down, even for a second."

I consider that while I drive. "Sarah, I need to ask you something." I turn left onto her street. "You were at that party the night Zac and Grace—"

"Got busy? Yeah, I was there."

"Help me out. I thought Grace liked *me*. Far as I knew, she went out with Zac twice and told him, 'Thanks, but no thanks. I really want to be with Ian.' That true?"

Sarah nods. "Definitely."

I pull up in front of her place, a big single-level house with a monster pickup truck in the driveway. "So how did they hook up?"

She spreads her hands and shakes her head. "Ian, you know how these things go. We were all drinking and dancing and getting silly. Zac kept putting the moves on Grace, and even though Grace kept shooting him down, that didn't stop everybody else from teasing them."

"Teasing them?"

"Oh, yeah. Miranda was about to go nuclear. Everybody knows she wants Zac McMahon *bad*. But Zac wouldn't even look at Miranda. No challenge, you know? The more Grace told him no, the more Jeremy kept taunting him, 'You gonna take that shit, dude?' and the madder Zac got."

"How'd they end up going off together alone?"

"Miranda threw beer in Grace's face because Zac wouldn't look at her. Like that's Grace's fault, right? Grace took off. Jeremy elbowed his lord and master, told him Grace just left. I knew right away he was gonna chase her." Sarah collects her wet gear and hits the unlock button on the car door. "He had this look, like a lion after a zebra, you know? Thanks for the ride." She calls out over her shoulder and closes the door.

I drive home. I throw the car into park, cut the engine, and sit there while the rain dances on the windshield, trying not to squirm when I think of Grace. God, I was such an ass. I don't get it. I just don't get Grace. It's like she's daring me. I can't be seen with her. She knows this. She even offered to find other transportation to take my dad's pictures. She put herself out there in the cafeteria today with the food and the Tylenol, and I...I let my head fall to the steering wheel. I really am an ass. She was there for me. She was there because she thought I might need the pain reliever and braved all that shit for me.

I find my dad in his office behind the garage.

"Ian, have you seen the work Grace is doing? Look at these." On the wide-screen flat panel, Dad enlarges an array of thumbnail images.

They're not just pictures. Grace must have Photoshopped them or something. She changed the sailfish my dad tiled at the bottom of a pool into a 3-D image to make it look like it's leaping out of the water. In another shot, she blended a spilled glass of whiskey into a shot of kitchen counter tile so perfectly that it was hard to tell where the borders are. "Look at this one," he breathes like he just uncovered buried treasure. I guess he did in a way. "This would be great on the website's home page." He points to the custom tile work he designed around this huge bathtub. Grace managed to find real flowers like the ones painted on the tile, arranged them so they seem to grow right out of the tub.

Yeah, okay, so Grace is ridiculously talented. Doesn't change anything, I decide with a loud sigh.

Dad shoots me a look. "Am I boring you?"

"Not really," I say and shrug.

"Then what's bothering you?" Dad swivels his chair around to look at me. "You're not worried about the tests, are you? Ian, I'm sure it's just a precaution. You'll be fine."

I sit on the corner of his desk. "No. I mean, yeah, but that's not all." God, it's like I'm constipated. "It's Grace. She thinks we're friends now. You know, after last week."

"Weren't you friends before you cleaned lockers together?"

"Yeah, I guess. But now she thinks we're more, and we can't—"

"Why can't you?"

"Because we *can't*, Dad. Not now. Not after what—"

Dad flings up a hand to cut me off. "Do not tell me you're ashamed to be near her because she was raped."

I turn away. Pace. Scrub hands through my hair. "Um, well, yeah—"

"Ian, I thought you were a bigger man than that."

"Dad, you don't get it. Zac is—"

"I don't care about Zac. I care about you." He stands and catches my shoulders, gives me a little shake. "You're better than that. We raised you better than that. Forget about Zac. How do *you* feel about Grace?"

I squirm out of his grip, my face burning. "I don't know."

"Bullshit."

Did my father just curse? I gape at him until he waves a hand in frustration, and I cave. "Yeah, okay, I like her. But I can't go out with her. The guys—"

"Again I don't care about the guys and don't understand why you do. You like her. She likes you—or so you think. Why does all that other stuff matter to you?"

Guilt slithers around my gut. "It's a betrayal, isn't it? Grace says Zac hurt her. Zac says he did what every other guy in his position would have done—tried to score and got lucky. Being friends with one of them betrays the other person."

Dad paces away, sits back in his chair, and stares at the floor for a long moment. "Then I guess you have to choose." He shrugs. "For what it's worth, any man who 'tries to score' with a girl he's not even dating isn't much of a man in my eyes." He shoots me one of those you-know-better looks.

I look away. Pretty sure I don't know a damn thing, except that I'm the man in the middle again.

———————

Alone in my room I roll onto my bed and stare at the ceiling, replaying everybody's words again and again. What Sarah said about Grace letting her guard down—she's right. Can't believe I didn't notice that. That first day of locker cleaning time she wouldn't work on the other side of the hall because she was afraid to put her back to me.

Me?

I'm harmless.

Except to mailboxes late at night. I slap hands over my eyes and curse. I replay every moment from last week. Suddenly the tough chick costume makes a lot more sense. From the first second we met, Grace looked at me like I was about to shove her against a wall. I thought she was looking at me with lust in her eyes, and it's actually fear. More proof that I know nothing.

Can't do this anymore. I leave my bed, power up my computer, and check my email. Coach Brill sent some stats from last week's drills camp. I open the message, wince at the gaping blank space next to my name, and skim the others. Jeremy improved in cradling, but he's still weak—no surprise there. Kyle really leaped up in passing and scooping, and of course, Zac's percentage of saves and clears is high. But so is the number of personal fouls.

Interesting.

I click the link that goes to the team's website, access the video files. The coaching staff archives game footage we study for retrospectives. I play a few. And then a few more. I stare at pictures of him taken during the game I got hurt in. Oh, he got penalized in this game too? I click the video and there it is—*game face.* That's what Grace called it. Sarah said Zac looked like a lion going after prey.

Here's the link for the footage taken at the game between us and Holtsville High School. The game Grace mentioned, the game where Zac put a player in the hospital with a fractured skull.

I remember this. The guy shifted. It was a legal hit. But I click Play anyway. I fast-forward to that play, watch it once, twice, a third time in slow motion. Kyle's scrambling for the ball with two players from Holtsville, but he's taking a beating. Zac leaves his crease, tries to add power. The other team's attacker scoops the ball, lowers his upper body, and *bam.* Zac makes contact, and the guy hits the deck, already unconscious. It was legal. I play it again frame by frame, and there it is. Right before contact, right when the other player shifts to chase the ball, Zac *raises* his hands and hits the other guy in the face. The other player definitely shifted, but he was trying to scoop. Any hit while the ball is loose is illegal. Zac should have broken off the attack, at least lowered his hands. Instead, he raised them. It's subtle, but it's there. I let the video play out in slow motion and see a glimpse of that game face Grace described.

Zac raised his hands. He hit that player hard enough to send him to a hospital, and he did it on purpose.

I turn off my computer and shove away from my desk with a curse. What if Zac did what Grace says he did?

I'm afraid to answer that question.

Chapter 25

Grace

I didn't run.

That's a point for me, but then I remember this isn't a game.

I lock myself in a bathroom stall and text my mom.

Grace: Pls pick me up. Ditching rest of the day.

Mom: What happened?

Grace: Ian. Stabbed me in the back. Panic attack.

Mom: OK. Be there in 15.

I struggle to slow my breathing, but the pressure in my chest is obscene. Breathe in, hold it, slowly exhale. Repeat. One hundred. Ninety-eight. Ninety-six. Sweat forms under my hair. My stomach cramps up. It'll pass, I assure myself. It'll pass. Ninety-four. Ninety-two. It'll pass.

It finally does.

Counting backward doesn't help. Counting at all doesn't help. Why do these things keep attacking me? There is no way Zac McMahon gets panic attacks. I leave my little cocoon and pace the girls' bathroom, sweat dripping between my shoulders. A minute ago I was cold. I grab my gear and hurry to the closest exit just as a clap of thunder splits the sky and the rain starts. I don't mind the rain. It feels cool against my red skin. It hides the tears that stubbornly insist on filling my eyes despite my refusal to cry.

I stand in the rain for who knows how long, and finally Mom drives up.

"Grace, you're soaked to the bone."

"Mom." My voice cracks. "Take me home."

"What did he do?"

"He…oh, God, he was savage. I bought him lunch, and he…he wouldn't touch it. He was afraid he'd catch an STD." The burn, Jesus, the burn in my throat, in my eyes is impossible to hold back. The air backs up in my lungs, and Mom's voice, calm and soft, talks me through.

"Grace, count and breathe. Come on, honey. You got this."

"I thought he was different," I push the words out between gasps that rip me apart. "I liked him."

"I know. Breathe. Hold it. Slowly blow it out."

It feels like weeks before Mom pulls into our cracked and rutted driveway. The faded yellow paint on the house looks like a sad shade of vomit in the rain. One of the gutters is clogged. Water pours over the edge like Niagara.

"Go get a hot shower. I'll make lunch."

Ugh. Food.

Shivering, I hurry upstairs. I look like a zombie from some bad movie. Makeup runs down my cheeks, drips onto my arms in black splats. I strip out of my clothes, toss them into the corner of the room, and run the hot water. I replay everything that happened today and power through the burn behind my eyes. The hot shower thaws the ache in my limbs but makes the gash in my heart bleed harder.

I'm such an idiot. I believed him. Believed *in* him. I even worried about his headaches and dizziness. Damn it, I like him. I really like him. How did this happen? I swore I wouldn't let a guy get under my skin, and in one week, just one week, Ian burrowed in there like a freaking parasite. As the hot water restores sensation to my extremities, an ache in my heart begins, and I mourn the numbness. Before last week I did okay living without friends, living with all the hostility. How do I go back to that? How do I pretend I'm immune to ridicule when it comes from Ian?

The burn behind my eyes moves to my throat, and I swallow hard. God, I hate crying. Hate it with a passion, and that makes me mad. Mad is good. I can deal with mad. I turn off the water and viciously towel-dry my hair, my mind circling around everything that happened. Would it suck less, hurt less if I didn't understand *why* he was so mean today?

Maybe. Maybe not. I don't know. All I know is he's a pathetic excuse for a man, and the fact that I know this and still like him is really pissing me off. What the hell, just what the hell was wrong with how I looked today? Why does he care if I wear eye-black like the football team? It's my face. It's my body. I can dress it up or down however I want. Why is that such a hard concept for guys to accept? All that crap Jax said about dressing to be noticed—being noticed is fine. But being noticed isn't the same as being ridiculed, insulted, ostracized, shamed. Being noticed isn't an open invitation to guys to do whatever they want to me. Jax is a jerk, so you almost expect jerklike thinking, but Camryn? She's a girl, and for some reason, the girls are worse. I heard the stage whispers when I walked into lit class this morning.

I pull on a pair of comfy sweats and a flannel shirt, tug a comb through my hair. You know, I totally get why schools have uniforms now. Maybe the entire town—no, no—the whole country should have a dress code. Everybody wears the same damn thing so nobody's a slut, nobody's a goth, nobody's a jock or a hipster or a nerd. No pressure! No responsibility! One size fits all!

I don't know. Is that what Ian's problem is too? He likes me and can't stand that other guys are looking at me that way? Ugh, it's like the stupid *Shrew* play. Everything always circles back to ownership. *My* wife, *my* woman, *my* girlfriend, *I saw her first*, *my* love—*mine, mine, mine.*

I fling myself back to my bed with a muffled scream. People need to wake up, open their eyes, and get a clue. I'm not anybody's property. I lie on my bed, staring at nothing in particular, stewing over the stupidity that surrounds me when a strip of fabric catches my eye. I cross to my closet, run my hand down the satin gown Kristie sent over last year. She and my dad wanted to throw me a lavish sweet sixteen party, but on *their* terms. No black lips, no eyeliner. Just yards and yards of Pepto-Bismol pink.

The dress had a poof skirt and sleeves. Formal dresses haven't had sleeves for years, but somehow Kristie managed to find one that does. Worse, she bought it without even asking me first. I tried it on, refused to model it for my dad, who immediately called me ungrateful. Of course, the party never happened.

If they'd bothered to ask me what I wanted, I would have pointed to the blue sheath with the sparkles. I would have had my hair done in a fancy updo with flowers or maybe more sparkles. I'd have had revealed a little skin, maybe bared my shoulders—

The idea comes out of nowhere and hits me between the eyes. It's so much awesome perfection that I can't believe there's no little lightbulb over my head. Oh, God, it's perfect. It's crazy. It's bold. It'll likely get me kicked out of school.

I'm totally doing it.

———

My chest hurts. Anxiety and exasperation just started their third round in a brawl for control over my body.

Exasperation is winning…so far.

The school is empty. It's just me and a few security guards outside. Mom dropped me off before her run today, and the first buses haven't arrived yet. Just inside the main entrance, where the only lights on are the ones that illuminate the trophy cases lining the hall, I scope out the best position for what will probably get me suspended. Detention at least.

Somebody left a chair by the auditorium doors. That'll work. I unzip my pack, pull out the yards of pink fabric I prepared last night. I cover myself head to toe and pin a strip over my face so that only my eyes are visible. I drag the chair to the center of the main hall, climb on top, and wait. The lights come on. It's showtime. A few minutes later I see them. Lines of students snake out of buses and come at me with their forked tongues and poisonous glares, and my stomach flips over. I swallow hard, willing the burn in my throat to go down instead of up. I thought I knew what it meant to be afraid, but this? Oh, God, this is insane.

It's not too late.

Nobody's seen me yet.

I can go, just stuff all this cloth into a trash bin and pretend I never saw it before. I can flee to Europe, tell everyone I'm a celebrity's daughter. It would be so easy—

That's right. It would be *easy*.

This is *right*. The doors open, and some students skid to a halt when they see me. I ignore the looks, the laughs, the finger-points. My legs twitch, but I lock them together. When a guy walks past me, I nod and say, "You're welcome."

"Who is that?" some students wonder out loud. Others know. "It's the slut. Ignore her."

Students move past me, some rolling their eyes, pretending they don't see me. To each guy, I say, "You're welcome. You're welcome. You're welcome."

Through the open doors, I see Ian, Kyle, and Jeremy about to walk in. I roll my shoulders, straighten my spine, and raise my voice. "You're welcome! You're welcome!" A small crowd is log-jamming the hall now. Some students are waiting to see what I'll do next. Others still can't figure out what I'm doing now. But nobody asks the question. Nobody asks me what they should be thankful for.

They don't care.

The lacrosse players come in. Ian skids to a dead stop when his eyes meet mine.

Bright eyes, he calls me.

"Holy crap," I can actually read Jeremy's lips from here. Beside him, Ian's dark eyes pop wide, and then they roll toward heaven. The permanent lift on his lips fades into a flat, disapproving line, and now I feel a jolt of pride jump into the fray still going on in my belly. I'm *glad* he disapproves. That was my goal. Now I need to raise the stakes. I want to make people uncomfortable. I want them to squirm.

I want Ian to squirm.

"You're welcome. You're welcome." A few guys actually circle back for seconds, laughing and shrugging because they don't get it. Nobody gets it.

Jenson Stuart, a sophomore on the wrestling team, is the first one to ask the question. He stops in front of my chair, looks up with a frown. "What am I supposed to be thanking you for?"

"For saving you from committing rape. You're welcome."

Jenson shifts his weight, looks around, and laughs once. "Whoa, back up. Are you calling me a rapist?"

"You're a guy, right?"

Jenson puts his hands on his hips. "Yeah. So?"

"Everybody knows one look at a female body sends a guy's hormones surging, and your weak little bodies just can't handle it. And then you do things you regret but blame it all on girls."

The humor on Jenson Stuart's face transforms into outrage. "What did you say?"

"You heard me."

"I ain't weak, bitch."

Weak is the only word that registered in that whole sentence? Really?

Ian jumps between us, hands up to pacify Jenson—interesting how he runs to my rescue today but had no problems squishing my heart yesterday.

"Grace, chill. Jenson, just ignore her. She's pissed at me."

Ignoring them both, I continue my speech. "Girls should cover up—cover everything up so boys don't lose control of their own bodies. It's our duty."

Jenson shakes his head. "I don't get it. I can control my body just fine."

"So why do you all keep blaming the girl every time a girl is raped?"

"I don't!"

"Sure you do! Every time you treat a girl like a slut, you're blaming her for your reaction."

"I don't even know you!"

Oh my God. Boys. "Forget me. I'm talking about all girls. Ask yourself how you talk to us, how you talk about us. Do you use words like *my girl*, like we're property? *I gotta get me some of that*, like we're yours for the taking? *I'm hungry, get me food*, like we're servants? Is that how you dis the girls in your life? Then you're part of the problem."

"What problem?" Jenson throws up his arms, and I am grateful. I'm actually grateful when Ian steps up again.

"Dude." He shakes his head. "Just go to class. This isn't about you at all. She just wants to make a scene."

"Crazy bitch."

"Another label? Slut, bitch, anything else to add?"

"Yeah." Ian whips dark eyes to mine. "How about out of line?"

"There is no line. The line got blurred when Zac attacked me in those woods." Where is he anyway?

"Grace, I see what—"

"Oh, you see, huh?" I cut him off. "Tell me, Ian. Are you undressing me with your eyes?"

"What? No!" He doesn't even acknowledge the pat on the back from Kyle.

"You said I get off having every guy in the school think I'm sexy. You said I look hot. Is there anything sexy about this outfit?" I demand. "Well, is there?"

He blinks up at me, probably wondering if he should call the school nurse, see if she's got a straitjacket handy.

"Look. You can't go around calling every guy in school a rapist."

"Oh, I can't? Why not? Every guy in school feels so justified calling me a slut."

"I never called you that."

My eyebrows shoot up. "Really? Not once? That's great, Ian, but what did you do when your friends said it?" I wave a hand toward Jeremy and Kyle. "Did you set them straight? Did you stand up for me? Or did you just stand there and laugh and tell them the food I give you has STDs?"

"Okay, but—"

"There are no *buts*. There is no reason you can give me that makes that right. Go tell your sisters they asked for it. Tell your sisters why it's *their* fault when someone calls them a slut."

"I wouldn't let my sisters leave the house dressed like you," Ian retorts.

"*You* wouldn't let them? Are you their master?"

"Hey, if you don't like being called a slut, maybe you shouldn't cry rape," Jeremy cuts in, his freckles blending in with the flush on his face.

"I didn't *cry rape*. I *was* raped!" I shout back.

"Maybe girls shouldn't drink themselves drunk if they care so much what happens to them!" Kyle says.

I shout louder. "Maybe boys should stop making excuses for—"

"Miss Collier, what do you think you're doing?"

Heads swivel. Mouths form O-shaped gasps. I turn, and there's Mr. Jordan, arms crossed, lips pressed.

I clear my throat, pull in a calming breath. "I'm protesting, Mr. Jordan."

"What exactly are you protesting?"

"The way everybody in this school shames girls based on our appearance."

"A lofty goal. Are you aware that other students are insulted by your attire?" He turns, indicates Khatiri standing nearby, big sad tears rolling down her face. Khatiri's family came here from Afghanistan, but she doesn't wear the native garb. No. Oh, no, no, no! I clasp my hands to my heart, climb off my chair. "I'm so sorry. I wasn't trying to ridicule. I was using a *burqa* to make boys see how they treat us—"

Khatiri steps closer to inspect the fabric I'm wearing over my head. "This is more like the *niqab*, and it's a religious custom, not military. The *burqa* is a symbol of oppression the Taliban forced on women. My mother was beaten for wearing what you're wearing because part of her face showed."

I look away, sick that I made Khatiri cry. "I'm sorry."

The bell rings, and the rest of my audience scatters, chattering, laughing, and pointing as they go.

"Mr. Russell, don't you have a class to get to?"

"Oh. Um. Yeah." Ian doesn't move.

"Miss Collier, I'll expect you in my office at dismissal."

I roll my eyes in disgust and stuff my costume into my backpack. Khatiri disappears into the girls' bathroom. Jeremy and Kyle have deserted Ian, so he follows me down the main corridor, and as soon as we're out of Mr. Jordan's line of sight, he grabs my elbow and spins me around. "What is going on inside that head?"

"My head's perfectly fine." I twist my elbow, and in a second I'm free of his hold, crouch into a fighting stance, dare him to touch me again. Ian immediately puts up his hands. "What's it to *you* anyway?"

He shifts, looks away. "I don't know."

I have no patience for him right now. I stride down the hall, but he jogs to catch up. "Just…well, you said you hate the way everybody's treating you, so why do you start more trouble?"

Start more trouble? Of course, that's what he'd think. "Because there's no changing certain people's minds once they're made up. You taught me that," I sneer at him. "But maybe I can get other people to *see*."

He gasps like my words just made him bleed. I hope they did. And I hope the wound gets infected too.

I turn onto the main stairwell. It's still crowded, even though there are only a few minutes left before the late bell. We fall into line and climb to the second floor. "If *people* are gonna treat me like crap anyway, I want it to be for a good reason."

Ian winces at my not-so-subtle inflection and leans closer. "I'm sorry I hurt you."

I turn east on the second floor and wave my hand. "No. You're not. You *had* to hurt me. That's what boys do when they're scared of a girl. They hurt her."

He blinks and opens his mouth to deny, closes it, and then offers me this excuse. "I have reasons."

"You have *excuses*. Weren't you listening?" I wave a hand back in the general direction of the main entrance. "Religion, government, the media—everybody tells you it's never *your* fault. You're just an innocent guy minding your own business, and these women, these females *beguile* you with their looks." I make spooky fingers to emphasize the word. "Guys are so dumb. You actually believe this crap. You waste half your lives trying to prove to everybody and their mother how tough you are, how strong, how manly, and then say crap like, 'Ooo, baby, you make me so hard,' because there's absolutely *no way* you can control your own body."

Ian stops walking, stares at me. "When did I say that to you?"

"You didn't," I admit and then stop to look him dead in the eye. "What you did is so much worse."

The late bell rings, and we both ignore it, facing off in the center of the second-floor corridor, where we had bonded over a couple hundred lockers. "I said I had reasons," he repeats, shoving his hands into his pockets.

"And I said you don't. You know what I think? I think you got scared." I drill a finger into his chest. "Your spine turned into Jell-O the second you walked in here yesterday."

Ian rolls his shoulders. "My spine is just fine."

"And you know what's even worse?" I barrel right over his lame defenses. "You're afraid of shit that's so unimportant. It's ridiculous. Talk to me when a guy you know for years, a guy you think is nice enough to date a few times turns ugly when you tell him you'd rather be with his friend instead of him."

Ian takes a step back like I shoved him with both hands. The color fades from his face.

"Talk to me when that guy hears you tell him no, hears you but waits while your head spins and your stomach churns, waits until you fall over and then pounces and tells you nobody gets to say no to him. Talk to me when he takes your clothes off and shoves himself inside your body and your limbs are too numb to stop him. Talk to me when he leaves you there, alone, unconscious, and bleeding and then puts pictures of what he did to you online. Then you tell me about your *reasons*."

Ian takes another step back. Then another. I stalk him, keeping pace.

"Talk to me when your friends drop you. Your parents can't look at you. And then you meet someone you could maybe care about, someone you think is different, someone who knows what's right but won't do it because it's too hard, someone who stands up in front of everybody and joins in the fun. Then you tell me about your reasons."

I stand there, glaring and panting against the tears fighting to fall—I'll be damned before I let them fall—while Ian just stares with his mouth open. "You know what, Ian? I'm *glad* you weren't there that night. You probably would have joined in, made it some kind of a team-bonding ritual."

His hands come up to his face, cover his mouth. When he shuts his eyes, it's in defeat. I've got him. He knows I've got him. Whatever reasons he had, I guess they're not worth the breath needed to say them.

A teacher steps out of a classroom. "Get to class, you two."

I don't need to be told twice. I leave Ian there, my words echoing down the hall.

Chapter 26

Ian

Grace's words burn my damn ears. I walk away, but it doesn't help. I swear I still hear her. I get to math class five minutes late, earn a reprimand from my teacher and a few glares from classmates. It's like…like she fucking branded me or something. I slam my books down, slouch in my seat, seething while Mrs. Patterson starts talking about derivatives.

Where does she get off, talking to me like that? What the fuck does she think she's doing, saying all guys are rapists? Lucky Jenson didn't deck her for saying that crap. Just because I don't want my sisters to get hassled doesn't mean I *own* them. And I never called her a slut either. Okay, so I didn't really stick up for her. I should have. I defended her when Jeremy and Kyle hassled her, but Zac? Different story. She doesn't get it. She doesn't understand what I lose if I admit I like her.

I like her. Goddamn it, I like her a lot.

I even like the way she dresses. The black and all the hardware? It's hot. There! I admitted it. It's hot. She's hot. Does that make her a slut? I don't know, and I don't care. I slide my hand into my pocket, feel for the stud I've been holding onto because it's hers.

There's nothing wrong with Grace. Nothing except for one thing, and that's Zac. He got to her first. And now she's off-limits, and it's either her or—

"Mr. Russell, what is the integral of secant squared?"

Um. Holy shit. "Um. What?"

"What is the integral of secant squared?"

"Yeah. Uh, tangent x?"

"Are you asking me or telling me?"

"Telling you."

"Final answer?"

I nod, gulping.

"You forgot the plus C."

"Oh. Right." I look down at my notebook like I actually give a shit.

Mrs. Patterson turns back to the board, writes out some theorem or something, and I go back to brooding. Grace's words are tattooed on my goddamn eardrums. What the hell's wrong with calling a girl your girlfriend if that's what she is? Okay, okay, *I gotta get me some of that* is just crude. But nobody really talks like that, except maybe Jeremy, but that's because he's still sexually twelve. And if I ever told my mom, *I'm hungry, get me food*, she'd—

Whoa. Wait. Oh, God. I remember the night Zac and I got drunk. He shouted up the stairs, and his mother got out of bed to make us something to eat. He never even said *thank you*. I squirm in my seat. I don't know if I ever said thank you either.

The pen in my hand cracks. I stare at it for a long moment, finally drop it on top of my book. I don't know what to do. *Fuck!* That's a lie. I *do* know what to do. I just don't know if I can do it. The thing is, all this shit? It's not about Grace, not really. It's all about Zac. He leads, and we follow. Why?

I don't know.

Nobody's ever *not* followed.

My mind replays that night last week at the Pizza Hut when we had our bet going. When that girl Addie caught Zac hugging my sister, he didn't look sorry like "Hey, it's not what it looks like!" He looked annoyed like "Did I just blow a sure thing?" My head aches, and I'm dizzy. I know I should go to the nurse because sitting in a dark room and doing nothing beats sitting in math class, but I have to work this out.

The game when I got my first concussion, I hit the ground hard, got the breath knocked out me. I couldn't breathe. I had to blink a few times to clear my vision. Sound was just formless noise, and I remember wishing I could blink my ears too. There was a moment when I was rolling around the field, trying to reboot my entire body when Zac left his crease and hit the player who had hit me, and though my brain was getting sloshed around, I'm pretty sure I saw it—the expression Grace keeps trying to grab with her camera, the expression Sarah called *hunger*.

It was in his eyes.

Thank God Zac has my back. That's what I remember thinking at the time.

You probably would have joined in, made it some kind of a team-bonding ritual.

I don't care what Grace thinks. I am not what she says I am.

I'm *not*.

———————

The third-period bell finally rings, and I book it to gym class. The locker room is buzzing with guys ranting about Grace's demonstration this morning.

"Did you see it?" Zac asks me with a smile.

I pull my shirt over my head and nod. "Yeah. Ringside seat. Where were you?"

"Late. Got lucky with that girl from the Pizza Hut, remember?"

"Addie."

"No. The other one. Jess."

The other one was mine. Son of a bitch. I tug a Laurel Point HS T-shirt over my head to hide my disgust.

"She snuck me into her room, and I fell asleep."

"Dude, you stayed all night? You are the man!" Some kid I don't know holds his fist out, and Zac obliges him with a bump.

That's when I see it. Zac's iPhone tucked into his shoe.

Zac's got an audience now. Won't notice if I play around with his phone. "Zac, can I borrow your phone?"

"Right there, bro." He points to the shoe and then holds his hands up to his chest to describe the size of the girl's tits.

Chest. I mean *chest*.

I grab the damn phone, unlock it. He has no password. I scroll to his media files and find the video he took of Grace in the woods that night.

Whoa. There are two. I text both to myself and then quickly send a text to my dad to report my dizziness. I'm about to put the phone back, and then something occurs to me. I go into his sent messages history and delete the one I sent with the videos attached.

A second later my phone buzzes, and Zac gives me the dumb-ass look. "Why did you need my phone if you've got yours?"

"Mine never works in the locker room," I cover fast. "Weird."

Fortunately the bell rings before he can ask me any more questions.

Thinking about what's probably on the unwatched video on my phone causes time to come to a complete halt. Decades later gym is finally over, and I'm free. I check my phone. Three messages wait for me—the two I sent from Zac's phone plus one from my dad.

Dad: If you want to go home, leave. Already squared it with the nurse.

Excellent. I tuck the phone in the pocket of my jeans, fold the jeans, clean shirt, and underwear, and take the pile with me to the showers. I don't like prancing around the locker room wrapped in a tiny towel. Five minutes later Zac catches up to me when I dump my wet towel in the bin.

"Dude, your head okay?" He's got his phone out. I freeze for a minute. I'll be damned. He checked up on me.

I shake my head. "No, I'm going home. I've been dizzy for hours."

His lips thin, and his jaw tenses. "I should have knocked that number-twenty-three punk out."

"Zac, it was a clean hit."

"Still. Nobody messes with my crew."

I drop my eyes, cursing silently. Grace sneers in my head. *"It's not supposed to be easy. It's right."*

I make it home by a little past twelve and go straight to my room. Nobody's in the house. That's good. I sit at my desk, watch the first video. It's short, less than a minute, and the video quality sucks, but it was still enough to convince the whole school Grace Collier is scum after Zac posted it on Facebook and tagged her. But the second video is longer, about six minutes. I play it once. The video quality still sucks. It's dark, Zac's hand on the phone shakes. But the sound quality is dead on. I hear everything. The same sounds are on both videos.

Except they're *not* the same sounds.

I play it again. Six more minutes.

By the third time, my hands clench. Six more minutes.

The fourth time, I'm shaking.

Six minutes.

In case you're wondering, that's how long it takes to hate my best friend.

I drop my phone on the desk and stare at it for hours but it never tells me what I should do. I rake my hands through my hair, cursing. I need advice. I need to talk to someone, but who? If I talk to Jeremy or my dad or my sister or my coach, I know exactly what each of them would say and I still wouldn't know what to do.

I can almost hear my dad's stupid flip-calendar speech, preaching about my loser friends, about how I'll never be anything worthwhile, and all I can think is, I'm not what Zac is.

I grab the phone, shove it deep in my pocket, where I swear it tries to burn its way out, and drag myself downstairs. Need to think. Need to—Jesus, don't know what I need. I shrug on my sweatshirt and hit the street, running until my lungs scream.

Chapter 27
Grace

After the worst day at school—I keep thinking one day can't possibly top the day before, but I'm always wrong—I get a text message, which is weird because I have no friends. I unlock my phone, see the message is from my dad, which is even weirder because he never texts.

Dad: Don't forget Kody's party. I don't want you disappointing him.

Whoa, what?

When have I ever disappointed him? I love the little guy, even though his parents are jerks. I put up with all this Ian crap just to make some money for his gift. Besides, the party was canceled.

Wasn't it?

Grace: Party officially back on for Sat?

The burn in my throat is back. It's an old friend now. The thought makes me laugh once. I *do* have a friend. His name is Phlegm.

The phone buzzes again.

Dad: Of course it's on! You knew this. Why are you playing games?

I throw my phone at the wall. It lands on the carpet near the stairs with no damage. It's the cellular equivalent of a middle finger. She uninvited me. Kristie actually uninvited me. And she probably told my dad *I* was the one who didn't want to come.

Mother of God, she really does hate me.

Why? What did I do? She was my teacher. We paid her to give me dance lessons, not seduce my dad. She's the one who trapped him, getting pregnant a few months later. I didn't do any of this. I drive my fist into a sofa cushion and scream. Everything that's happened—it's *her* fault, not mine. All of it—the insults scraped into my mom's car, the shunning at school, the harassment, losing my friends, Ian. If I hadn't been so upset, so angry at her, would I have let Zac hug me and kiss me and listen to me cry? Would I have seen through his pathetic seduction attempts? Would the warning bells have gone off if I didn't let myself get so drunk?

Oh, God.

Something rolls over me, into me, through me, something heavy, too heavy to bear. I collapse onto the sofa because I think I know what it is. Oh, God, I know what it is. *It is my fault.* Mine. I let this happen. I should be hanging out with Lindsay and Miranda right now in Miranda's basement, watching movies and picking out our prom dresses, and Ian and I—

I can't, I just can't do this anymore. I run to the kitchen. The semester abroad brochure is stuck to the refrigerator with a magnet, but Europe's not far enough. I need to run.

I need to go where nobody can reach me again.

There's a high shelf in one of the cabinets where my mother keeps all the bottles of booze people bring over yet never drink. I think maybe they just mate in the dark and form little bottles, so I stuff a few into my pockets—who cares what kind? It doesn't need to taste good.

It just needs to make me numb.

The woods are cold and dark and smell like a cemetery. Leaves crack under my boots, and I click on the flashlight I grabbed, smack the bottom a couple of times. I don't know how I got here—the scene of the crime nobody believes happened—but I did. I stretch out on the damp ground with my back against the railroad tie. Yeah. *That* railroad tie. I open the first bottle, swig whatever it is. Rum. I shrug. Like I said, it doesn't matter. The remains of a lot of parties litter the site—empty cans, bottles, plastic six-pack rings, and *ugh*, a condom. How many girls like me are out there—girls who got too drunk, wore the wrong clothes, said the wrong thing, and ended up sitting right here, staring into a bottle?

The train whistle blows. I pick up somebody's empty beer bottle, hurl it against a tree, and something twists in my chest when it smashes into a million pieces because I'm jealous. I'm actually jealous of it. I stand up, chug more rum, find another beer bottle, and throw that one too. I line up a whole six-pack on the railroad tie, try to see how fast I can throw, reload, throw again. The arc of light from my flashlight glints off all the pieces, kaleidoscope designs, and I wish I could be one of them instead of me.

But I don't break like glass bottles. I bend and twist and—and I *feel* everything that's thrown at me, and I'm tired. I just want to shatter so I never have to feel anything again.

Another gulp of rum and I see it.

A large shard, all jagged edges and sharp points in the center of the light beam like it's on stage.

Seductive.

I pick it up, fondle it for a minute, glide it against my skin. It's cold and smooth, and with just one flip of my hand, I figure it'll bite. It'll hurt. But it can't be any worse than what I feel right now, and when it's done, I'll be done too.

I adjust my grip on my piece of glass, my passport to freedom, and shut my eyes, imagining it, imagining the peace, the end of the pain, just…an end. I grip it harder, and a jagged edge reveals its teeth. My hand shakes, and my breath hitches.

No.

I drop the shard, fall to my knees, and cover my face.

"Jesus H. Christ, you scared the shit out of me."

I swing the light beam around, and Ian steps into my clearing.

Maybe there's a God. Maybe there isn't. Something got him here just as I'm ready to break, and I wonder, *Is he here to save me or smash me himself?* He's not happy—that's clear. His eyes have shadows, and his face is tense. I pick up my bottle and chug, then stretch out on the ground against a tree.

"What are you doing, Grace?"

I lift my eyebrows at his painfully obvious question and don't bother to answer. I swallow another drink, feel it burn a path to my stomach. A few seconds later he takes my bottle, swallows some, makes a face.

"Can I sit?"

I go still. Me wearing my kick-ass boots, drinking in the woods alone with a boy, and he wants permission to sit? *Are you completely insane?* every cell in my body screams at me, but I shift over a bit because it just doesn't matter. What can he possibly do to me that hasn't already been done? He crouches beside me, leans against my tree, and passes back my bottle.

"So why didn't you do it?" He picks up my piece of glass, tosses it far out of the way. I mourn the loss as I follow its trajectory and swill more rum when it plops somewhere behind a shrub.

Why didn't I do it? Damn good question. How can I possibly explain it? I wanted to. I still do. But there's something else I want more. Need like I need air to breathe. "In your family, you have any old cur...curmug—" I know this word. I glance at my bottle. Rum works fast. Good.

"Curmudgeons?"

"Yeah, them. Got any of them who love to tell you how hard their lives were when they were our age?"

Ian's dark eyes go wide for a second, so I know I'm totally not making sense, but he plays along. "What, you mean like having to walk to school in the dead of winter?"

Exactly like that. I nod, excited. "In a foot of snow."

"Barefoot," he adds, lips twitching.

"Uphill."

"Both ways." We say at the same time and share a laugh that doesn't last long because—well, because we're sitting in the woods doing our best to *not* talk about the real reasons we're sitting in the woods.

"Yeah, my grandfather's like that, and by all indications, my dad will be in about five more years."

I shake my head. "Your dad's pretty great."

Ian takes back the bottle. "You only met him the one time. Trust me, he gets worse."

"No, he's really great. He came to help me when one of the home owners got out of line with me."

Ian whips his head around. "Whoa, hold up. Who got out of line? When was this?"

"Oh, it was the day Zac sprang you early from slut training camp." I wiggle my fingers at him like they're filled with the power of all those slut cooties. "You were supposed to be there but ditched me to hang with your bro." I steal the bottle back, swallow more rum. "Wish my dad was like yours. He doesn't stick up for me anymore."

"Yes, he does. I was there when he almost kicked Jeremy's ass."

I snort. "That was easy. But he doesn't back me up when it's hard. Kristie uninvited me to my brother's birthday party." I slap a hand to my mouth. I didn't mean to say that. And I want my glass piece back right now, but it's gone like all of my friends.

"No way." He grabs the bottle out of my hands.

"Way." I grab for the rum, but Ian holds the bottle out of my reach. "Kristie called Sunday night, told me the petting zoo people double-booked, so the party was off and not to come. Then today my dad texts me, says to make sure I don't forget the party and disappoint my brother. Like I'd do that?" I want more rum, but Ian won't give me back the bottle.

"That why you're sitting in the woods, drinking, and staring at pieces of glass?"

I shrug, and he changes the subject. "Okay, so tell me what this has to do with relatives who had hard lives?"

"Oh, right." I hold a finger to my lips. "That's me."

"You?" Ian gives me an eye-roll. "Uh-huh."

"I'm ser ous," I say and laugh because such an easy word tangles up my tongue. I climb to my feet. Whoa, not so easy in high-heeled boots. I'm not drunk enough—not nearly drunk enough. I pull out the second bottle I stole from the kitchen, open it, gulp some down, and remember my manners. When I offer some to Ian, he only shrugs.

"Why are you a crazy old curmudgeon?"

I laugh and fling out my arms, spilling some of the—what is this? Whiskey. "That's my life. Every day it gets harder and harder." I swallow another sip, let out a loud belch, and quickly cover my mouth. I blink at him for a minute. "Oh, jeez! Gross." I crack up laughing, and it's this strange rasp that isn't happy at all. And then it's gone. "The worst thing, the very worst thing that can ever, ever, *ever* happen to a girl happens to me, but I'm still here. And I think it can't ever get worse than that, right?

It just can't." I try to walk, but the trees pitch and look like they're about to fall. I grab one to hold it up. "Only it *does*. Every damn day it does. I'm walking barefoot, in the snow, uphill, and let's see what else we can throw at her, you know? And the worst part is I don't see half the shit coming at me until I feel it." My voice cracks, and I slide back down to the ground. Great big tears roll down my face, and Ian's jaw drops. "I completely and totally suck at life and just don't want to feel anymore."

"Grace, I'm sorry. I am so fucking sorry."

"You keep saying that, but then you keep doing crap that needs apol-apol-gies."

"Okay, why don't you give me that bottle? You're slurring and wobbling on those damn heels."

I move the bottle out of his reach. "I'm not drunk." To prove it, I gulp down more whiskey.

"Yeah, you are."

"If I were drunk, you'd be on top of me."

Ian jumps to his feet, grabs the bottle out of my hand, and smashes it against a tree. "Shut up. Just shut the fuck up." He shouts at me, but his voice trembles.

I blink up at him for a second. Wow. He is seriously pissed off. "Aw, what's the matter, Russell? Don't want to catch one of my STDs?"

"Grace, I mean it. Shut. Up."

I climb back to my feet. "When I opened my eyes and saw you, I thought I was safe." I wipe the tears off my face because they're pathetic. "You hurt me the most of all." No, *I'm* pathetic.

He lowers his eyes, shoves his hands into his pockets. "Yeah. I'm sorry for that. I had reasons—"

"Excuses. Not reasons." I shrug like I don't care, except I do care. I care way too much, and God, it hurts.

Ian winces like I just cut him with my piece-of-glass friend. Where did it go? It sailed way over there, behind that…that—what is that? I squint at a bush or a tree or a weed—who knows?—and almost fall forward.

"Grace. Grace? Whoa, easy. I got you."

I feel so light. I look down and find Ian's hands holding my arms, holding me up. I stare into his eyes, at his lips. His hands tighten on my arms, and I think I'm closer to him than I was before, close enough to just reach out and trace the line of his cheekbone. Abruptly he clears his throat.

"Grace, tell me something. If you had that picture of Zac, the one of his game face, how does that fix any of this?" He waves his hands at my bottle.

Whoa, abrupt change of subject. I'm dizzy. My shoulders sag. Aw, crap. I really wish I had my piece of glass. "It doesn't. I already got it. You saw it, 'member? You snagged the camera, scrolled through the card. That was the first time you were mean." Was it the first time or the second time? There are so many times, and they're starting to blur together. Just one big ball of tangled-up meanness. "Piece of glass. Want it back."

"No. What's wrong with the picture you took?"

I swat at his hands, but he doesn't move. "Police said it's not enough evidence to convict. It was a waste of time. Feudal."

"Futile?"

That's what I said. "Zac wins."

Ian opens his mouth and then closes it. He opens it again. "I'm sorry."

I laugh. He's funny. He's so tall and cute. "I thought you were diff'ent."

That makes him mad again. "You don't know what you're saying."

"I know 'zactly what I'm saying." I lean closer. I want to mess up his hair.

His eyes pop. "What the hell *are* you saying?"

What would it feel like? My fingers through all that dark hair? His hands on me? His lips on mine? Oh, wait. Almost forgot I already know what that feels like. How could I almost forget that part? It's my favorite part. "I wanted you to ask me out. For ages I wanted that, but you never noticed me."

"Yes, I did."

"Didn't do anything about it then."

"Yeah, well, I notice you now."

I snort. That's only 'cause I'm drunk and falling in love with sharp pieces of glass. I'm tired. I'm so tired. My eyes feel like they've been weighted down, so I just put my head on his shoulder and shut them for a moment. Suddenly Ian's arms wrap around me, and he hugs me…tightly.

"I should have asked you out." he says with an extra squeeze. "I definitely should have asked you out."

I snort again 'cause seriously? I'm supposed to believe that?

"Grace?"

"Mmm." With my head on his shoulder and his breath warm on my cheeks, I sigh. This is all probably just a dream. I zone out, content to be warm and pretend Ian's really here.

"Grace?

Damn it, why am I dreaming so *loud*?

"Will you go out with me? See a movie or something?"

"Sure, dream Ian. I'll go out with you. Get your shots first. Anti-cooties, slut vaccine."

His arms tighten around me. "Shut up, Grace."

"Dreams don't yell at you."

"I'm not a dream, Grace."

"Should be."

He sighs, and his breath tickles me. "Grace, look at me."

Lift my head? I don't know if I can. But I try anyway because I like to have nice dreams and haven't had one in forever. My head feels about two sizes too big and a hundred pounds too heavy and *whoa!* There are two of him. He scooches down a bit, so he's eye level with me, grasps my head between both hands, and I smile. "Thanks."

"No problem. Are you looking at me, Grace? Do you see me?"

"Yep, both of you."

"Jesus." He rolls his eyes. "Timing sucks, but you need to hear this. I believe you. Did you hear me, Grace? I believe you."

It takes my brain a second or two to catch up to my ears, and when it does, I finally shatter like one of those beer bottles and fall into a million jagged pieces. Only he doesn't let go. He never lets go.

We stand like this forever until I can breathe without sobbing, blink without crying.

"You are so fucking strong, dealing with all that crap, and I don't know why it took me so long to see—Well, I do know why, but that doesn't matter because now I see. Now I know. You're a goddamn warrior." Ian kisses me right on my forehead, and damn it, it's so right, so perfect. I don't ever want to move, not even to tell him I'm not any of those things. I'm just a girl who got mad.

Really fucking mad.

"Grace?"

"Mmm."

"Glad you didn't do it. The glass, I mean."

"Would have been easy. Not right."

With his arms still wrapped around me, Ian jerks like I electrocuted him. And then I'm falling, and while I'm falling, I'm thinking, *I knew this was only a dream.*

———

"Grace."

Something keeps hitting my face, and I bat it away. Somebody laughs.

"Grace, come on. Open those bright eyes."

Ian? Oh, God. I blink, and he's smiling down at me, one hand holding mine and the other cradling my face. What—I glance around, discover I'm in his car. The woods. The booze. The piece of glass. I gasp, sit up, and shut my eyes. *Shit, shit, crap!*

"Grace, look at me." The hand on my face shakes me a little, taps my cheek again. My eyes fly open because the tone of his voice tells me he's pissed off.

"Nothing happened. Okay? I promise you. Nothing happened."

How did he—I just nod.

"Gimme your key."

Key? I pat my pockets down. I think I stuffed it into my back pocket. I shift, struggle with uncooperative limbs, and finally fish it out. Ian takes it, leaves the car. I curse and bury my face in my hands. What the hell was he doing in the woods? The passenger door opens, and I almost spill out of the car all over his shoes. He sighs and scoops me up at the knees like I'm a sick child.

"I got you."

Oh, God, you have no idea. I shut my eyes and sink into the sensation because it'll probably never happen again until I'm in college where nobody knows Grace the slut. I jolt when I feel softness against my back.

I'm on the sofa in our living room. Ian tosses my key on the coffee table, flicks on a lamp, grabs my feet, and unzips first one boot, then the other. Even with the booze numbing my neurons, I feel a tingle. He pulls me upright, peels off my leather jacket, tosses it on a chair, puts my boots in the corner. There's a blanket on the back of the sofa. I pull it down, but he's right there, smoothing it over me, tucking it around me. God, that feels so amazingly good. I force my eyes open—I don't even remember closing them—but Ian's gone. Damn. I close them again, try to remember all the shitty things he did so I won't miss him so much, and…and then I remember the amazing thing he just told me. It wasn't a dream?

"Grace."

"I'm not sleeping." I wrestle my eyelids open.

"Okay." Ian's back, and he's laughing. There's a tall glass of water in his hands. He pulls me upright again, holds out his hand with a smirk.

Pain relievers.

I smile at the irony, pop the pills, swallow some water, and settle back down. "Don't go," I whisper.

He looks at the door, brow wrinkled, lips tight. My heart cracks another centimeter, but I don't say anything. I figure I already gave him enough chances. He kneels next to me, reaches out with his thumb to make tiny circles along my cheek, and if I weren't already down, I'd have melted into a puddle. My eyelids are so heavy, but if I close them, I might miss something. I imagined this moment for ages, how it would play out, what circumstances would lead up to it. He shakes brown hair out of his dark eyes, licks his lips, and I swear I can smell chocolate.

He lowers his eyes, and I almost protest until he says my name. "Grace? I really want to kiss you."

My lips tingle, and I can't tell if it's anticipation or something else. "You can." His eyes snap back to mine, a little wider. He looks, just looks at me for so long, the tick of the clock on the wall ticking louder, louder, *louder*, and just when I'm sure he's going to laugh and tell me he was only kidding, he shifts to sit on the sofa beside me. He cradles my face in both hands, and my heart kicks into a higher gear. He leans down, angles his head, and I forget to remember why I hate him.

"Not until you're sober."

I close my eyes so he won't see the disappointment, but my mind plays back the day we kissed in front of the lockers. He tasted like chocolate, and I want more. Because who can eat only one chocolate kiss? My fingers dig into his wide shoulders—funny, I don't remember wrapping my arms around him—and tug him back hard enough to make him grunt. There are hard muscles under soft skin, warm hands and hot breath, galloping heart rates and heavy limbs. An hour ago I didn't want to feel anything again. Now I feel everything, and it's still not enough.

"You're not making this easy, Grace."

"You really believe me?"

Ian nods, his eyes pinned to mine. "Yeah, I do."

"Why? Why now?"

He abruptly stands up, runs a hand through his hair, and I pout. I wanted to do that, but I forgot. "Grace, there's something I need to do, and then I'll be back, okay?"

I turn away, blood going cold. He won't be back. And tomorrow he'll twist the knife a little deeper. Maybe it will punch through to the other side, and all this will finally be over.

He makes an odd choking sound, and before I can figure out why, he falls to the sofa next to me and hauls me against his chest. "No. Damn it, Grace. No. Don't do that." His arms are like steel walls around me.

"Do what?" I murmur flatly into his chest.

"Think what you're thinking."

"What am I thinking?"

He grips my shoulders, holds me away, and looks me straight in the eye. "Things like 'Oh, guess he just wants to find out if I'm as easy as Zac says.' Or worse like 'Wonder how Ian's gonna stick it to me tomorrow.'" I lower my eyes, and he hugs me tight again. "Grace, I know you already gave me a lot of chances. Give me one more. Please? Just one more. I have to take care of something. But tomorrow I'll tell the whole school you're my—"

He breaks off abruptly, and I look at him to figure out why. He looks so confused that I almost laugh. "What?"

"I don't know what to call this. You. Us."

"Us?" My jaw drops. We're an *us* now?

"Yeah. I mean, you were so pissed off about the way guys *own* girls, remember? I don't want to piss you off by calling you my girlfriend."

Holy mother of God in heaven and baby Jesus too. "You…you're saying you want us to be together?"

He smiles, relieved. "Yeah. Together." And then he quickly asks, "I mean, if you still want that too. A lot changed, and I get that. But not this."

I want. Oh, God, I want. "What about your friends, your teammates? What about lunchtime when they won't let me sit at their table?

What about the next time one of them thinks he can take a ride on Grace? Will you ever be able to look at me and not see Zac all over me?"

His jaw twitches, and when he talks, his voice is tight. "One step at a time, Grace. Just tell me you'll still be here."

"Yeah. I'll be here, Ian."

He smiles, shifts me off his lap, adjusts my blanket, and walks to the door. At the front door he looks over his shoulder. "Grace. Remember what I said. I believe you."

Oh, yeah, I remember. Those words feel even better than a kiss on the forehead, and *that* really curled my toes. After all that's happened to me, after all the times and creative ways I've been hurt, how can one boy get me to believe in fairy tales?

Chapter 28
Ian

No! Zac, stop. I don't want to.

Inside my dad's Camry, with my hands choking the steering wheel, I try to cool down, but my temper's about to boil over. The way Grace stared at the chunk of glass—it still makes me shiver, and that pisses me off. It's the way she should look at *me*. She did look at me that way once. But I couldn't deal, so I ripped the heart out of her chest and squished it in front of the whole team, in front of half the damn school. I catch my reflection in the rearview mirror and shake my head. Can't even say I saved her life. No, she did that herself before she even knew I was there. She fought her demon and won.

Oh, God, I'm sick. Help me, Zac. I feel so sick.

Zac's video is on replay in my head, and I just sit here shaking like the useless bobble head on the dashboard. I slash out a hand and send the stupid thing flying.

I know what I have to do, knew it before I went to the woods this afternoon. Doesn't make it easy. The team will suffer for this. Probably have to skip the All Long Island Tournament. Seniors could lose scholarships. My concussed brain could still heal. There's a chance I could be fine. But if I do this, none of us will play. I'll lose everything—my friends, my team, my shot at an athletic scholarship.

I pull out my phone and stare at it for a long moment, then play the video again. I think about Zac helping me pass my midterm and covering for me after I dented the car, about his total confusion when he admitted he tried to score with Grace because she was drunk. "Isn't that what those parties are for? You'd have done the same thing if you'd been there!"

No! Zac, stop. I don't want to.

I would have stopped. I swear I would have stopped.

Nobody gets to tell me no.

I suck in a big breath and do what I should have done the minute I watched this damn video—text Coach Brill, attach Zac's video to the message. After a beat I tap out a quick message warning him to view it alone. It's not much, but I want to protect Grace's privacy. The next call I make is to the detective who questioned me the night I took Grace to the hospital.

"How did you obtain this video, Ian?" Detective Buckley asks when I tell him what's on it.

"I took it off Zac's phone."

"You took it. In other words, you helped yourself?"

"Yeah, but—"

"Ian, email me the video, and I'll see what I can do, but—" he trails off, and I get what he's not saying. As evidence goes, it's not much.

My phone buzzes with a text message. Coach Brill orders me to meet him in his office *now*. I start the car and drive back to school, my stomach twisting tighter with each mile. It's dark when I get there, but the team's still out on the field, running practice drills. I turn my back and start the long, lonely walk to the locker room. The smell of sweat and other funk never goes away.

I'm really gonna miss it.

My phone's tucked securely in my pocket. I pace, shoes squeaking on the tile outside the coach's office.

I didn't tell Grace about the video.

I wanted to.

I thought about it half a dozen times.

I wanted to be her hero. Wanted her to throw her arms around me, all gushy with gratitude.

But I didn't.

I have no reasons, just excuses. After all the shit I said and did, she still likes me. Why? There's no reason for it. I don't have half the female population cooing about how drop-dead gorgeous I am. I'm nowhere near as smart as Zac. I have no clue what I want to do with my life. And oh, let's not forget the dent I put in the car because I didn't think it was a big deal to drive when I was buzzed. I'm a real fucking prize. She deserves more than me. She deserves a warrior like her.

The doors open with a clang. I freeze halfway through my pace path, quiver like a three-year-old after a nightmare. Cleats clack, and suddenly Zac is standing right in front of me. "Russell? What the hell, man? You look like you've seen a ghost."

A strangled laugh escapes. Yeah. I guess I have.

He heads to his locker, strips off sweaty gear. "Seriously, dude. What's up with you?" Behind him, the rest of the team files in, but I ignore them.

I swallow hard. "Zac, I asked Grace out."

Zac's face comes apart—eyes pop, jaw drops, nostrils flare. "What the hell did you say?"

"I asked her out. I like her. I liked her first. You shouldn't have moved on her at all. But you did, and that's done."

Zac paces away, hands apart. "I don't believe what I'm hearing. That skank is trying to ruin my life, and you want to slow dance at the prom with her? Are you tripping, man?"

"Zac—"

"No! No, man. I forbid it."

I blink. "You what?"

"You came to me, said what you had to say. Now it's my turn. I forbid it."

"I'm not asking your permission."

"Then what the fuck are you asking for?"

"The truth!" I shout back. "What did you do to her? And don't feed me the party line about how she asked for it."

He stops pacing, slowly turns to face me, and crosses his arms. "I don't like your tone. *Bro.* You're supposed to be my friend. First you tell me you're hot for a girl I already did—who wasn't that good by the way—and then you ask me a question that's not even a question."

The guys all stop what they're doing and watch. My blood's heating up. "*Wasn't that good?* That's funny." I laugh once. "Not what you said after the party. Not what you said on Facebook when you posted that little video tribute."

Zac laughs. "Ian, you got it bad, don't you? Okay, look. All that was just talk. I was hoping for an encore, you know?"

"An encore. Uh-huh. How'd that work out for you?"

The smile switches off. "You are really pissing me off." He takes a few steps toward me, and I shift sideways. He looks at me in horror. "Look at us. Is this what you want? We been friends for years, and now we're about to fight over some—"

"Don't say it, man."

"What, slut? Whore?"

"Zac, tell me what you did to her."

"I banged her, man. That's it, and it wasn't worth it since all she did was lie there—"

"What did you just say?" I angle my head. He admitted it. He just admitted she was unconscious. "What happened to your first story? She was totally into it, and now all she did was lie there. Which one's true, Zac?"

He stands there, face red, eyes shocked. For the first time since I met Zac, he doesn't have a witty comeback. Matt and Kyle exchange a worried look. Jeremy inches his way closer.

"Zac. Just tell me. I'll go with you to the cops. This doesn't have to—"

"The *cops*? Jesus Christ, are you out of your mind?" He rubs a hand across his mouth. But his face changes. I've never seen Zac scared before...until now.

"I know what you did. Zac, *I know.*"

His eyes fill with regret, and his shoulders droop. "Ian. I don't know how it happened. I...Christ, I just couldn't stop."

Holy fuck. "It'll be okay. We'll—"

The breath whooshes from my lungs when Zac whips around to plow his fist into my gut. I fold in half, and he follows up with another fist to my face that sends me sprawling into the lockers. My vision goes blurry, and when I taste blood on my tongue, my old pal Zac leans over me, eyes blazing. "You found it, didn't you, Russell? Where is it?" He pats my pockets, finds my phone, and drops it to the floor, smashes it with his cleats. "You want to go to the cops with no proof to back up your little story? You want this team to see how you rolled over on a brother? You do that."

The regret I swear I saw in his eyes a second ago is gone. Just like the bonds of friendship. I scramble to my feet and land one punch to Zac's jaw before Jeremy gets my arms pinned behind my back. The rest of the team closes in. "She said no, Zac. She told you no, but you didn't listen."

Zac laughs. "I never heard no, man. All I heard were moans."

"You did. You said nobody gets to tell you no, and then you fucking raped her."

The smile drips off his face, and a second later he's got a fistful of my shirt in his hand. "You weren't there, Russell. Your phone is in pieces. So where's your proof? Huh, *pal?*"

"With the police. And with Coach Brill."

When Zac's face pales and his grip on me goes slack, I twist the knife a little deeper. "Zac, you don't really think my phone had the only copy of that video, do you?"

"What video?" Matt asks. "What the hell's he talking about, Zac?"

I stomp on Jeremy's foot, break out of his hold while Zac slumps to a bench, his face white. "The video he took while he raped Grace. She said no. She said to stop. But he said nobody gets to tell him no. And when she passed out, he forced her. Why'd you keep it, Zac? You're such a smart guy, why did you keep it?"

As soon as I ask the question, the answer comes to me. A trophy. Zac needed a damn trophy.

"No. No, that can't be right, man. Tell him! Tell him that's not right," Kyle demands.

"He's lying!" Jeremy shouts. "He just wants to do her himself."

Kyle stares at me. "Russell, what the hell are you saying?"

"Kyle, I wouldn't lie about this. Zac would. He did."

With a roar, Zac lunges for me, shoves me into a locker, and before I can get my hands up to defend myself, he lands a blow that rings my bell. I slide to the floor and curl into a ball as his fists pound my face, a cleat lands in my side. Shouts and screams fill my ears. I can't move air and the way my head is ringing, and I know I've just suffered my last concussion. I spit blood and blink, but it's no good. I'm fading. I stare up into Zac's face, but the Zac I know isn't here anymore. It's Grace's *game face*, Sarah's *hunter face*, and when he brings his fist back for the punch I know will kill me, I keep staring at him because I want him to know that I see what he really is.

That's when a huge paw closes around Zac's fist and hauls him off me. Coach Brill looks down at me and roars at the team, "Call 911!" he shouts at the blur on his right. "What did you do, Zac? What the hell did you do?" He shakes Zac like a rag doll.

Wasn't easy. But I did it. I shut my eyes and slide under the gray.

––––––––––

"You could stay home again today," Mom reminds me for the twelfth time since they let me out of the hospital.

"Mom, it's fine. Really. Just help me get the sling on." I'm banged up pretty good. Luckily my ribs are just bruised, not cracked. Keeping my arm immobile really helps the pain.

She frowns at the ugly purple stain on my chest and winces just as somebody taps on my bedroom door.

"What?"

The door opens. Grace stands on the other side, and her bright eyes laser right on to my manly ripped chest and not the bruise.

Definitely not the bruise.

"Um, your dad said I could come up, but I—" She points back downstairs.

"No, it's okay. Come on in. Mom, could you give us a few minutes, please?"

She smooths the hair out of my eyes and gives me *the look*, and my face burns. But she leaves, shutting the door behind her.

"Ian. You sure you're up for this?" Grace sits on my bed, her knees bouncing—the only outward sign she's terrified. I don't know why. She's faced a hell of a lot worse.

I slowly sit next to her, trying not to wince, and put a hand over her knee. "Well, I thought about Europe. Semester abroad program, but—" I grin, and she rolls her eyes and grabs my shirt, helps me wrestle it on.

"I didn't mean school. I mean, us."

Us. That's why she's scared. "Never been more sure of anything." She turns those bright eyes on me, and I can see the words mean something to her. They mean something to me too. She nods and smiles. I squeeze her knee, lean in, and kiss her until the pain fades away.

She pulls back, slips the sling over my head, tucks my left arm into it. I try not to breathe. Then I try not to squeal like a girl when she tightens the straps.

"Okay?"

"Yeah," I squeal.

Damn it.

She looks around my room, and it hits me. This is the first time she's been up here. "You built all of these?" She asks with a jerk of her thumb toward the shelves over my desk that hold my *Enterprise*—the aircraft carrier, not the starship—and my *Falcons*, the Navy jet and the *Star Wars* ship, plus an assortment of cars I think are cool.

"Yeah. Told you I like building stuff."

She nods and stares at her toes. She's not wearing her superhero costume today, and I kind of miss it.

"Ian—"

"Grace—"

We both start at the same time and then laugh. Awkward.

"You go first," I offer.

She nods once, bites her lip, and tries again. "Thank you." She shrugs, laughs once. "I know that doesn't cover it all. For going up against your friends, for finding that video, for going to the police, even for saying you believed me. And then you got beat up for me." She slips a hand into my hair and gently rubs my head. "You got another concussion. I know what that means for you, and I'm so, so sorry."

I shut my eyes and enjoy the feel of her fingers against my scalp for a minute. When I set her straight, she'll probably take off. But it's the right thing to do. "Grace, I appreciate the thought, but don't thank me. Truth is I didn't do this for you. Or…not *only* for you."

Her hand freezes against my head.

"I couldn't live with it, Grace. Even if I never found the video, I couldn't live with the way Zac was treating you." I reach up, wrap my free arm around her waist. "I didn't see it. Not until you made me look. God! I *hated* you for making me look." She pulls away from me, but I keep going. I need to say this. I need her to get it. "The way Zac treats girls—our server at Pizza Hut, my sister, even his mom—girls are just here for his convenience, and after a while I started to hate him for that. Grace, I started to hate myself. I don't want to be that guy. So I guess that's why I did it."

Her mouth falls open, and her eyes go misty.

"Aw, hell, don't do that."

She laughs, wipes her eyes. "I will if I want to. I even stopped wearing black eyeliner in case."

I nod. I'd noticed. "I like the way you look without all the makeup." I whip up a hand when she opens her mouth to argue. "You know, when I was waiting for Coach Brill in the locker room the other night, I kept wishing I could be the hero for you. Save you." Grinning, I remember how she battled Miranda and even a stupid piece of glass. "Hell, you don't need a hero. You just save yourself. You know what you *do* need, Grace?"

She spreads her hands apart, shakes her head.

"You need a guy who *gets* you."

She swallows, licks her lips, and my brain almost fries. "Is that you?"

"God, I hope so."

She smiles and leans over, presses her lips to mine, and for a minute, I don't feel any pain.

"Is your dad mad at me for all this? No team, no scholarship and all that?"

I shake my head. "I don't know. He's been weirdly quiet about everything the past few days."

"Oh."

"I've been thinking though." Thinking's pretty much all I can do right now. "Mechanical engineering. A lot of the state schools have decent programs."

Grace stands, takes the *Enterprise* off my shelf. "You'd be able to build real stuff."

"Yeah, stuff that comes from my mind instead of from a kit. Plus, the tuition is a lot cheaper than at the private schools. Besides, scholarships were never a guarantee." I shrug and then wince. Bad idea.

She puts the model back and flips her hair behind her shoulders. "I think it's a great idea. Did you tell them yet?" She jerks her chin toward the door."

"No. No way. I don't need to hear another lecture about my math grades and how I threw away any shot at an athletic scholarship. I did what I did, and that's done."

"Ian," she says and holds out her hand to me. I take it and slowly stand up, facing her. "You should tell them."

"Yeah. Maybe. I don't know." I glance at my alarm clock. "Come on. We should go. Don't want to be late."

She snorts out a laugh, and we head outside where my dad's got the car running and waiting. The drive to school is quiet and uncomfortable and way too fast.

Dad pulls up in front of the school. "You sure you're up for this?"

"Why does everybody keep asking me that? Dad, I'm fine. No headaches. My ribs are trussed up tight. Besides, I've got my own personal bodyguard with me." I grin at Grace in the backseat. Nobody can get through her. The girl is fierce.

"Okay. Go straight to the nurse if you feel dizzy. I won't be far today. I can be here in ten minutes if—"

"Dad. Relax. I'm good." I open my door. Grace opens hers. She's got both our backpacks because even though I feel good, I can't quite manage the weight yet.

"Ian?" Dad powers down the window.

"Yeah?"

He stares straight out the windshield. "Proud of you. Never been prouder."

A lump the size of Coach Brill's fist suddenly forms in my throat. I nod. "Thanks," I manage to croak out. He starts to power up the window, but I raise my good arm to stop him. "Dad, if you have some time today, look up the SUNY mechanical engineering programs, okay?"

His jaw drops, but he quickly closes it. "Mechanical engineering. Okay. Okay, I'll do that."

As Dad drives off, Grace slips her hand into mine. "See, that wasn't so bad, right?"

"I guess. So are you ready for this?" I squeeze her hand.

"Not even a little."

I pause in my climb up the steps. "Did you get hassled? You said people were cool to you the past few days."

Grace shakes her head. Her hair's wild today, tumbling down her back. Even though she's not wearing the ass-kicker boots, it's okay. I've still got my souvenir stud in my pocket.

302

"No, pretty much everybody was cool. Mrs. Kirby apologized for the whole *Shrew* class thing."

I nod. That's good. "Come on. Let's get this over with." I tug her hand, and we head into the school together. Heads swivel. Mouths fall open, but most break into grins.

"Ian, how you feelin', man?"

"Better, thanks."

"Good to have you back, Russell!"

I grin and nod. Grace's hand twitches in mine. After a few minutes I get why.

People are still ignoring her. Until we get to her locker.

"Khatiri, hi."

The girl at Grace's locker turns, grabs Grace in a hug, and squeals. "Oh, I'm so happy for you both. And glad you're okay, Ian."

I nod. "Thanks."

Khatiri's smile fades. "Um, Grace." She tugs a folded square of paper from her pocket. "I was asked to give you this, and this time I'm doing it in person. Uh, something about you switching phones with your mom?"

Frowning, Grace nods and reads the note. "It's from Miranda and Lindsay." She looks up at me, and those bright eyes of hers sparkle with tears. "She says they're sorry and want me to sit with them during lunch."

She folds up the note, and then her eyes snap up to Khatiri's. "Wait. You just said 'in person.' Why?"

303

Khatiri bounces on her toes. "Um. Yeah. The last time I had a note for you, I chickened out. I left in a place I knew you'd find it."

Grace's eyes go round. "The photography book! That was you? Oh my God."

Khatiri stares at the floor, shifts on her feet. "Yeah. Sorry."

"No, no, it's okay." Grace opens her arms and hugs Khatiri. "Thank you."

"Did it help? I mean, did you call?"

"Yeah. Yeah, I did, and it helped."

Grace and Khatiri smile and hug again, and I have no freakin' clue what the hell is happening here.

"Okay, well, I'll leave you two to, um—See you later." She waves a hand from me to Grace and takes off.

I lean over to whisper in Grace's ear. "What the hell was that about?" But she only shrugs.

"Tell you later."

Before I can say anything, I spot Erin Specht heading this way and resist the urge to pretend I don't see her.

"Um, Grace? Just hang here for a minute, okay? There's something I need to do."

She nods, and I take off. "Hey, Erin! Wait up." Erin glares at me like she wants to strangle me with the strap on her backpack, and I swallow hard. "This won't take long. I just wanted to say I'm sorry." Her mouth falls open, so I keep going. "It wasn't cool, the way I treated you. It took me a while to figure that out and even longer to man up and apologize for it. I hope you can forgive me someday. So. That's it."

She says nothing. But her eyes fill with tears, and she presses her hands to her mouth, nodding vigorously. My eyes pop when she hugs me for a moment. Christ, that hurts. Then she pulls back with a watery smile, waves, and leaves.

"What the hell was that?" Grace demands when I go back to her.

"Um. Don't hate me, okay? That was Erin Specht. I finally grew a pair and apologized to her."

"For what?"

Where the hell do I start? "Tell you later. Come on. Bell's gonna ring."

The morning passes in a blur. By lunchtime my ribs ache, and the bruises on my face pound. I grin because Grace will probably have her bottle of pain relievers handy. In the cafeteria I watch Miranda and Lindsay approach Grace. I move closer, ready to step in if I have to. But Miranda just wraps her arms around a shocked Grace. After a minute Grace hugs her back.

Girls are so weird. I shake my head. If it were me, I'd tell her to get lost.

Grace sees me and frowns. "You're pale. Here," she says and fishes out the bottle of pills.

I laugh.

"What?"

"Nothing." I wrap my free arm around her. "Just like the way you take care of me."

With a grin, she wriggles free and points to a table. "Sit there. Take the water. I'll get food."

I do as I'm told because I wasn't lying. I really do love the way she fusses over me. As I crack the seal on the bottle of water and drown two capsules, shadows cross my table. I look up, find Kyle, Matt, and Jeremy standing around me, looking tense.

I brace, and my eyes almost cross from the pain. Kyle puts up his hands. "Relax, man. We're here to apologize."

This should be good. I wait, but they just stand there, staring at their feet, the ceiling, out the window—anywhere but at me.

"So," I say and then clear my throat. "Is there any word?"

The guys look ill. "Yeah. Zac's officially off the team. Cops arrested him yesterday, but everybody's saying it won't stick. Coach is still considering whether to punish the whole team." Matt shoves his hands into his pockets.

"I admitted I was the one who called Grace that name in front of her dad, not Matt," Kyle adds. "Maybe he'll just bench me instead of all—" His shoulders sag like he already knows there's little hope of that actually happening. "What about you? Are you like…permanently injured?"

I nod. "Looks that way. Besides the bruises and sore ribs, Zac gave me another concussion—my third this year. I'm done, guys. I can't play again."

Matt winces, puts a hand on my shoulder, squeezes gently. "Really sorry, bro." Then he snaps straight up like somebody shot him. I follow his eyes. Grace strides toward us, carrying a tray of food. She's got on the warrior face—the face that says, *I dare you to say something*, and when the guys all shift their weight and clear their throats, I get that they're here to apologize to *her*, not me.

She slides the tray across the table and sits down, glaring at each of them in turn. Kyle clears his throat. "Um. Grace? We just wanted to say we're sorry for hassling you." He smacks Jeremy's head.

"Um. Yeah. Sorry."

Grace shuts her eyes for a minute, and when she opens them, the attitude is gone. She slides the tray closer. "You want some pizza?"

Kyle grins and beats Jeremy to one of the slices. "Sure. Thanks." All three of them grab chairs, and in minutes the tray is a sad reminder of lunch past. Again, I'd have told them to get lost, but my girl's a bigger person than I am. I swallow a grin. She raises her eyebrows, and I just shake my head and laugh.

Good thing she can't read my mind, or she'd hurt me for that *my girl* thought.

Chapter 29
Grace

I pull over to the curb, kill the engine, and put my head on the steering wheel. A hand brushes my hair.

"Panic attack?"

With my head still on the wheel, I turn, peek at Ian. "No. Just immense dread."

He shakes his head with a laugh. "After everything you been through, you're gonna let a kiddie party break you?"

I shrug and practice my deep breathing technique, thoroughly enjoying Ian's fingers dancing through my hair, and finally sit up.

"Better?"

"Oh, yeah." I lean over to kiss him gently. It's only been a few days since the attack in the locker room. He's not allowed to drive until his doctor is sure he won't have seizures or dizzy spells. "How's your rib?"

He's not wearing the sling, but I know he's still in pain.

"The rib's fine. But honestly? I'm a little dizzy." He winces a bit, and when I pull back to examine him for myself, he quickly adds, "I think I'm just rocked by how good you look."

I press a hand to my flapping heart and glare at him in horror. "Oh, God, you actually dig the pink."

"Oh, yeah. This?" He traces a finger around the pink leather studded gauntlet on my wrist. "Nice touch."

"Well, it matches the sweater set."

"You in a pink sweater set. Your dad's gonna faint." He nuzzles me, kisses my cheek, and I feel the tension pour from my limbs.

"Could be worse," I point out. "I could have added pearls."

Ian laughs. "You ready?"

"I guess." We open our doors.

"Gift?"

I grab the wrapped boxes from the backseat, join him at the curb. "Check."

"Fighting spirit?"

I roll my shoulders and crack my neck. "Check."

"Okay. Before we go in, need to tell you something." Ian runs his hands up my arms to rest on my shoulders. "My take on all this? Your dad messed up, and he knows it but can't accept it."

I give him an eye roll. "Come on. It's not nuclear physics."

"It's kind of a guy thing. We're like...programmed to protect our girls. And I know you hate the whole ownership thing, but you can't fight DNA."

"Yeah, so? What's your point?"

"He failed, Grace. You got hurt, and he can't face that."

I stare at him for a moment. Oh my God, are guys seriously this moronic?

"Look, I was in the hospital waiting room that night. He rushed in, screaming for names. One of the detectives had to take him outside, calm him down. He messed up, Grace. He knows it. Give him a chance to stand up like you did for me."

I shrug. "Okay." I push open the gate to the backyard. "But if Kristie says one word about my attitude, I'm dropping her."

"There's *my* warrior woman."

"Oh, you're just asking for it now."

Ian just grins. We walk through the backyard gate, and a minute later Kody attacks me, fueled by a sugar high. "Grace! Grace! Is that for me?" He grabs at the boxes in my hands.

"Happy birthday, little dude."

Next to me Ian coughs and shakes his head once. "Jeez, do *not* call him that."

"I'm five now, Grace. I'm not little anymore." Kody pouts, and I laugh.

"I'm sorry. Let's see." I tug him to my side, measure his height against mine. "Oh, wow. You've definitely gotten taller. Look how high you are!"

"Whoa." Kody's eyes go wide. "Come on, come see the snake. It's so cool and not slimy one bit."

"Oh, God."

"Mom! I got more presents!" Kody runs off with his treasure.

Kristie, a pitcher of some red juice in her hand, turns with a flip of sleek blond hair and spots me by the gate. The smile freezes on her face, and her eyes dart across the deck to my dad, who's pricking hot dogs sizzling on the grill with a giant fork. Dad follows Kristie's glance, puts down the fork, and joins us. "Kody's already overloading on the candy. He's really excited." He gives me a kiss on my cheek and turns to Ian, oblivious to my uncomfortable smile. "Ian. How are you feeling, son?"

"Better, Mr. Collier. No headaches."

"Good. I want you to sit down, take it easy. Any dizziness, any problems, you go right inside and lie down for as long as you need, okay?"

"Yes, sir."

Dad smiles and then looks at me. The smile stays, but it's not as bright now. "Glad you made it, Grace."

I don't roll my eyes, but I hold up my hands in surrender. "I know Kristie told me not to come, but I promised Kody, Dad. I hope it's okay that I'm here."

Kristie and some other moms have their heads together, pretending not to look at me, and I swear I can see the question marks in their eyes.

With a loud sigh, he shakes his head. "Okay, come with me. This is going to stop right now." He grabs my hand, tugs me to the grill. "Hey, Mike. Do me a favor and man the grill for a bit? I need to take care of something."

"Sure, man." Mike, a bald guy with a goatee, grabs his beer and picks up the giant fork.

"Grace, would you and Ian wait for me inside? I'll be right there."

I exchange a glance with Ian and nod. We step through the sliding door, sit awkwardly on the family room sofa. He adjusts his position with a wince, and I grab a few throw pillows and stuff them behind his back. "Better?"

He shrugs. We sit silently, my knees bouncing until Ian puts a soothing hand over one. A minute goes by, then two. Then the door opens with a soft swish.

"Kirk, I don't see why we—"

"Humor me."

Dad and Kristie step into the room, his hand at her back, practically pushing her along. She nods once. "Grace."

"Kristie."

Dad ushers Kristie to the love seat, then drags a chair over to sit between us, leaning over his knees. "Honey, Grace says you told her not to come today."

"What?" Kristie feigns surprise. "Oh, I'm sure there's been a misunderstanding."

Here we go. "Bullshit—" I am ready to brawl, but Ian squeezes my knee hard.

"Grace."

"Dad, Kristie called me and said the petting zoo people double-booked and there'd be no party. She was just going to do something informal after school one day, and I should make other plans." This is hopeless. A complete and total waste of time. He'll just believe her, defend her like he always does.

"Kirk, that's not—"

"It *is*, Kristie. I heard you." Dad cuts her off. Kristie just deflates like a stuck balloon, speechless. "I was in the garage when you were on the phone. I didn't say anything because I know *why* you did it."

He reaches over to squeeze her hand, and my heart pinches hard enough to make me gasp. I catch Ian's eyes, jerk my head. It's time to leave. It's never been clearer that I don't belong in my dad's rebooted life. I don't have a K in my name, and I look terrible in sweater sets. But Kristie looks at me for the first time since she entered the room. "Grace, I'm sorry I lied to you, but you don't understand how sick and…and well, *tortured* your father has been since you were assaulted."

"Tortured," I repeat, numb. I don't understand. He hasn't said anything to me about it except to criticize my outfits.

"Kristie, I—"

"No, Kirk. She needs to know." Kristie puts up a hand to stop Dad but keeps her eyes on mine. "He isn't sleeping. He's been sick. I found him hiding in the garage, sobbing."

"Over me?" I still don't understand. I reach for Ian, and he takes my hand, holds it in both of his. I swing my gaze to Dad. "But you blamed me."

His mouth falls open to deny, but he can't because it's pure truth and he knows it. "Oh, God, I did, and I'm sorry for that, Grace. I know it's not your fault. I know that." He spills out of his chair, kneels on the floor in front of me, snatches my hand from Ian's, grips it hard. "It was *my* fault, Gracie. Mine. I wasn't there. I haven't been there for a long time." He stares at me and I see the regret in his eyes, but what the hell good is regret? I wish I could just hold up my arms up so he could scoop me up and lift me high where I always felt safe and adored, and I can't because those days are long gone and we both know it.

"You couldn't even look at me." My voice cracks.

"You're right, Grace. I couldn't look at you. But not because I'm ashamed of you or the way you dress. It's because there's so much pain in your eyes, honey. When Keith has a nightmare or Kody gets a bump, I can kiss them, give them a hug, and tell them everything's gonna be fine. But this—Grace, I don't know how to fix this. There's nothing I can do to make you better, and that kills me, Grace. It *kills* me." He clutches both of my hands in his, and I feel them shake.

It's a long time before I can talk. "That's not true," I finally say. "You can tell me you still love me and nothing will ever change that—not Kristie, not the boys, not the way I dress, and not this."

His eyes, the same as mine, widen behind his glasses. "Did you…do you—oh, honey, please tell me you don't think I stopped loving you."

I shrug. I can't because that's exactly what I think and what I've been thinking for a really long time. How could I not? I've been replaced.

My dad makes an odd choking noise, and suddenly he's hauling me up and into his arms. "No. Aw, no, no, baby, no. I have loved you since the second I learned there'd *be* a you, the very second."

Pretty words, but actions speak louder. I try to make him understand, but the lump in my throat is makes it damn hard to talk. "Dad, come on. You criticize everything about me from my clothes to my grades to my college plans. I'm not allowed over here without an appointment. You coach soccer and coordinate vacations, and I get a five-minute phone call once a week. I was even uninvited to the party today. I don't *matter* anymore, so what am I supposed to think?"

He lets go of me, sinks to the sofa, looking beaten. "You *do* matter. You always have and always will." He turns to Kristie, sitting with her head down and her eyes wet. "And you're right. A phone call once a week makes me a…well, a telemarketer, not a dad. We'll spend more time together—just you and me." He sends Kristie a look full of meaning, and I snort. He's never defended me to Kristie, not in all the years they've been together.

Kristie looks from him to me and swallows. "Grace, I know you hate me. I'm not going to make excuses for what's already happened. But I really love your dad, and I know you do too. For his sake, can we start over?" She manages half a smile and extends her hand.

Can I do this? Just forgive all the crap that's happened? I stare at my hand, imagine every frown, every criticism, every hurt feeling slip through my fingers like grains of sand. When it's empty, I take her hand. "Okay, we can try, starting with no more trying to change how I dress." I tug at my sweater. "I really hate cardigans. And pink."

Her eyes widen, and then she grins a watery smile. "Stay there. I'll be right back." Kristie runs up the stairs. I shoot a questioning look at Dad, but he just shrugs. A minute later she runs back down the stairs, carrying a shopping bag. "I bought you this weeks ago but was afraid to give it to you because I didn't want to upset your dad."

I open the bag, pull out a black T-shirt. The collar and sleeves are fastened by metal rings all the way around. It's perfect. "Why give it to me now?"

"It's your style, Grace. You own it," she says with a little shrug of apology directed at my dad.

"This is awesome. Thanks."

"Good, can I borrow this? I really love it." She runs a hand over my sweater, and we laugh a real laugh, the first time that's happened since dance class all those years ago.

Dad wraps us both in a hug. "I love you. I love you both so much." We stand like that for a long moment, and then he pulls away, wiping his eyes. "We should get back." He takes Kristie's hand, holds out his other hand to me.

"I need a minute," I tell him. They smile and leave us.

Ian gives me a slow clap and then opens his arms for me. I move into him, hold him—not too tight. I let it all go—every last bit of resentment. "You ready to head back out there now?" he asks after a long hug and a kiss to my forehead that still makes my knees weak.

"Almost." I shrug off my cardigan, slip Kristie's new T-shirt over the other half of my twinset, and rip off the price tag. "There. Now I'm ready."

Ian's gaze runs up and down over my body. "Nice. Might look better without the pink sweater under it."

Shrugging, I take his hand, grab the cardigan. "Too cold. Come on."

Outside on the deck I pause for a second, pull out my camera—mine, not the school's. I shoot the blur of shrieking kids, laughing adults, and way too many weird animals. Kody tugs me over to pet a snake. Chairs are dragged over to the table for us. Dad shoves a loaded plate into Ian's hands, and Kristie admires my wardrobe adjustment. Ian snatches my camera, captures a shot of my dad and me just as Dad tells his friends, "This is my daughter. You know, she wore a *burqa* to school?" I blink in shock. I had no idea he'd even heard about that.

I stare at the picture on screen—me looking fierce with my kick-ass T-shirt and pink sweater, while Dad looks down at me with pride in his eyes. I print the picture as soon as I get home and stick it to my mirror, right next to the one of me with Ian kissing my forehead.

I grin at myself in the mirror. I didn't break.

Author's Note

When I was researching this novel, I learned about a courageous photographer whose work both haunted and inspired me, so I named my heroine Grace in her honor. Visit project-unbreakable.org for more information about Grace Brown and to view the compelling work she's doing. Her photographs made me understand how victims of rape aren't just victims of rape. They're victims of bullying and shaming and even the justice system.

I wrote *Some Boys* to shed light on this tendency to defend rape because the men and sometimes women who commit it *aren't* monsters in masks hiding in the bushes. After no other crime does society turn on its victims the way it does when the crime is rape. And with the rise in social media, victim-blaming is going viral. It's my profound hope that readers will recognize the rape myths they once believed were facts and change the way they think about and talk about rape.

A young girl attends a party, has too much to drink, and is the victim of rape. She endures medical exams to collect evidence. She identifies her attacker. And the battle lines are drawn. The police ask her humiliating questions about her habits, her past relationships, her conduct. If her attacker is anyone other than a masked psychopath, his friends, teachers, or coaches rally to defend him by calling her a slut, taunting, threatening, and even harming her.

This is not fiction. What happens in *Some Boys* is in the news every day. It's what happens to 20 percent of college women and 4 percent of college men. It's what happens every two minutes to somebody in America.

If you're the victim of sexual assault, I urge you to contact your local crisis hotline or go to www.rainn.org for help.

You're not alone.

It's not your fault.

Some Boys Discussion Guide

Questions about Some Boys

1. What do you think is the main theme of *Some Boys*?

2. In the opening scene, we learn Grace's friends have turned away from her. Why do you think they did this?

3. Each chapter in *Some Boys* alternates between Grace and Ian. What did you think about the ways Grace thinks about boys? What did you think about the ways Ian thinks about girls?

4. Why do you think Ian searched Zac's phone?

5. During lit class, Grace class is reading *The Taming of the Shrew*. What similarities do you see between Grace and Shakespeare's Kate?

6. Throughout the story, Grace is criticized for the way she dresses. Why does she wear her costume? Why do you think Ian doesn't like it?

7. How would things have changed for Grace if she'd accepted her mother's offer of that semester abroad?

8. Throughout *Some Boys*, decisions by main characters Grace, Ian, and Zac are questioned. What about decisions made by supporting characters? Which decisions were good, and which were bad? Explain.

Questions about You

1. How do you think you'd respond if it were your friend who'd been raped or accused of rape?

2. Rapes like Grace's have occurred in towns across our country like Steubenville and Maryville. In what ways has reading *Some Boys* changed the ways you think about how rape crimes are investigated? How would you change the law?

3. Also in the news frequently is the subject of *rape culture*. What do you think rape culture is, and how do the events in *Some Boys* support the existence of such a culture? How do you think rape culture can be eliminated?

4. Which lesson in *Some Boys* most influenced you?

5. How do the events in *Some Boys* change the ways you might approach intimacy?

Acknowledgments

This was such an emotionally hard book to write, and I owe debts of gratitude to a number of people for helping me through it. Hugs and kisses to all my guys, Fred, Robert, and Christopher, who'd catch me sobbing over my keyboard but wisely would not interrupt me. To John Grebe Jr., a big high five for helping me with the lacrosse scenes. To Lauren Gilbert and the Sachem Public Library, thank you for the countless sources you provided while I researched rape and those who commit it.

To all the members of the Long Island Romance Writers, RWA Chapter 160, *roars*! Thank you for your support, advice, cheerleading, and sanity preservation as I wrote this story while I honored my commitments to our chapter.

Enormous thanks to Aubrey Poole, the Sourcebooks team, and my agent, Evan Gregory, for giving me this shot at the hat trick—three published novels! A dream come true. Loud shout-out to the Sourcebooks design team for the amazing cover and not hating me (too much?) for my nitpicks. Extra-special thanks to Alyssa-

Susannah, better known as *The Eater of Books*, and to Amy Del Rosso, *Lady Reader's Bookstuff*—and all book bloggers because without your passion for books, my stories would never find readers. I can't thank you enough.

Thank you to Jeannie Moon and Jeff Somers for providing not only emergency readings of the manuscript but the feedback it desperately needed to take it to even greater heights than I could have managed alone.

Love and gratitude and all the chocolate to my Twitter friends for your continued guidance, humor, and support, and to my Book Hungry ladies, Kelly Breakey, Abby Mumford, Blake Leyers, and Karla Nellenbach, for your cheerleading, feedback, and senses of humor.

About the Author

Powered by chocolate, Patty Blount writes technical information by day and fiction by night. On a dare by her oldest son, she wrote her first novel in an ice rink. Her debut novel, *Send*, was inspired by a manager's directive to use social media. Passionate about happily-ever-afters, Patty frequently falls in love with fictional characters only to suffer a broken heart at the closing of each book. When she's not reading or writing, Patty enjoys hanging out with her family on Long Island and hearing from readers who love her characters as much as she does.

Read on for a sneak peek of Patty Blount's *Nothing Left to Burn*

Chapter 1
Reece

Dear Dad,

I promised Matt I'd do this. I know it'll piss you off, but
a promise is a promise, and I can't let him down.

Baring your soul wasn't as easy as I'd thought. There was so much I wanted to tell Dad. Remind him about all those times he'd said no, every time he'd made me feel less important than my brother. Every time he'd made me cry and wish I were Matt instead of me. There were *years* of pent-up resentment that could fill entire reams of paper, yet I'd managed to scrawl just a few lines. Somehow, the right words were impossible to find—if they existed at all.

I folded the crisp white sheet of paper into thirds, then folded that in half, tucked it carefully into my pocket, and thought about abandoning this entire pointless idea. But I had no other options. I sucked in a deep breath, tried to ignore the pounding of my pulse, and left the car.

It was time.

At the entrance where the roll-up doors were all the way up, I stopped and took a good look around. Red trucks gleamed in the light.

I could hear guys busting each other's balls, laughing hard and cursing loud. The slight scent of mildew tickled my nose when the April breeze blew my way. The fire station was every little boy's fantasy, including mine. But I learned a long time ago that it did no good to dream.

Then I saw Amanda Jamison, packing nylon rope into a bag, and just watched. In her station uniform, the lean muscles in her long limbs flexed when she strode to a truck to stow the bag. I knew Amanda from school. Knew the blond hair she wore scraped viciously back and twisted into a knot at her neck was straight and smooth, reached past her shoulders, and smelled like lemonade. Knew I had no shot with her. She'd never said so much as "hi" to me.

She'd had a thing for my brother.

She caught sight of me, turned, and didn't notice her rope bag tumble out of the truck. "Matt? Oh God. Matt."

Matt. My shoulders sagged. Okay. No turning back now. I swallowed hard and walked into the house where I had never been welcome. It took only three steps for recognition to fill Amanda's eyes. Or maybe it was revulsion. The two often went hand in hand where I was concerned. Mom says people just didn't *get* me. I figured that's because Dad always told them I was strange.

"Excuse me." I cleared my throat. "Could you direct me to the chief's office?" I took out my completed application from the bag on my shoulder, and her eyes popped.

"*Reece* Logan," she said with a sneer, and I jerked in surprise. Apparently, she *did* know me. She'd come to Matt's funeral; she and a few other kids from junior squad. Hard to believe that was four months ago. She'd hugged my dad, kissed my mom's cheek, and walked right past me. I figured that meant she'd heard all about my father's version of the accident that killed Matt—and believed it.

When she glanced over her shoulder at a group of guys in turn-outs checking the equipment on Truck 3, I knew exactly what she was thinking. She probably hoped they'd pick me up and toss me out of the station for her. I saw the way her eyes scanned me from head to toe. She was cataloging. Indexing. Comparing me to Matt. When I held out my hand, she looked at it with disgust all over her face.

I swallowed hard, searched for something, *anything*, to say. "You came to the funeral. You and Gage."

She squeezed her eyes shut, and when she opened them, they were wet. "Yeah. We did."

"Thanks for that. It was…hard." I laughed once, a short uncomfortable huff of air, and then shrugged. Understatement of the century, but what the hell are you supposed to say about your brother's funeral?

"Amanda? Problem here?"

She whipped around to face the tall, thin man standing in the swath of sunlight. He took a step closer, and I recognized him. Mr. Beckett, the chem teacher from school.

Her face hardened. "Right. Hard." She picked up the rope bag she'd been packing and shoved it back into Engine 21. She slammed the compartment door, and I had the feeling she wished it were my

331

head. I figured she didn't want to know there was someone who looked this much like Matt, sounded like Matt, walking around while Matt couldn't. When she stalked off to talk to Mr. Beckett, I knew I'd underestimated her hatred, but I couldn't let that stop me.

"Hey!"

She whipped around. "What?"

"Chief." I waved the sheet of paper at her. "Please."

She pulled in a deep breath and ground her teeth together. "Go home."

I laughed bitterly and shook my head. Hell, hers would probably be the nicest greeting I'd ever get in this house. I stepped around her, strode to the door that led from the apparatus floor to the inner offices, and prayed I'd survive this, even if it was only long enough to keep my word to my brother.

Chapter 2
Amanda

He stood with the sun shimmering at his back, and I stopped breathing.

Matt. Oh my God. Matt.

The blood rushed from my head. The gear I was packing squirted from my hands, hitting the ground with a dull thud. I watched, dizzy, as the ghost in front of my eyes stepped out of the glare and became a living thing. Not Matt. Tall, maybe even taller than Matt, same toast brown hair, same piercing brown eyes. But where Matt's eyes used to glint with a bit of mischief, this boy's eyes held something else.

Pain.

My heart gave a long slow roll when I realized who this was.

Reece Logan. Matt's brother.

Oh crap. I shot an uneasy glance over my shoulder where the guys on Truck 3 checked their equipment, but the lieutenant wasn't with them. And then I remembered he wasn't onshift on Wednesdays. Is that why Matt's brother was here—because he knew his father *wouldn't* be? I looked away, really wanting to avoid getting sucked into somebody else's family drama, but it was too late. He drifted closer to me, stood so close I could feel the anxiety radiating off him in waves.

Damn it, when he spoke, he even *sounded* like Matt, but without the laugh in his voice. Frowning, I looked at him again. Now that I could see him up close, I noticed his face was more angular, his lips thinner than Matt's, and there was a tiny scar running through one eyebrow. When he took out a completed application from the bag on his shoulder, my mouth unhinged. He said something about Matt's funeral, and I swear, I'd have blasted him between the eyes if Mr. Beckett hadn't picked that minute to walk in, crinkling a bag of potato chips.

He saw me talking to this boy and immediately frowned. "Amanda? Problem here?"

Crap, crap, shit. Mr. Beckett had a strict no boys rule.

I quickly got rid of Reece and turned to my foster father. "Sorry about that."

He upended the rest of the chips into his mouth, folded up the bag, and put it in his pocket with a frown. "Who was that boy?"

I shrugged. "A new volunteer."

"Do you know him?"

Don't lie. Do not lie. No lying is another rule. "His father's a lieutenant here."

Mr. Beckett's eyebrows shot up over his glasses. "Really? He certainly didn't look twelve."

I shook my head. "He's not. He's in my grade, so he's probably sixteen."

"I wonder why he's volunteering now. What changed?"

I didn't wonder. I knew. "His brother got killed back in December."

"Ah. How tragic." Tragic—yeah, but Mr. Beckett's expression relaxed. "But are you sure you don't know him personally? You seemed extremely upset speaking to him."

Oh, I knew Reece Logan. But I shook my head. "I never spoke to him until today." Not a lie. "I know the lieutenant, and from what he says, he and his son do not get along. I don't want that drama spilling over onto my squad."

Mr. Beckett pressed his lips into a thin line and looked down at me over the rims of his glasses. "I'm not comfortable with you continuing here if there's going to be drama."

Oh God. The blood in my veins froze. Junior squad was all I had—he couldn't take that away from me. I shook my head firmly. "There won't be. I won't let that happen."

Mr. Beckett considered that for a moment and finally smiled. "Okay. Just be sure you keep things entirely professional with that boy."

I nearly cried with relief when Mr. Beckett turned to leave.

"Oh, by the way…I came in to tell you I can't pick you up tonight. Can you get a lift?"

Yeah, from a boy. "Sure. No problem. Thanks, Mr. Beckett."

"What's on the agenda tonight?"

"Uh, we're doing PPE."

He flashed a wistful smile. "Oh, that's a fun one. Okay, have a good class. Don't let that boy's drama become yours."

Oh, count on it.

After Mr. Beckett walked back to his car, I finished checking the equipment on Engine 21.

"Man, got a minute?"

I looked up and found Neil Ernst, our instructor, standing behind me, his face tense. Immediately, I snapped up straight.

"Sure, Lieutenant. What's up?"

He waved a hand toward the parking lot, so I followed him out through the bay doors. He shoved his hands in his pockets and stared at the ground.

I started to sweat. This was bad.

"Um, yeah, so, the wife and I are moving to Florida. She's got a really good job waiting down there, and yeah. We're leaving Long Island."

I was nodding like I totally understood, but all I kept thinking was *what about us?* I took a deep breath. "What about J squad?"

Neil shrugged. "Chief's still making up his mind. He'll probably ask Steve Conner to take over for me."

I was still nodding like some lame bobblehead toy. "Okay, so congratulations. Or good luck." Or whatever.

"Yeah, thanks. Um, so I just want you to know I think you're one of the best damn cadets we've ever taught here. I hope you'll continue. When you turn seventeen, you're eligible for full volunteer status."

I knew that. I was planning to, assuming the Becketts didn't ship me back into the system. "Uh, thank you."

"I mean it, Man. You've been a great leader, a great assistant, and you really know your stuff. Whoever the chief puts in charge of J squad, I know you'll be his greatest asset."

My face burned under the praise, but it made me happy to hear. I worked my ass off for the squad, for LVFD. It was nice knowing that was appreciated. "So what about tonight's class?"

"Oh, um, yeah. So that's why I told you our plans. I can't stay tonight. We've got some hotshot real estate agent coming by tonight to appraise our place. Says she can get it sold like that." He snapped his fingers. "So I told the chief I couldn't do tonight's class. But you can. You've done PPE before—so has everybody else. Just run the practice drills, and you'll be fine."

Still nodding. "Yeah. Okay."

Neil held out his hand. "Thanks, Amanda. For everything."

I shook my instructor's hand. That was the only time I could remember him calling me Amanda. To everyone here, I was Man— short for Mandy, but a way of making me feel like one of the guys.

That had been Matt Logan's idea.

While I watched Neil Ernst walk away, my eyes got stuck on Engine 21. It had been right there. That's where I first met Matt Logan, two years ago. I'd been standing behind my foster father, trying not to shake in my secondhand shoes.

"Hey. Can I help you?" he'd asked and smiled in a way that almost melted me into a puddle.

"Hi." Mr. Beckett shook his hand. "This is Amanda, and she'd like to join the junior squad. Right, Mandy?"

I think I may have nodded or something. I know I hadn't been able to manage the powers of speech. Matt Logan was gorgeous, and I wasn't allowed to talk to boys.

Like I said—it was a foster house rule.

There were a lot of them. Don't become a statistic. (There was a ton of scary statistics about foster kids.) Don't use drugs. Don't steal. Don't lie. Don't defy. Don't skip school. I learned most of those at my first foster house. Mrs. Merodie's. I didn't last long there, because there was one really big rule I didn't know about until after.

Don't love your foster parents.

"You're in luck," Matt had said. "We're having our meeting later. Come on. I'll get you started." He'd led us upstairs to the chief's office, Mr. Beckett signed the forms, and a few minutes later, I was officially a junior squad cadet. Mr. Beckett promised he'd be back later to pick me up and left me there, having a private panic attack. What if he didn't come back? Where would I go? Who would take care of me?

"We meet here every Wednesday night and Saturday morning. Bring a notebook." Matt led me into the conference room, where three boys sat with their feet on top of the table at the front of the room. "Guys, this is Mandy. She's our newest cadet."

I remember trying not to cry when all three boys eyeballed me. They were so different. One looked like he was twenty, tall and hairy and muscular. Another looked like a fire hydrant—short, wide, no neck. And the third boy was a scrawny kid who looked young enough to still believe in Santa.

Max, the muscular one, had stood up, walked over to me, and put his hand on the wall, trapping me. My heart had started racing. He leaned in close, too close. "I'm Max. Anything you need, you tell me."

Beside me, Matt's tone suddenly went ice cold. "Max. Cut the *playa* act."

Max shot up one finger, ordering Matt to wait a minute, his eyes never leaving mine. "How old are you?"

I didn't answer. I couldn't remember. Max was standing so close, I could count the whiskers that lined his jaw, and the way he smelled...God!

"She's fourteen, Max."

White teeth flashed. "So am I, so that's perfect."

My eyes popped. He was *fourteen*? Steroids. It was the only explanation.

Suddenly, Matt was standing between us. "Off limits."

Max's lips tightened, but after a short glaring contest, he nodded and went back to his seat at the front table.

Matt led me to a seat and handed me a huge textbook.

"Logan!" Lieutenant Neil Ernst had barked from the doorway. "A word, please."

Matt headed into the hall with the lieutenant, and I tried not to shift and squirm under the stares from all those boys. A few minutes later, he was back. "Special assignment, cadets. Mandy passes all her practicals, or we all fail. Got it?"

"What? That's bull—"

"Tobay. This is a squad. She is now our sister."

Max sucked on the inside of his cheek. "Copy that."

The kid who was shaped like a hydrant had shaken his head and muttered something that sounded like, "Be easier if she was a guy." His name was Ricky, but everyone called him Bear, for obvious reasons, I suppose.

Matt angled his head. "Then start treating her that way."

A few minutes after that, Gage Garner walked in. The fact that I was a girl had no impact on him at all. He nodded, shook my hand, and settled in to take notes. I didn't have a notebook. Matt ripped some blank pages out of his and slid them to me. "Got a pen, Man?"

I shook my head, so he took one from his pocket and slid it over. "Can you talk?"

Startled, I blinked at him and nodded. "Yeah. Sorry. Um, thanks."

He grinned. "Oh good. I was starting to worry."

Lieutenant Neil Ernst began his lesson. It had been about fire suppression. I learned later that all of the boys, except for Kevin, the scrawny kid, had begun J squad when they were twelve. They had two years of training over me. "Don't worry, Man," Matt had said. "We'll get you up to speed fast. Right, guys?" There was a second or two of hesitation, but they all nodded. Whatever they felt about me didn't matter; they liked Matt Logan. Respected him. Listened to him.

I had been *Man* ever since. Matt made me one of the guys that day, made me part of a family, a *brotherhood*. He gave me something that was *mine*, something I could keep no matter what foster home I landed in. And now, he was dead, and everything had changed. Our lieutenant was moving away, the boy responsible for Matt's death wanted to join my squad, and Mr. Beckett wasn't sure he wanted me to stay. I realized I didn't have a damn thing.

The PA system crackled into life. "Jamison, chief's office. Jamison to the chief's office."

I hightailed back inside and upstairs and wondered how much longer I'd get to be *Man*.

SEND
Patty Blount

All Daniel Ellison wants is to be invisible.

It's been five years since he clicked Send, five years since his life made sense. Now he has a second chance in a new town where nobody knows who he is. Or what he's done. But on his first day at school, Dan sees a kid being picked on. And instead of turning away like everyone else, he breaks it up. Because Dan knows what it's like to be terrorized by a bully—he used to be one.

Now the whole school thinks he's some kind of hero—except Julie Murphy. She looks at him like she knows he has a secret. Like she knows his name isn't really Daniel.

TMI
Patty Blount

Best friends don't lie. Best friends don't ditch you for a guy. Best friends don't post your deepest, darkest secrets online.

Bailey's falling head over heels for Ryder West, a mysterious gamer she met online. A guy she's never met in person. Her best friend, Meg, doesn't trust smooth-talking Ryder. He's just a picture-less profile.

When Bailey starts blowing Meg off to spend more virtual quality time with her new crush, Meg decides it's time to prove Ryder's a phony. But one stupid little secret posted online turns into a friendship-destroying feud to answer the question: Who is Ryder West?

GONE TOO FAR

Natalie D. Richards

Piper Woods can't wait to graduate, to leave high school—and all the annoying cliques—behind. But when she finds a mysterious notebook filled with the sins of her fellow students, Piper's suddenly drowning in their secrets.

And she's not the only one watching…

An anonymous text invites Piper to choose: the cheater, the bully, the shoplifter—popular kids with their dirty little secrets. And with one text, Piper can make them pay.

But the truth can be dangerous…

Praise for Natalie D. Richards:

"I predict readers will want more and more from her. I know I do!" —Jennifer Brown, author of *Hate List* and *Thousand Words*

"Her novel has the feel of a high-stakes poker game in which every player has something to hide, and the cards are held until the very end." —*Publishers Weekly*